WEATHER OVER MENDOZA

Printed in Australia
First Printing: November 2022
Shawline Publishing Group Pty Ltd
www.shawlinepublishing.com.au

Paperback ISBN 978-1-9228-5066-9
eBook ISBN 978-1-9228-5071-3

A catalogue record for this work is available from the National Library of Australia

WEATHER OVER
MENDOZA

JOHN MICHELL

Dedicated to Captain Sir Thomas Moore, whom ever so briefly I loved and admired from across the sea.

PREFACE

Weather over Mendoza is a fictional novel featuring at its core a man reflecting on a past that has now caught up with him. Although set in a Cold War spy fiction framework, the narrative's espionage references are broad brush leaving the meat of the story to be found in the surrounding text.

The primary inspiration to write such a book came from the fact that I was living in Moscow in 1991 and witnessed first-hand the collapse of the Soviet Union. That momentous event variously impacted vast numbers of people, creating a fertile setting for writers of fiction. The result in my case is a tale of reflection, of a man plunged into crisis and reliving his life in the rear-view mirror.

My main character, Adrian Ashton, has made many mistakes, some dreadful. Like the fictional Adrian, most folk in the factual world will also have made mistakes. It is this concept of generally good personality occasionally overcome by bad that I wanted to explore when devising the extenuating factors shaping Adrian. The aim is to leave readers pondering a philosophical question: is it just and right to think the worst of Adrian, or is there reason to be sympathetic to his plight?

John Michell
Australia, Spring 2022

DISCLAIMER

This book is a work of fiction. Comments or actions attributed to public figures are inventions or loosely based on historical events. In the latter case, summaries and accounts provided are not intended to be of academic quality, accuracy or balance. Otherwise, any character's resemblance in the book to any individual living or dead is purely coincidental.

Nor does the novel attempt to document in depth the complex evolution of Soviet political and intelligence structures. This deliberately superficial treatment has led to some minor misrepresentations in order to avoid lengthy and unwieldy explanations of no relevance to the storyline.

By the author of *The Far Grass*

CHAPTER 1

Should he have pushed harder to go in 1964 at the time of Carstone? That was the question, especially now it had turned midnight and was Sunday 27 February 1994, six hours until *The Sunday Exegesis* article destroyed him. Thirty years earlier the Politburo ministers in the Kremlin had flatly refused. Bad timing politically, they said. The agent code named Mendoza must try to see it out. And after Feodor's skilled hatchet job on Carstone had seen the American gassed and later pronounced dead on arrival at London's St Thomas' Hospital, the matter of Adrian Ashton's defection never arose again.

Still, at the time Adrian was miffed by the perceived indifference to his safety on the part of the Soviet political leadership. Worse, it smacked of the KGB going along with the Politburo's edict demonstrating yet again that Lubyanka, Feodor aside, did not rate him as an agent. Even then, Feodor's becoming his benefactor was born of duty rather than a clear-eyed assessment of his spying worth.

Adrian was seated in the void of his London flat's bay window. A Walther PPK pistol lay on the table along with an unopened letter, the weapon pushed to one side as if he were fearful of it. Adrian's life flashed before his eyes. He could scarcely believe that his current, terrifying dilemma courtesy of *The Sunday Exegesis* was entirely of Feodor's making.

***

attributed to me without my knowledge.' Adrian smiled at Hardwicke in a no hard feelings sort of way. 'Beyond that, I'm not at liberty to say more. The truth is I've probably said too much as it is.'

Adrian sensed rather than saw Hardwicke's determination mount, recognising the journalist was an especially dogged character.

'So, you refuse to comment on the allegation that you are Mendoza?' Hardwicke said, jutting forward his jaw as he spoke.

'That's correct.'

Hardwicke confidently withdrew a larger wad of paper from his carry bag, at least six pages thick. He held the papers triumphantly in the air, just as Adrian had predicted. But the entrapping evidence was worse than feared.

'This is the body of the statement to which I refer,' Hardwicke said. 'If you flick to the last page you'll see it is signed by a man called Feodor Kozlovsky, Feodor Timofeyevich Kozlovsky to be precise.' Hardwicke smiled smugly. 'He was a KGB officer who made at least two rushed visits to England using various aliases when you were under threat, one in 1954 and another in 1964. You will know him well. You first met him in 1944 during the war when he escorted you out of Nazi Germany and eventually to Moscow. After you were trained by the Soviets and returned to London, he kept a close watch over your spying affairs.'

Adrian tried to stay impassive despite the wobbly panic rising from the pit of his stomach. *No, no*, he thought, horror-struck that his benefactor should be Hardwicke's informant. *Feodor would never betray me.*

'Oh, come on,' Adrian said, feigning exasperation. 'Some former KGB nobody on the make is your star witness? Give me a break. In the current climate these guys would sell their grandmother if they thought it would earn them a buck.'

Hardwicke laughed coldly. 'Nice try, Mr Ashton, but no kewpie doll, I'm afraid. Personally, I find the details of Mr Kozlovsky's 1964 visit to England the most interesting. He has stated, in a sworn document remember, that at the end of 1963 the CIA obtained information indicating a Soviet source in MI6 had compromised an operation in Nicaragua conducted by MI6 earlier in the year on the CIA's behalf.' Hardwicke paused for effect, letting Adrian stew. 'But by end-1963,' he continued, 'MI6 was in a terrible bind and fiercely discounting the possibility of more spies among its number, what with the Soviet announcement the preceding July of Kim Philby's defection to Moscow, hot on the heels of a cavalcade of other British traitors dating back to the early 1950s. Given that, in mid-January 1964, the CIA sent one of its internal investigations people to London specifically to run checks. His name was Kevin Carstone and his brief was to ascertain who of three possible MI6 officers, you being one of them seeing as you led the Nicaraguan operation, might be the Soviet mole. According to Feodor Kozlovsky, this Carstone soon reached the conclusion that you were the guilty party, the Soviet agent. You apparently hit the panic button and begged your KGB controller at the Soviet embassy here in London to do something. You even demanded to defect.'

Adrian shook his head, all the while dying a little inside. *'Feodor, Feodor,'* he moaned silently. *How could you do this to me? After all this time and all we went through together.* 'You're engaging in fantasy,' he told the journalist, trying to dismiss Hardwicke's claims and end the conversation.

But Hardwicke was far from finished. 'Your controller,' he said, ignoring Adrian, 'was so concerned with what the American Carstone had learned and its effect on you that he sent an emergency message to KGB headquarters in Lubyanka: *Weather over Mendoza.* It was a code meaning you were in imminent danger of discovery. The gravity of the situation prompted this Feodor chap to come to England to personally deal with the problem.'

Hardwicke's eyes set hard as he beaded Adrian. 'And the solution conjured by this Feodor fellow in 1964,' he said, 'was to murder Carstone and make it look like suicide. Feodor Kozlovsky told you all about this, Mr Ashton, but you did nothing. That makes you an accessory after the fact to the death of Kevin Carstone.'

Hardwicke studied Adrian, searching for a facial expression indicating he was about to admit everything. The journalist's smug smile returned. He was congratulating himself, believing the forensic precision with which he had put the concluding accusation was responsible for the slump in Adrian's shoulders. But Hardwicke did not know that, rather than yielding to acid questioning, Adrian's devastation came from Feodor's abandonment of him, after fifty years of rock-solid trust.

Adrian forced himself to return Hardwicke's stare, it slowly dawning on him that his visitor was searching for corroboration, however flimsy, for Feodor's claims. Then the story would be ready to go. A horrible thought engulfed Adrian. If Hardwicke didn't already know about Sara from Manchester, he soon would; and she knew it all. To be sure, the CIA agent Kevin Carstone had not passed on Sara's information to MI6, the every last detail she sold him all for a measly eighty quid, chiefly because Feodor staged his suicide before he could. But shortly before he died Carstone did give both the American ambassador and CIA station head in London a summary of Sara's revelations. The MI6 hierarchy, however, anxious to avoid another spying scandal had warded off Carstone's confidants, painting their second-hand information as hearsay incapable of amounting to proof, especially as it originated from a prostitute.

But it was also clear to Adrian that Hardwicke had the scent of a scoop in his nostrils. It was only a matter of time before he contacted either the ambassador or the former CIA station head. Then he'd beat a path to Manchester where he'd try to find Sara and grill her, just as the MI6 management should have done in 1964 if it hadn't been so hell-bent on denying the presence of another spy in its ranks.

Wretched pessimism gripped Adrian. Hardwicke was bound to locate Sara, and she was sure to spill the beans for the right price. For a moment Adrian tried to hope that Sara was dead but couldn't stomach the awful possibility. *Maybe she's immigrated to Australia?* he wondered instead, able to live with that and building his grasping hope on the stories he used to tell her about his upbringing there. But in his heart of hearts Adrian knew he was indulging in wishful thinking. Someone as tenacious as Hardwicke could still track down Sara on the other side of the world.

Hardwicke's voice broke through Adrian's mounting despair. 'You can either come clean and cooperate with us,' he said, 'in which case we'll go as lightly as we can. Or you can decline to help and we'll get after you, boots and all. Your choice.'

Adrian desperately wanted to be alone to think, to plot how best he might find a way out of this mess. In any event, he knew the journalist was lying about going easy—not when there were all sorts of prestigious industry awards in the offing.

All of a sudden a vision of Sara came to Adrian, clear as a bell. It was the day in February 1964 when he rebuked her after she told him that Carstone had also used her services, and he foolishly believed her. Most of all, Adrian remembered Sara's soaring anger and how in no uncertain terms she told him their relationship was over. Resentment and fear caused Adrian's decorum to desert him. 'Get out of here you obnoxious hack,' he shouted. 'I wouldn't give you the shit off my underpants you contemptible bottom feeder. Now piss off.'

The hitherto silent security guard stepped in between Adrian and Hardwicke before shepherding his client towards the door. Hardwicke stood on the threshold. 'You're a traitor, Ashton,' he seethed. 'And I fully intend to see you're held to account. Be in no doubt of that.' Hardwicke sniggered. 'I'll even personally deliver you a complimentary copy of the paper on the Sunday when we publish the story, to your door at 6 am on the dot.' He laughed malevolently. 'Until then you'll just have to sweat.' With that, Hardwicke turned heel and marched from the flat, leaving the door ajar as he went.

***

For fully a month afterwards Adrian grieved for Feodor, feeling like a yawning gap had opened in his life exposing him to an Arctic wind. Some days he wept or drank too much or didn't eat; and other days he did all three. His torpor was broken by another ring on his intercom just before Christmas. It was the postman with a registered letter, which obliged Adrian to walk downstairs to sign for it. Otherwise, it would have lain scattered in his building's dank foyer along with the rest of the mail he had not bothered to collect.

The light brown envelope bore the stamp of the Swedish postal service, giving away that the correspondence was from Feodor. For the first time in weeks Adrian smiled. Feodor always spoke English with a guttural accent. During his fallow period from 1947–53 he'd been exiled to the Soviet embassy in Stockholm. Thus his standard play was usually to pretend to be a Swede whenever in an English-speaking environment. Occasionally, for reasons of tradecraft, he would vary the guise, using Danish, Norwegian or even Czech identities—but never German.

'Not after the Nazis,' Feodor used to say. 'Not after what they took from me.'

The letter was addressed to *Comrade Mendoza*. Adrian recoiled before realising the egregious security breach was nothing of the sort, not now that Feodor had revealed everything to Roger Hardwicke from *The Sunday Exegesis*. Inside his flat Adrian stared at the letter, unwilling to open it. He knew what it contained. It was Feodor explaining why he'd betrayed him.

CHAPTER 2

Adrian lived in London's trendy Notting Hill, just off Kensington Church Street. Although born and bred in Australia, he had stayed in England after the war at the behest of the Soviets, something that was no great sacrifice given the trauma of his antipodean childhood. When Boxing Day 1991 formally marked the Soviet Union's collapse, Adrian spilt no tears for the behemoth; he was long assimilated into British ways and unaware that Roger Hardwicke and *The Sunday Exegesis* were to come.

Adrian was an enigma, a recluse who didn't like to live reclusively. So, sustained by his MI6 pension, he lived an inner city life without actually participating in it. This natural reserve accounted for his dearth of friends and had certainly won him few admirers when working in MI6, even if most of his co-workers did not understand his reticence stemmed from his uncertain upbringing. And now in February 1994, at nearly seventy-two, the leopard wasn't about to change its spots.

In contrast, Adrian was far more outgoing with Sara on the occasions when he used to journey forth to Manchester to see her. Particularly amazing was that his affection did not wane after she told Carstone all she knew.

'Always on the job, our Sara,' Adrian had since quipped whenever consoling himself. 'When she wasn't selling her body, she was selling her mind.' But he wasn't quite so sanguine about the fallout from Carstone sounding the death knell for their relationship; he had pined for Sara every minute of each and every following day. Most of all, he missed the times when she was of a mind to kill two birds with one stone, the occasions when in addition to the succour she sold him she was also prepared to tolerate his sexual dysfunction—his *oddity* as he termed it—and pretend to be Heidi.

***

Adrian's career as a Russian agent could best be described as disappointing, dashing the high hopes the Soviets initially held for him. This did not sit well with some in the Soviet security apparatus and inevitably there was talk of being rid of him. The high-water mark of Adrian's spying was undoubtedly the exercise in 1963. He liked to think of it because he could still savour the taste of its success, a triumph made even sweeter by the fact that Kevin Carstone came along the next year and spoiled everything.

The 1963 accomplishment had its genesis in August 1962 when Adrian was made the director of MI6's Central America section, a backwater job of fringe importance reflecting, like the KGB, MI6's low regard of him. Adrian's appointment, nonetheless, did come at a time when the Americans had their fingers deep in the Nicaraguan pie. For the preceding six years, a moderate president had ruled the Central American country. In this relatively tolerant environment, communist elements backed by the Soviet Union had emerged. By 1962 these movements, most prominently the so-called Sandinistas, were challenging the established order in Nicaragua and threatening to destabilise America's southern sphere of influence. Alarmed at this, the US elected to provide support to the president's younger brother, a hard line pro-American individual who headed Nicaragua's National Guard. The American endgame intended for the younger man to supplant his elder sibling as president.

But October 1962 saw the advent of the Cuban missile crisis. For thirteen days the US and Soviet Union teetered on the brink of nuclear war. Eventually, the American President John F. Kennedy stared down his Soviet counterpart. On receipt of a face-saving US guarantee not to invade Cuba, the Soviets withdrew, taking their missiles with them. But privately shaken by the near calamity of an all-out nuclear conflict, Kennedy was now wary of the US being seen to overtly undermine a benign Nicaraguan presidency. Faced with the White House's concern, the CIA's solution was to enlist the assistance of MI6 to establish back channels through which support for the Nicaraguan leader's younger brother could be delivered, secretly and deniably.

MI6 was leery of the idea, fearing that one misstep could land the UK in the middle of another US–Soviet flashpoint. It tried to deflect the CIA, telling it that Central American affairs were too peripheral for MI6 to be of much assistance. But the CIA stomped its foot, knowing that as the junior partner in the Western intelligence alliance the British service really had no choice but to comply.

Somewhat irked at being railroaded, MI6 made Adrian the head of operations, when usually an abler officer would be allocated the task. And while entrusting Adrian with the job no doubt reflected MI6's frustration at being forced to do the CIA's bidding, for the KGB it was an opportunity begging to be exploited—once all in Lubyanka got over the shock of Adrian's selection, that is.

Thirty-two years on, Adrian well remembered the day in late October 1962 when he reported the unexpected development to his KGB controller.

'You've been what?' the handler asked, trying unsuccessfully to mask his disbelief.

Adrian had grown used to his controller's low expectations over the past many months of reporting to him. Even so, he stiffened, offended by the man's surprise.

'You heard me,' Adrian replied tartly. 'The CIA wants to institute regime change in Nicaragua. But what with Cuba and everything, the White House is demanding prudence. So MI6 has been asked to help. Some of our people have already gone to Nicaragua to open a station in our embassy and begin the ground work.' Adrian puffed himself up to full height, all five feet seven inches of him. That's why he'd been a tail gunner for the Australian Air Force during the war, because his size allowed him to fit into the Lancaster bomber's notoriously confined rear gunner's turret. 'I will personally be establishing networks through which cash and weapons will be funnelled to the president's younger brother.'

The lights burned late into the night in KGB headquarters on Lubyanka Square in Moscow upon receipt of the controller's flash report. For eight long years Adrian as Mendoza had been an underperforming asset. But now his good fortune had at last delivered something tangible. Debate raged. Certain hawkish elements argued this was an opportunity to expose America's perfidy and win back the high ground lost on Cuba; others countered that if another crisis came to a head it could spiral out of control.

Finally, a commanding voice spoke. It was Adrian's benefactor, Colonel Feodor Timofeyevich Kozlovsky. 'There are factors commending both arguments,' Feodor said. 'But each looks too short term. We need to take a strategic approach to Mendoza's Nicaraguan assignment.'

All around the table knew that eighteen years earlier, in 1944, the younger Feodor had escorted the agent Mendoza, then a downed Allied airman, through Nazi Germany and occupied Poland all the way to the Soviet line on the Lithuanian border. The monumental feat still sparked awe such that, save for his banishment from 1947–53 during the bureaucratic wars over the KGB's formation, people in Lubyanka invariably hung on Feodor Timofeyevich's every word.

Yet those discussing Mendoza were also aware that the KGB kopek counters, unmoved by Adrian's recent stroke of luck, were again agitating to be done with him. Few present, however, fully appreciated the primacy Feodor attached to protecting Adrian, the abiding duty seared deep within him during the 1944 epic escort exercise.

'Mendoza's elevation to MI6 Assistant Director General,' Feodor declared, directing the full force of his natural authority to defending Adrian from the latest initiative to cut him adrift, 'takes good strategic advantage of his Nicaraguan opportunity. His promotion will grant him access to MI6's most sensitive material, generating the enhanced return on investment our financial people are demanding, now and for years to come.' The post of Assistant Director General was not as grand as it sounded but it did place Adrian on the bottom rung of MI6's senior executive.

A day later, Adrian's controller instructed him to take a hands-on approach to the Nicaraguan campaign.

'Don't go sitting in the embassy issuing orders,' the Russian said. 'We want you to be seen out and about leading the operation, such that in London and Washington you become the face of it.'

Adrian gulped slightly, which his handler, a decorated war veteran, rightly interpreted as trepidation. 'You need not worry about the Sandinistas assassinating you, if that's your concern,' the controller said sharply, resisting the urge to say what he really thought, 'we will be taking steps to ensure your wellbeing.'

***

So it was that Adrian spent the first five months of 1963 in the Nicaraguan capital of Managua directing the activities of the MI6 station hastily set up in the British embassy.

The advance security assessment had forecast a volatile theatre of operations and urged extreme caution, which was code for saying: *Be careful or you could get killed.* Adrian's willingness to lead from the front, while spurning the protection of the small military unit sent to safeguard the MI6 operatives, mightily impressed his colleagues. Inevitably, as the Soviets intended, news of this daring reached Adrian's MI6 bosses in London. Adrian warmed to his task, regularly donning a white flannel suit and, as if Graham Greene's Man in Havana, travelling from the capital to meetings with shadowy figures in the distant and dangerous cities of Ciudad Antigua and Granada— dangerous of course only for those without the might of the Soviet Union at their back.

Soon the supply networks were established and functioning well. The CIA began to offer compliments with neither it nor MI6 aware the Soviets were withholding information from the Sandinistas in order that Adrian's creations should prosper. Of course, the KGB had the wit to ensure the communists infiltrated two or three of Adrian's startups, a measure designed to prevent even the keenest MI6 or CIA nose from smelling a rat. Eventually, in May 1963, the president's younger brother, aided by National Guard loyalists, deposed his elder brother as head of state.

Mission accomplished, Adrian returned to London to a warm reception. Hints were dropped that he could do well to apply for the Assistant Director General promotions soon to be adjudicated. To be sure up on the top floor of MI6 headquarters there was some surprise at Adrian's stunning success, as there had been when reports of his intrepid leadership began to filter back to London. But when the Foreign Secretary's American counterpart made mention of his pleasure with the outcome, Adrian's contribution in particular, any reservations among the MI6 management abated.

Adrian was elevated in August 1963. He spent the following weekend in Manchester with Sara, where she teased him good-naturedly for the bounce in his step. And when Adrian got defensive—he was taking himself a little seriously at the time—Sara was at pains to restore his celebratory mood. To that end, she devoted a full two hours on Sunday afternoon to pretending to be Heidi, all for the very reasonable asking price of six pounds.

***

Adrian studied the minute hand of his watch, tracking its inexorable progression towards 1 am on Sunday 27 February 1994, only to grimace and abruptly return the timepiece to his shirtsleeve. He was thinking of those heady days in August 1963 and how his time in the sun was short-lived. But there was no denying that soon enough he was back to his usual pedestrian ways, while people on the top floor could be heard muttering he'd just got lucky in Nicaragua. And then, Adrian thought, along came Carstone in 1964 and the terribly stressful time that ensued. It was probably a mistake, he decided, not to have objected after his request for defection was denied, especially once Carstone's sniffing around had turned into hot breath on the back of his neck.

But to rock the boat was not Adrian's way and in any event the error was excusable. By 1964 he was forty-two and convinced he was past his prime, even if now he acknowledged the absurdity of this. It was time and place, Adrian told himself, an unwarranted fear he was too old to start a new life in a country he had visited only the once, long ago for nine months from September 1944 until June 1945 when the Soviets returned him to the British, trained and ready to go. So after Carstone had been taken care of, Adrian stayed in place for the duration.

And just how did Adrian Ashton manage to remain an undetected Soviet spy in MI6 for over three decades? Well, as Feodor was wont to say whenever Mendoza's name arose in Soviet intelligence councils, his low-key approach was helpfully distinct from the typically flamboyant Soviet assets who had gone before him. And no question that Adrian's staid personality and everyday performance were significant factors in him going undiscovered. But to attribute his survival solely to these personal characteristics would be to ignore Feodor's key interventions, first in 1954 during a particularly tricky situation threatening to stymie Adrian's entry into MI6 and again in 1964 at the time of Carstone. In addition, of course, there was also the 1944 miracle in Nazi Germany when Feodor had prevailed against nigh on impossible odds.

Adrian, therefore, had plugged away in his usual sedate style until eventually March 1987 rolled around. MI6 rules clicked in, those mandating that officers must retire on achieving sixty-five years. Adrian's last act as an active KGB agent was to meet Valentina, his only female controller, outside St John's Wood tube station on the night he left MI6. With a tinge of faint praise, she thanked him for his service, while handing over an envelope. Adrian was not at all pleased on later counting his termination payment to find it amounted to a paltry 2,500 pounds. He thought it very light on considering he had been a faithful servant of socialism ever since his Marxist conversion at the feet of Heidi, in 1944 while hidden in the house she shared with her husband in the outer Berlin suburb of Kladow.

CHAPTER 3

The Avro Lancaster bomber H for Harry banked sharply. But too late. The German flak had caught its starboard wing, taking out both Rolls-Royce engines, causing the aircraft rapidly to destabilise. Flames licked along the wing towards the plane's fuselage illuminating the kangaroo stencilled on its forward section. 'We'll have to bail, boys,' the pilot bawled into his intercom, the urgency in his voice enhancing his unmistakably Australian twang. It was mid-February 1944. A-wing, 433 squadron, Royal Australian Air Force was aloft over Siemensstadt in the Spandau district of Berlin, its twenty-first sortie in the RAF Bomber Command raids on the German capital dubbed the Battle of Berlin.

The pilot never made it. Nor did five others of H for Harry's seven-man crew. The forward section was well ablaze by the time the plane pitched forward and started to nosedive. The poor devils had no hope. Only Adrian Ashton, the tail gunner, had sufficient time to scramble from his turret and plunge into the freezing night sky. Adrian could not have known it but by the time his parachute opened he was above the Wannsee area on Berlin's outskirts. Featuring the Greater and Lesser Wannsee Lakes along the eastern bank of the River Havel, the area was an idyllic water playground just the width of the river from the leafy Berlin suburb of Kladow, a rural hamlet a mere seventeen kilometres from the centre of the German capital.

Adrian watched his comrades perish, the Lancaster exploding in a ball of flame as it plummeted to ground off in the distance. Icy tears stung his face, his dismay turning to palpable grief. Adrian and the others in H for Harry all knew the laws of probability were working against them from the moment they lifted off that evening. But the young men were buoyant, lackadaisical and naturally optimistic in the customary Australian way. Theirs was a mutually reinforcing capacity to deny the grim reality that, after flying twenty previous missions, the crew's chances of survival reduced exponentially each time they went out.

For Adrian especially, his crewmates were more than comrades-in-arms; they were his family. Mind you, on first joining the Royal Australian Air Force, the RAAF, he didn't fit in immediately. He was an introverted boy, a product of a government-run orphanage system that had conditioned him to speak only when spoken to. But after a time, particularly once the recruits had been sorted into bomber crews to train together—H for Harry in Adrian's case—the group bond developed. Adrian came to enjoy the ironic nickname of Rowdy the others bestowed on him and the many boisterous drinking sessions that went with it. Jimmy, Pete, Bluey and Dingo were just some of the rough diamonds that Adrian grew to trust, value and love.

The birch pine forest in which Adrian came to earth was thankfully not dense. Cushioned on landing by a bed of pine needles, he lay panting on the ground amazed that somehow he had managed to escape the cramped tail gunner's turret as the blazing plane steepled out of control. He tried to tell himself to be grateful. Even so, there was no escaping the terrible loneliness and guilt that Adrian felt for surviving when the others in H for Harry had not.

Suddenly Adrian heard male voices speaking loud and excited German, causing instincts of fear to jangle. He recalled with chilling clarity the intelligence briefings at RAF Binbrook in Lincolnshire, 433 squadron's home base, warning of the threat posed to downed flyers by irate German civilians. Adrian lay as still as possible, knowing that a group of men out at this time of night would be searching for airmen lucky enough to survive being shot down. But then came the sound of a barking dog. Resignation and fatalism took over, paradoxically easing Adrian's tenseness. The search party would find him soon enough. Lying back in the pine needles and accepting that capture was inevitable, Adrian wondered if his short life was to end just one month before he turned twenty-two. In particular, he thought of Melbourne in the state of Victoria, his birthplace and Australia's southern-most mainland capital city.

***

Adrian was born in a discreet private hospital in one of Melbourne's better suburbs in March 1922—the runt of his father's litter as it turns out. Some years later he was told that his natural parents had christened him Adrian Bolton Ashton, but since died of lingering complications associated with the Spanish flu pandemic. To be sure, his birth parents had selected his given names. But Adrian never knew the surname of Ashton had been randomly allocated as a means for concealing that his father was a wealthy industrialist and his mother a housemaid at the industrialist's family home. And although the story that his birth parents were dead was fanciful, the deception was effective enough. Perhaps intuitively understanding the truth of his abandonment from a young age, Adrian seldom gave much thought as to the identity of those who conceived him.

Within an hour of his birth, Adrian was removed from his mother's breast and whisked to a grim state-run home for bastard children in the tough inner city suburb of Port Melbourne, where wet nurses weaned him throughout infancy. On turning five he was transferred to another government orphanage in Carlton close to Melbourne's general cemetery, one offering basic primary schooling. The Carlton orphanage in fact provided Adrian's earliest life memories, of eating porridge for breakfast all year round, lights out at 7 pm and bouts of bed-wetting—not to mention the teasing of other boys for his small stature, pale complexion and protruding ears.

to a responsible authority rather than beat him to death. But Adrian also knew there was a very real possibility he could fall into the hands of the Waffen-SS, the feared military arm of the Nazi Party. In which case the foreboding gnawing at him, that the end of his life was imminent, would soon be realised.

The large black and tan dog crashed through the low-set undergrowth. In the cold moonlight, Adrian could see its bared teeth. 'Britischer flieger,' he screamed, causing the dog to stop with its head inclined to one side, tongue lolling from its saliva-dripping mouth as if the animal was astonished by Adrian's revelation. All Australians flying for Bomber Command had been trained to say the German for *British airman* if captured, owing to the possibility that some German civilians might confuse Australia with Austria leading to all sorts of nasty complications involving mistaken perceptions of persons turning their back on the Fatherland.

***

Adrian had joined the RAAF in 1940, aged eighteen. For the preceding three years he'd worked as a labourer in a rope factory in the inner Melbourne suburb of Footscray. Lodging in a spartan boarding house nearby, it was a lonely time. Adrian had left Hester House a terribly damaged boy, making it difficult for him to find friends, male and most certainly female. Added to which almost all of the rope factory workers were older men with whom he had little in common. But in the absence of any alternative, Adrian stuck at it until one day out of the blue he saw a pamphlet calling for volunteers to join the RAAF.

Much to his surprise, his application was successful, a function of the fact that Adrian's size made him an ideal recruit for an air force at war and desperately short of tail gunners. For the institutionalised Adrian to again be living in dormitories with males of his own age represented a return to what he knew best and, despite the dark memories of Hester House, he relished the familiarity.

In June 1943 the seven-strong H for Harry bomber crew, Adrian its tail gunner, was posted to RAAF 433 squadron. Shortly after the young men travelled to the United Kingdom along with other squadron members, journeying first by train to Perth in Western Australia before making the perilous, radio silence flying boat dash across the Indian Ocean to Ceylon, on to Karachi—then part of British India—before finally landing exhausted in London.

Eight months on Adrian was lying on the floor of the Wannsee forest with a large black and tan Rottweiler dog standing over him. A voice called the animal to heel, leaving Adrian free to search in the dim light for a glimpse of the approaching search party. When he saw them, his heart sank; not one of the men was in uniform. There were in fact ten civilians in the group. To a man they screamed excitedly on sighting Adrian, two of them roughly pushing him into a clearing. A young, strapping man began to slap Adrian's face, his ferocity increasing with each blow. But then another man calmed the assailant, repeating the German word *informationen* as he did, revealing to Adrian that his captors wished to interrogate him.

'Sprichst du Deutsch?' the man who halted the assault said as he stepped forward from the shadows. He was older than the rest and clearly the group's leader.

'Nein,' Adrian replied, that single word exhausting his limited stock of German, obliging him to continue in his mother tongue. 'I don't speak any German.'

To Adrian's amazement, the man responded in near perfect English. 'Tell me your exact target tonight.'

'The Siemens and Halske plant in Siemensstadt,' Adrian said. It did no harm to say this. By now the Germans would be well aware of Bomber Command's intentions.

'And your name?

'Adrian Bolton Ashton, sergeant, serial number 35895, 433 squadron, Royal Australian Air Force,' Adrian offered in standard name, rank and serial number response. 'I'm actually an Australian,' he added after a pause, as if in afterthought.

The man nodded briefly, showing no surprise at Adrian's aside. 'What is the next target and when will the raid take place?'

'I don't know.'

The man turned and made a come hither motion with his hand. 'Horst,' he said. Horst was the young athlete who initially slapped Adrian. The older man muttered something in German. Horst immediately clenched his fist, drew it back as if cocking a slingshot and struck Adrian a crushing blow on the nose. The force of the punch dropped Adrian to his knees, blood dripping to the forest floor like large droplets of ink. Two men dragged him to his feet.

'I'll ask you again,' the older man said. 'When is the next raid and what is the target?'

Adrian could taste the blood leaking from his nose, and his eyes wept blow-induced tears. He was desperately fearful now. The next Bomber Command mission was likely to target Berlin's already damaged rail network in a last-ditch attempt to achieve its total destruction. And while he knew that much, on the question of timing he was less certain. Bomber Command's high casualty rates had led to a sharp reduction in the frequency of raids from the virtually nightly sorties of December 1943 and January 1944. Adrian's best guess was the next attack would take place in early March. But he was in too much pain and fear to compose an answer that gave nothing away and in the end, as his mind whirled, did not answer the question.

'Horst,' the older man commanded again after a short wait. Horst's blow this time was to Adrian's solar plexus. Adrian doubled over, writhing in pain and fighting for breath, prevented from falling to the ground only by the strong arms of the two men holding him upright.

'The Waffen-SS,' the older man whispered in Adrian's ear, 'is always appreciative when we have extracted a little information from the downed airmen we hand to them. They pay us well for our trouble. You will regret very much refusing to tell us what we want to know; the SS will not be half as civil.'

With that, the older man barked orders to his underlings. Adrian was frogmarched 100 yards from the clearing to where a lorry with an enclosed rear tray section was parked. Unceremoniously, his captors threw him into the back of the vehicle. Three men joined him, sitting on bench seats, weapons in the form of clubs and pitchforks at the ready.

'Heil Hitler,' the lorry driver yelled before climbing into the front cabin and starting the engine. The confirmation that his captors were Nazi sympathisers came as no surprise to Adrian.

CHAPTER 4

Adrian resided at Hester House in Ballarat from the age of eight, after arriving there in 1930, until 1937 when he was discharged—once a boy had completed his third year of secondary schooling he was expected to strike out alone into the world. The Victorian government had built the facility during the prosperous 1920s as a school for homeless boys. Although staffed by civil servants, from the outset it had operated along the lines of a military cadet boarding college. Apart from a matron and the headmaster's secretary, all the staff were men, mostly from uniformed services backgrounds. The boys were introduced to parade ground assemblies, marching in formation and other harsh discipline. Cold showers for wrongdoers in Ballarat's freezing winter were a much-favoured form of punishment, closely followed by endless hours of standing to lonely attention on the rain-swept parade ground. And although Adrian found he could tolerate the occasional indignity in the midst of frigid winter, it was the summer months he really hated. In particular, the flies that bred in the sheep dung on the nearby countryside tormented him, attacking his nose, ears and eyes and forever forcing him to fight for his food. This experience would later be a significant factor in his decision to remain in England after the war, that and the fact the Soviets wanted him to be their spy in MI6.

For all of Hester House's mindless discipline, however, and the misery of Ballarat's summers, over his initial four years of residence Adrian grew accustomed to the daily regime of life. He found that routine gave him structure, where previously he had none, and slowly instilled in him a sense of purpose and belonging.

But shortly after turning twelve in 1934 Adrian's world changed. A man who enjoyed the proto-military title of Corps Commander, and much authority in the eyes of the boys, called Adrian to his Hester House office. 'Now that you've embarked on your secondary schooling,' he said, 'we're thinking of training you as a stable hand. It'll be an introduction to work, for later on when you leave here.'

Adrian wasn't sure what this entailed but since there were no stables at Hester House understood it would involve activities away from the Home. 'Around horses, do you mean?' he asked.

'Well, I'm not talking about assisting in the birth of the baby Jesus,' the man replied acerbically. 'Yes,' he said more reasonably, 'around horses at the Argyll stables at Wendouree, on Sundays after morning chapel.'

Adrian knew of the nearby suburb of Wendouree, famous for its lake and botanical gardens, having been there on a handful of school excursions. He was at once excited.

'Yes please, sir,' he gushed, too enthusiastically for his own good as it transpires, 'I would love to work at the stables.'

Noting Adrian's response, the man leant back in his chair and rubbed his stomach. His business-like manner now seemed to have morphed into something sinister.

'There is a problem, though,' he said after a considered pause. 'Mr Argyll can take only one boy. Yet there are several others also eligible for the placement.' The man stroked his chin as if deep in thought while Adrian looked on, his wish to be chosen for the task causing him to ignore the way in which the man was looking at him. Finally, the man spoke. 'Perhaps if you're nice to me, I could see my way clear to select you. What do you think?'

Adrian was confused. He was always polite to the Corps Commander and wondered what the man was getting at. 'What should I do, sir?' he blurted, knowing from the moment he uttered the words it was a question he would live to regret.

'Why don't you shut the door and come and sit on the edge of the desk, here on my side? So that we can talk more easily.'

Adrian did as bid, the sense that all was not well starting to consume him. But owing to the Home's fearsome discipline, he was unable to deny the order. The man began to stroke Adrian's thigh. Frozen with fear Adrian watched mortified as his elastic-banded short trousers were slid down below his knees, while simultaneously the Corps Commander began to unbutton his trousers with his free hand. Adrian's next conscious memory was of being forcefully spun around, glimpsing as he turned a jar of Vaseline on the desk and the man's fingers dipping into it. Then followed the feeling of sticky dampness as the lubricant was applied. The urgent pushing from behind soon became excruciating pain after which the man began to grunt in increasingly beast-like snorts. How long it went on for Adrian wasn't sure. But finally the man stilled, breathing heavily with his head resting on Adrian's shoulder. Then roughly he pushed Adrian away and handed him a napkin.

'Here, you little slut,' the man rasped, his voice still hoarse with sexual desire. 'Wipe your arse. You're leaking shit, blood and custard everywhere.' As if in a trance, Adrian did as directed. 'You can start at the stables next Sunday. But if you tell anyone about this, you'll regret it for the rest of your life. Understood?'

***

In the back of the lorry in the Berlin countryside in February 1944, the battered and bruised Adrian recalled his rape as a twelve-year-old. These memories usually entered his mind like an unwelcome visitor until such time as he could suppress them. But now the flashback loomed large, vivid and immovable. With his life hanging in the balance, it seemed that no defence mechanism could obscure his sense of humiliation.

By association, Adrian thought of the bullying prefects at Hester House, older boys who delighted in telling him he was nothing more than a discarded bastard child. Much as with his rape, however, Adrian had always denied the truth staring him in the face, a subconscious device to avoid the stark reality of his rejection. But with the emotional trauma of his boyhood somehow bared by his capture by the Germans, the festering wound that was the dual indignities of his rape and abandonment had become a deep and poisonous well of resentment.

Anger tore at Adrian's heart. He raged at his birth parents, his unknown conceivers who deposited him into a state-run orphanage system, one unable to protect him from debilitating spoilage before spitting him out like a piece of unwanted garbage. He also railed against the fascist Nazis poised to torture and eventually kill him. But for all that, Adrian saved his most profoundly bitter hatred for the smugly superior Andrew Argyll, Chantelle's dressage training partner and the son of the owner of the Ballarat stables.

Adrian did not see much of Chantelle initially. She was older than him by five or so years and rode trackwork Mondays to Fridays, exercising the horses that Andrew's father trained to race. It was in the period after Adrian's thirteenth birthday that Chantelle first started to appear on Sundays, when she and Andrew began to practise jumps routines on a specially constructed course near the stables. Adrian would watch her from a distance, never fully able to understand the tingling he felt. By then the shape of her bustline was prominently pronounced, the sight of it leaving Adrian feeling quite stupefied. And if that wasn't bad enough, Chantelle's rounded flanks now filled out her riding jodhpurs with such perfection as to often cause him to grasp at his genitals over the top of his work fatigues. This only compounded matters. From day one, and daily thereafter, the parsons at Hester House chapel had told the boys that to touch their penis other than for urinating and washing was guaranteed to send them blind and condemn them to a life in hell.

Adrian's early adolescent infatuation would normally have ebbed away in time. But fate was destined to burn Chantelle into his psyche, indelibly so. It all stemmed from a time in 1936 when Adrian, by now fourteen, was in his last year at Hester House. It was a Sunday and he had just finished at the stables for the day. But not long into his trek back to Ballarat the wind picked up and rain threatened. Adrian made the snap decision to return for the old waterproof jacket he wore when working. Nearing the stables, he thought he could hear a whispered conversation. At first he imagined it was the wind, but then fragments of talking and muffled laughter became clearer.

Creeping inside, Adrian was astonished to find jodhpurs just like Chantelle's strewn on the ground, next to which lay a pair of women's white briefs also seemingly cast aside in haste. Adrian stared at the underwear, revulsion and lust rising in him in equal measure as the terrible truth began to dawn. Next thing he knew, he was gazing in fascinated horror at the rise and fall of the set of bare buttocks belonging to the thrusting male spreadeagled on top of Chantelle. Nausea rose in Adrian's windpipe spurred by Andrew Argyll's animalistic grunts of pleasure, sounds that distressingly reminded him of the rapist Corps Commander's raw gratification and the wicked pain it inflicted. Adrian watched on, trying to avert his eyes but finding he could not until freed by the briefly intense but pleasurable release of claggy moistness into his underwear.

The revulsion and lust Adrian experienced in the Ballarat stables were to become scarring memories. These were harrowingly incompatible forces: revulsion because thereafter it prevented him from ever having conventional sexual intercourse with a woman—the image of Chantelle's violation was too powerfully reminiscent of his own; and lust because the same image also stirred in Adrian an irresistible sexual need. Little did Adrian know that both bugbears would later form the basis of his sexual dysfunction, the blight on his life he came to call his *oddity*.

***

The shout of a German voice interrupted Adrian's painful recollection. One of his guards in the tray section was leaning around the outside of the lorry speaking to the driver in the front cabin. The vehicle began to slow. Soon it ground to a halt. Next there was a flurry of conversation in German involving the lorry driver and persons apparently on the road impeding the vehicle's progress. Torchlight was played inside the lorry's rear section. In the weak light Adrian could see fear and confusion on the faces of his captors. Shortly after strong arms vaguely smelling of fish dragged him from the vehicle, where he stood confused and unsure what was happening. A flash of light lit up the night sky, barely a second ahead of a loud bang. The rattle of small arms fire briefly followed and then there was silence.

Through the haze of the weapons discharge, Adrian could make out a man in a black hood urgently waving his hand back and forward on the fulcrum of his wrist, urging Adrian to run to him. Adrian hesitated, reluctant to leave the lorry until the man's intentions were clear. Exasperated by the delay, the man gestured into the dark. Two figures, both also hooded, moved forward, one lifting Adrian under the armpits, the other by the feet. The stunned Adrian did not struggle. As the men carried him into the birch forest, Adrian could see several shapes on the ground, one of whom was Horst, the strong young fellow who had twice punched him. An old hunting rifle lay by the German's side, blood seeping from a gaping wound in his chest.

Adrian was placed in a small cart that was usually horse-drawn, and covered with a canvas top. The two men who had carried him each took up one of the shafts. Two others walked behind, after a time taking their turn at hauling the improvised carriage. For Adrian, it was an uncomfortable two hours until the sound of lapping water could be heard. Next thing he was out of the cart and into a creaking dinghy. The party of five, Adrian and the four men who abducted him, headed north rowing across the Greater Wannsee Lake and into the River Havel, stopping periodically to listen for sounds of pursuit. It was another two hours before the river crossing was negotiated and they were moored at a timber jetty leading to a weathered on-shore boat shed. Adrian could not have known it but they were in the outer Berlin suburb of Kladow.

A sinewy man of about fifty wearing a Greek fiddler's cap was waiting in the darkened boat shed, his face smeared with what appeared to be camouflage paint. He silently handed money to each of Adrian's rescuers. One after another, at intervals of roughly five minutes, the four men exited the boat shed and disappeared into the night. Alone with Adrian, the man in the fiddler's cap held a forefinger to his lips. Placing his cheek on the back of his hands compressed at the palms to mimic a pillow, the man signalled Adrian should sleep. Adrian was exhausted and needed little encouragement, soon falling into a restless slumber.

On waking with the dawn, Adrian wondered momentarily where he was. The man in the Greek fiddler's cap who greeted him on arrival the night before sat on a chair near the boat shed door, apparently having kept guard all night. Again he held his forefinger to his lips commanding Adrian to be quiet before giving him some bread and a tumbler of cold coffee to go with it. An hour later the high-pitched whine of a piston engine announced the arrival of a small car, following which a man and a woman entered the boat shed. The male was tall and seemed about fifty, the woman possibly a little younger, of stocky build and no-nonsense deportment. Both wore hats pulled low over their eyes as a means for obscuring their features from full view.

A hushed conversation in German ensued. The woman proceeded to bathe Adrian's face, cleaning away the caked on dry blood caused by the blows he received while in the custody of the civilian search party. She left as a set of workman's clothes was produced into which the two men remaining motioned Adrian to change.

Adrian worried about being dressed in civilian attire. His uniform, in theory at least, offered a modicum of protection as an enemy combatant. But if found in civilian clothes he would be classified as a spy and summarily executed. He shrugged internally. His captors the previous night intended to hand him to the Waffen-SS. Had that eventuated, he would have been killed in any event. The tall man who arrived with the stocky woman briefly inspected Adrian before nodding curtly. It was time to go.

Adrian cautiously left the boat shed, fearful as to what awaited. He was ushered into the back of a Volkswagen sporting headlamps that gave the vehicle the resemblance of a startled bug and told to keep low. The car had been bought on the black market specifically to ferry Adrian about. It was probably stolen but the tall man had not bothered to ask. The trip took around twenty minutes, their destination a house of unimaginative design set in wooded grounds, a square box of rendered brick rising two levels to an apexed, slate-topped roof.

'Quickly,' the man ordered in accented English, once the car was inside the dwelling's perimeter and hidden from view. 'Follow me and don't stop to look about.'

Adrian was taken to a basement room and told to wait. Locking the door, the man returned upstairs where he peered furtively through the two large windows situated on either side of the house's front entrance. Satisfied that the arrival of the Volkswagen and its young passenger had not aroused interest, the man returned to Adrian in the basement, this time wearing a bandanna wrapped around his face.

'Klaus,' he said extending his hand, deliberately not revealing his surname.

Adrian apprehensively took Klaus's hand. 'My name is Adrian Ashton,' he said. 'I'm a flyer with the Royal Australian Air Force.'

'You are not British?' Klaus asked sharply in a mixture of surprise and alarm.

'No, I'm Australian,' Adrian replied evenly. 'My squadron flies for RAF Bomber Command.' But then his nerve deserted him. 'Why did you save me from the civilian group taking me to the Waffen-SS?' he blurted. 'Who are you? Where are we?'

Underneath his face mask, Klaus smiled briefly. The fact that Adrian was flying for the British had put his fears to rest. 'So many questions,' he said philosophically. 'All you need to know for now is that we are a group of German citizens opposed to Hitler and his murderous thugs.'

'And me?' Adrian asked warily.

'Our aim,' Klaus said, 'is to return you to England so that you might continue to fight the Nazis.' He rubbed his chin over his bandanna. 'But when that will be possible is not currently clear.'

Klaus, in fact, was a German communist. The group he headed, of necessity, indulged only in low-key resistance against the Nazis, activities like distributing anti-Nazi literature to factory workers. But if this made true his claim to belong to a group of Germans opposed to Hitler, his suggestion that his people would seek to facilitate Adrian's return to England was not.

Klaus's lie was all to do with a man called Ernst Thälmann, who was the leader of the German Communist Party and at one time a member of the German parliament, the Reichstag. But in March 1933, shortly after Hitler became Germany's Chancellor, Thälmann was arrested in a purge of parliamentary communists. Now eleven years on, Klaus had recently learned that Thälmann was about to be executed, the news delivered to him a week ago by a young German woman he'd never met before.

CHAPTER 5

At the time when Klaus received advice of Ernst Thälmann's impending execution he was taking coffee and butterbrezel at a café a short walk from his *zigarrehaus*—the tobacconist shop in central Berlin he owned jointly with his elder brother. Klaus was startled when the young woman sat at his table, especially as in his experience such pretty ladies usually kept their distance from older men. And when the woman whispered her name was Ilsa and she was delivering an urgent message from Moscow, Klaus's surprise became gut-wrenching fear.

'Ernst Thälmann,' Ilsa muttered, 'is soon to be executed. The order came personally from Hitler himself. You are instructed to capture a downed British airman as soon as possible. When that is done you should leave a chalk mark on the bottom step of the stairs leading into the Hausvogteiplatz U-Bahn. You will then receive instructions to hand the flyer to others who will contact the Waffen-SS to negotiate his trade in return for sparing Thälmann's life.'

Klaus could barely believe his ears. He tried to protest that even were he able to carry out such an order, he had no safe place where he could keep an airman until passing him to others.

'The direction has come from Ulreich,' Ilsa said, anxious to leave, 'with Stalin's express approval. You'll have to find a way.'

Werner Ulreich was a senior German communist, second-ranked only to Ernst Thälmann. Unlike Thälmann, Ulreich had managed to avoid arrest after Hitler banned the communist party in 1933.

He fled to Russia, where he now resided at the Lux Hotel on Gorky Street in central Moscow. The Lux was home to a plethora of exiled communists from around the world, those lucky enough to have escaped the purges of the late 1930s by the paranoid Soviet Premier, Joseph Stalin.

***

On returning to his home in Kladow, Klaus shared his dilemma with his wife, Heidi. It was she who later cleaned the caked blood from Adrian's face at the boat shed where he spent the night after being whisked from the clutches of the German civilian search party.

'You can't very well ignore a direction that carries Stalin's endorsement,' Heidi declared when Klaus canvassed the option of doing nothing. 'He is the leader of world socialism. These are difficult times, certainly. But if we are to serve the cause, we must have the courage to do what is necessary.'

In his own way Klaus was just as committed to socialism as Heidi. But he was somewhat more cautious. 'So what do we do,' he asked, 'to safeguard against the airman identifying us as and when he is handed to the Waffen-SS?'

Heidi thought about this. 'Put yourself in the shoes of the Nazis,' she said finally. 'Not for one second would the Waffen-SS expect us to keep a British airman hidden in our own home. The same applies if we use our real Christian names.'

'But when the airman discovers he has been used as a pawn,' Klaus interrupted, 'he will readily tell the Nazis all he knows about us.'

'Yes, that is true,' Heidi replied calmly. 'But remember the flyer will be with us only for a couple of days, kept locked in our basement and be out of sight. If we hide our faces, he will have virtually no idea where he is or who we are.' She watched Klaus, who was swallowing nervously. 'Therefore,' Heidi continued, 'he will give the Nazis only first names and vague descriptions, and an even vaguer outline of where he has been.'

'Surely that would still be enough to place us in danger?' Klaus protested, his agitation causing him to stand and pace the room.

Heidi held up her hand. 'Not necessarily,' she said. 'As I say, the airman will have little to go on. And even then, he won't be believed because the Waffen-SS always treats the first answer as a lie. Under Nazi torture, the airman will actually be forced to nominate false names and locations. By the time the Waffen-SS accepts he is telling the truth, both he and his memory will be further impaired. He might well be dead. Either way, we'll be protected.'

Klaus didn't know what to think. But he did accept it was his responsibility to carry out the task given to him by Werner Ulreich, especially as it had Joseph Stalin's backing. That onus eventually led him warily to accept Heidi's reasoning, while all the while the voice in his head was telling him that her thinking owed more to ideological staunchness than it did clever reverse psychology. It was, therefore, perhaps fortuitous that fate should contrive never to put Heidi's theory to the test.

***

That night Klaus slept fitfully, weighing Heidi's argument and wrestling with how best he might arrange the pick up. And when he did get to sleep in the early hours of the morning, his dreams were dominated by images of Ilsa, the young German woman who had made contact with him.

Naturally enough, Ilsa wasn't Ilsa. Her name was Christel Metternich and her bloodlines extended back to the eighteenth century and the noble House of Metternich. Christel was twenty-eight and had a twin sister, Wilhelmine. The twins hailed from Kiel where their family held a substantial stake in the Krupp shipyard. As Nazi supporters, the Metternichs had benefitted greatly from the contracts awarded to Krupp by the German Navy. The girls had joined the Hitler Youth in the 1930s, later training as nurses and later still volunteering for deployment to the Eastern Front.

It was at the battle of Stalingrad in Russia that things changed for Christel and Wilhelmine. Hitler regarded Stalingrad's capture as one of the key dominoes needing to fall in order to win the war, both for its strategic value and the propaganda coup entailed in taking the city bearing Stalin's name. In their own way, the Soviets agreed with this assessment. They fought with unimaginable ferocity, while all the while enduring unthinkable hardships. But they prevailed. By February 1943 the invaders were demoralised and exhausted. Christel and Wilhelmine were among the vast number of Germans to become Russian prisoners of war after the surrender.

The twins were lucky initially. Separated from their male colleagues, they were handed to a female Soviet guard detachment. True, they were beaten and given little to eat. But they avoided the rapes, and worse, regularly inflicted on German female prisoners—for a time at least. Frightened, hungry and huddling together like fearful kittens, Christel and Wilhelmine were bundled onto trucks along with other captured women—mostly Romanians and Ukrainians who had sided with the Germans—and driven nearly 500 kilometres to the southeast, to Rostov-on-Don. The Soviets had wrested Rostov-on-Don from the Germans around the time of the Stalingrad surrender. Despite widespread damage, the city's railhead was still functional. It was from there that the female captives were to be sent north to labour camps.

On reaching Rostov-on-Don, however, Christel and Wilhelmine's luck ran out when the female guard detachment handed the women prisoners to a Tatar unit. To a man, these were fearless warriors who had witnessed—and perpetrated—unspeakable depravities. Any shred of humanity the men might once have had was long gone.

In a matter of minutes, the younger women were separated from their older companions. The rapes commenced. Christel screamed as Wilhelmine was torn from her arms. Held by two laughing soldiers, she watched horrified as Wilhelmine was stripped naked and forced to lie on the frozen cobblestones. A man mounted Wilhelmine, followed by another, and then another. One of the two soldiers holding Christel wore a bayonet in a scabbard attached at his waist. As Christel slumped forward, exhausted and distraught, the men relaxed their restraining grip, engrossed in Wilhelmine's rape and content to let Christel kneel on the ground. Sensing their inattention, Christel summoned her last reserves of strength and courage to snatch the bayonet from the man's belt. Leaping forward like the gymnast she once was, she rushed to the man currently on top of Wilhelmine and buried the blade deep into his shoulder.

The Tatar soldiers shouted in alarm. One stepped forward and knocked Christel senseless with the butt of his rifle. She lay face down next to her naked sister, blood gushing from a cut above her left ear. 'Let's fuck the whore,' the soldier who clubbed Christel shouted to his comrades. 'Then I'm going to cut the bitch's throat.' By now the man Christel had stabbed was on his feet and clutching at his shoulder wound. With his trousers around his ankles, his limp penis was visible for all to see. Frustrated, angry and embarrassed by his predicament, the man hoisted up his garb and kicked Christel hard in the head before slumping to the ground, splitting open her cheekbone and causing a huge black bruise to form.

The wolf pack began to rip at Christel's clothing, only to freeze in war-intuited caution when the sound of a pistol shot rang out. Christel's attackers turned to see a man dressed in a NKVD major's uniform. The NKVD was a forerunner to the KGB and responsible at the time for Soviet Russia's foreign intelligence collection. It operated under Stalin's feared personal direction and exercised absolute authority.

The major was tall and fair, about thirty and held a smoking pistol aloft. But for his uniform, he could easily have passed for a German. After the triumph at Stalingrad, a Soviet plan had been hatched to insert agents into Germany who would assist in laying the groundwork for the ultimate prize, the Red Army's capture of Berlin. The NKVD major had been tasked with the job of finding suitable recruits from among the multitude of captured Germans. 'Place blankets around both women,' he ordered the soldiers, 'and bring them to my quarters.'

Christel and Wilhelmine were taken to the old rail administration headquarters. The building was heavily fortified and guarded by a contingent of hard-faced NKVD soldiers. Only those invited there could ever hope to gain access. The twins were placed in the former ticketing office, now divided into two sections. At one end stood a wooden desk with a field telephone on top. Three chairs complemented the desk, two on one side for visitors and one opposite made more comfortable by a cushion designed to support the occupant's back. Off to the side, files were stacked high in an open bureau. At the far end of the area a neatly made up army cot sat next to a bench on which a jug and ceramic bowl used for washing could be seen.

Christel and Wilhelmine sat on the two chairs across the table from the major. Female NKVD soldiers gripped their shoulders from behind holding them upright. The major placed the girls' military identification cards in front of them. 'Christel?' he enquired politely. It was all Christel could do to move her hand. 'The protector,' the major said in flawless German, the brief smile coming to his face disappearing as quickly as it had arrived. Without another word, he walked to the office door and barked a command in Russian. Within a minute, soldiers appeared with field cots identical to the camp bed on which the major slept. This was followed by the entry of a man wearing a white laboratory coat. The stethoscope around his neck revealed him to be a physician.

Still wrapped in their blankets, Christel and Wilhelmine were laid on the field cots. The doctor began to examine the twins, applying plaster bandages to the lacerations on Christel's head and cheekbone before liberally dispensing saline wash in and around Wilhelmine's private regions. On completion, he reported crisply to the major. The blond man swept the upturned palm of his right hand in an arc inviting the doctor to proceed. Taking a large silver injecting needle, the medico rolled Christel onto her stomach whereupon he lifted the covering blanket and injected her in the buttock.

The doctor departed. Shortly after, Christel began to feel the fog of pain lift. The major worked on a file at his desk, occasionally glancing up to see how Christel was faring. When he judged she was sufficiently awake, he directed his female soldiers to return her to the same chair on which she sat previously. This time Christel could sit upright without help.

The major stroked his cheeks with his index finger and thumb, as was his habit. 'The injection,' he told Christel in German, 'will wear off quickly. Listen carefully to what I say.' Christel did not answer—she had no alternative. 'My offer,' the major said, 'is to arrange for your return to the German lines as one of the lucky few who have escaped death or capture. The current injuries to your head and face will be helpful in that regard. But should you accept my proposal, you will recover soon enough once in Germany. And when you are well, you will seek an appointment to a military hospital in Berlin where there is always a shortage of nurses with your experience in treating war wounds. It is in Berlin where I intend that you will begin to work for us.'

'And my sister?'

The major raised his hand, causing Christel to shrink in fear. 'Do not interrupt me,' he ordered quietly. 'But since you ask, your twin sister stays here. Provided you serve us faithfully she will be well treated. But if you betray us in any way, shape or form she will be executed.' The major smiled resignedly. 'Although you probably don't know it,' he said, 'the defeat at Stalingrad marks the start of the German downfall.'

He looked at Christel's shocked face, silently marvelling at the effectiveness of the Nazi brainwashing. 'Yes, that's right. Despite what you've been told to think, Hitler and his disciples are done for. One day soon the mighty Red Army will take Berlin. As such, if your misplaced loyalty to the Reich compels you to go to the German authorities, please understand we will kill not only your sister but eventually you and the rest of your family as well.' The major stared at Christel with hard eyes, wanting to be sure she understood her position.

'May I ask a question?' she said timidly.

'One only,' the major replied. 'After that you need to make your decision.'

'How am I to work for you from Berlin? How do I know what I need to do and how should I report to you?'

'That's really three questions,' the major said with something approaching good humour. 'And I don't propose to answer any of them until I have your decision. If you wish, you and your sister can take your chances out there with my Tatarstan comrades. The alternative is to agree to become our agent in Berlin, in which case both you and Wilhelmine will have some chance of surviving.'

The choice before Christel was obvious. But she was a Nazi and like most Nazis more than a little fanatical. She wrestled briefly with her dilemma.

Major Feodor Timofeyevich Kozlovsky of the NKVD's Foreign Directorate, however, had chosen wisely. The files captured at the German field hospital spoke volumes as to Christel's Nazi credentials and, moreover, revealed she was Wilhelmine's identical twin, and the senior of the pair by one hour.

Feodor had struck pay dirt. As a behavioural science scholar, with postgraduate qualifications from a university in Frankfurt no less, he had long been fascinated by the study of twins. He knew that in the case of identical twins, more often than not the elder was the protector. This made Christel and Wilhelmine the very thing for which Feodor was searching. Staring impassively at Christel's sad face, he showed no emotion when finally she voiced her agreement to work for the Soviets.

CHAPTER 6

Back in his Notting Hill flat, Adrian recalled how for nearly three months he heard nothing more from the investigative journalist, Roger Hardwicke. With a yearning that had grown with each passing day, he willed for Hardwicke to be an empty threat, this despite his refusal to read Feodor's letter received prior to Christmas for fear of its content. But three days ago, on Thursday 24 February 1994, an unsigned note on plain paper arrived, crushing his vain hope. *The game's up Ashton*, Hardwicke's message read. *We're publishing next Sunday. I'll deliver a freshly printed copy of the Exegesis to your door by 6 am. Enjoy prison life, cocksucker.*

At the time Adrian was too disconsolate to give much thought as to where or from whom Roger Hardwicke had obtained his corroboration for Feodor's sworn statement; all that mattered was he had it. As it happens, the US ambassador in London at the time of Carstone was dead. Hardwicke discovered this on a cold Boston morning in December 1993. But the trip to Boston wasn't a complete waste of time.

'Charles Kilbay,' the diplomat's widow said as she and Hardwicke sipped tea, 'was an embassy colleague of whom Samuel spoke regularly. Sam and Charles were with this Kevin Carstone the night Carstone supposedly committed suicide. Sam said Carstone swore blue that the allegation of him assaulting a hooker in Manchester was a Soviet subterfuge. But when Sam and Charles went to the British authorities they refused to listen to them.'

The conversation meandered on, Hardwicke content to let the widow have her head. Eventually, he steered the discussion back to Charles Kilbay.

'He went rogue, you know,' the widow confided, now gossiping. 'Ran off with some coffee-coloured floozy from the Caribbean.' Many sly questions and a day later, Hardwicke exited the airport terminal in the Trinidad capital, Port of Spain. Charles Kilbay, the ambassador's widow had divulged, was the head of the CIA station in the American embassy in London at the time of Kevin Carstone's death.

A taxi took Roger Hardwicke to his destination, a white-painted timber house built for the stifling heat in the traditional colonial way. It was located adjacent to the famous Queen's Park savannah. A beautiful woman of about forty with flawless skin and a full-mouthed smile answered the door. 'Surely, sir,' she said cheerfully when Hardwicke asked to speak to Mr Charles Kilbay.

Charlie Kilbay, as he liked to be known these days, had his long grey hair pulled back in a ponytail. He wore an old Hawaiian shirt, board shorts and was barefooted. Over chilled coconut water, after declining a shot of vodka to go with it, Hardwicke volunteered he was investigating the death of Kevin Carstone for his newspaper. He did so on the pretext of an anonymous tip-off alleging British maladministration in the matter of Carstone's suicide, when in fact Hardwicke's spur was the ambassador's widow recounting how Kilbay was particularly disquieted by the British ready acceptance that Carstone had died by his own hand.

Kilbay was not unfriendly but a reflex habit of his secret working life compelled him to speak only on condition of anonymity. His pent-up frustration, however, was soon evident.

'You don't believe Carstone committed suicide?' Hardwicke asked softly after a time, his relaxed delivery belying the tension engendered by the question, that causing him to edge forward on his seat.

Kilbay scratched his head, choosing not to answer directly. 'There was this hooker in Manchester called Sara who Carstone interviewed one night in February 1964. No one knew her real surname; Carstone said she used Lnu, as in three letters. In the intelligence game LNU stands for last name unknown. Carstone claimed he was with her the entire night, questioning her about an MI6 officer she serviced, a guy called Adrian Ashton.' Kilbay smiled wryly. 'I'm guessing you know of Ashton and his history with the Agency?' Hardwicke granted that he did. 'It was Ashton who gave Sara the Lnu surname,' Kilbay continued. 'At first, he pretended to be a claims clerk with Lloyd's of London. But according to Carstone, Ashton later bragged to Sara that he was a Soviet mole in MI6.' Kilbay shrugged. 'Back in 1964, though, Sara's line of work made her an unreliable witness when you start talking legal proof. That was the MI6 argument, that any defense attorney worth their salt would have her evidence ruled inadmissible on character grounds quicker than you could blink.'

'And what about the allegation Carstone was elsewhere in Manchester that night, where he savagely beat another prostitute within an inch of her life? His billfold was found at the scene.'

'Yeah, yeah it was, but Carstone assured the ambassador and me it had been planted there by the Soviets to protect their agent, Adrian Ashton. Carstone stuck real rigid to his alibi that he was with Sara at the time the unfortunate girl was having the crap belted out of her. Frankly, I believed him.'

'But didn't the victim identify Carstone?'

'She did,' Kilbay acknowledged with a deep sigh. 'That was another reason why the Brits didn't investigate. They said the ID and the fact that Carstone left a hand-written suicide note proved the case against him.' Kilbay's brow furrowed at the memory of the British inaction. 'Early the following week,' he said, 'I examined Carstone's suicide note containing, among other things, his confession that he concocted the Ashton spying allegations as a smokescreen for his sexual perversity.' The slow shake of Kilbay's head was an admission of long-held uncertainty. 'The note looked genuine for sure and it did pass our checking mechanism. And there *was* mutual dislike between the two.'

'Did anybody question this Sara?'

Kilbay laughed sourly. 'MI6 didn't bother because they figured it was a waste of time for the reasons I just outlined. We in the CIA station in the embassy were in a difficult position. Your government had a standing rule that we were not to go near any British citizens, no exceptions. As such, our namby-pamby diplomats were telling us we had no jurisdiction to speak to Sara and to leave her to the local cops.' Kilbay pulled a face. 'So I had to bide my time. It was nearly a month before I was able to get up to Manchester.'

'Did you find her?' Hardwicke asked, just a tad too eagerly.

'Sure I did,' Kilbay retorted, momentarily annoyed that Hardwicke should doubt he would have. 'But not at the Dumbrille Hotel, which Carstone said was her base. A Dumbrille bellhop who came across with the help of a little inducement told me that something had scared her away from her usual beat and how she was now working the bars in the Northern Quarter.'

'So, what happened when you found her?'

'She ducked for cover. Conceded she once had a client called Adrian Ashton but deliberately used the past tense. Said she knew nothing about him; he was just another Joe. "Mutual decision," was all she would say when I asked why she was no longer seeing him. The way she was dodging around the mere mention of Adrian Ashton's name convinced me it was her past dealing with him that was scaring her.'

'And Carstone? What did she say about Carstone?'

'"Was he a sailor?" she asks when I give her his description. "I see lots of American sailors." I say no he wasn't lady and tell her she knows he wasn't. She then gets perky and starts cussing me.' Kilbay turned the palms of his hands upright. 'It was as plain as day I was wasting my time. Like I said, she was scared and weren't saying diddly-squat. Case over.'

And that was that. Kilbay and Hardwicke walked into the heat of the day, the former CIA man flagging down a taxi for the Englishman.

A vehicle blaring reggae music pulled up driven by a man wearing a Rastafarian beanie.

Hardwicke made to climb into the rear passenger seat only to turn back to Kilbay. 'I found your candour back there surprising, Mr Kilbay,' he said, inclining his head towards the house. 'Even if it was off the record, former intelligence officers are seldom so open with journalists like me.'

Kilbay thought about this. 'To be perfectly honest, I didn't like Kevin Carstone,' he said eventually. 'But when the CIA accepted the British finding on his suicide, I felt an injustice had been done, and still do. More to the point, Kevin died on my watch. I do believe the Soviets killed him and I also believe this Adrian Ashton was a Soviet agent—no Kim Philby mind, but a Soviet spy all the same. I'll take those beliefs with me to the grave. Good luck, Mr Hardwicke. I hope you can find Sara Lnu and get more out of her than I could.'

***

Arriving late into London, Hardwicke went to bed restlessly trying to fend off jet lag and the disagreeable thought he might have to publish the Adrian Ashton story using Charles Kilbay's unattributable beliefs as collateral for Feodor Kozlovsky's allegations. Still awake in the early hours, and desperate for the peace of mind needed to get to sleep, he pledged to settle for nothing less than a fully attributable source publicly declaring Ashton a traitor, and how that person had to be Sara Lnu. Only then would his investigation be the international sensation he so badly wanted it to be.

But four hours later, Hardwicke woke to the cold reality it was nearly thirty years since the Carstone incident. With that, his resolve failed him. Many of the people who knew Sara would be dead, have left Manchester or have failing memories, perhaps even Sara herself. 'There goes the British Press Award,' Hardwicke fumed bitterly, now convinced he would never find Sara, 'along with all the other kudos coming my way and the fucking job offer from *The Times*.'

Things did not improve on reaching *The Sunday Exegesis* office. 'Boss wants to see you,' the girl said bluntly. She had short black hair, tattoos and nose piercing, and was the editor's assistant. She had been waiting at Hardwicke's desk.

'And a very good morning to you too,' Hardwicke replied caustically. The girl walked off. 'Cunt,' she said as she went.

'What, pray tell, is this?' *The Sunday Exegesis* editor asked aggressively. The hardest of hard-bitten characters, he was holding an American Express credit card statement and had ruled a red line under one of the entries.

'I had to go to Trinidad at short notice,' Hardwicke said wearily. 'The flights were full but for first class. I used the corporate Amex to ensure I got the last remaining seat.'

The editor stared at Hardwicke, clearly unimpressed. 'And what did we find there in dear old Port of Spain,' he asked tweely, 'to justify this excess?' It was a rhetorical question because the editor was aware that Hardwicke had been chasing vital supporting evidence for the Adrian Ashton story. And like Hardwicke, he also understood the massive journalistic coup it would be to expose a long-time Soviet spy in MI6.

'You know as well as me that I spoke to the CIA fellow in whom Carstone confided just hours before he died.'

'I also know that all you got was an opinion, a hunch,' the editor interjected tersely. 'I've a good mind to spike this story unless we can get unimpeachable corroborating evidence. We risk being sued if we're not careful.'

'Well, we've got the Russian's sworn statement,' Hardwicke replied, 'this Feodor Kozlovsky. Surely that's worth something?'

'It is,' the editor agreed. 'And the fact that he took no money in return for making the statement is also a big help.' The editor looked keenly at Hardwicke. 'But why did he do that? Could it be he was just seeking revenge on an intelligence rival?'

Hardwicke shook his head, unable to answer either question. 'It took some time to find him,' he said instead. 'He wasn't very talkative at first. But once I showed him the KGB archive material and he took a good look at it, he began to open up, obviously convinced to change his mind by what he had read. His exact words were: "I'm eighty-two and dying and don't want to go into eternity with Mendoza fighting Adelaida for a place in my heart. It's now time to rescue Mendoza from his pain." I'm fucked if I know what he was on about but didn't want to interrupt him when he started to spill his guts. So spill his guts he did, all the way to the Moscow District Court.'

'Yet you never found out who Adelaida was.' It was a statement not a question. 'Perhaps Adelaida was another KGB spy?' Neither Roger Hardwicke nor his editor would know that Adelaida was Feodor Kozlovsky's wife, murdered by the Nazis in 1938. Nor would they ever learn that Adelaida was the daughter of an Argentine family who migrated to Germany before the war, a family that hailed from the west Argentine city of Mendoza.

'Nope,' Hardwicke said. 'When I asked him, he said no questions on Adelaida. So I shut up and he didn't mention the name again. He just wanted to give me chapter and verse on Ashton.'

The editor grimaced and put the credit card form aside before briefly staring at Hardwicke. 'Go to Manchester and start the search for this Sara, Roger. Find her, wherever she is in the world. The story will be defining for us both if we tell it properly. Find Sara Lnu and get her on the record.' The editor's eyes narrowed and became ice cold. 'I can only afford to give you to the end of January. Do absolutely whatever is necessary.'

Roger Hardwicke needed no encouragement to play dirty. But there were risks associated with unethical behaviour, not least censure from the peak press bodies that handed out awards for journalistic excellence. Fruitless weeks followed as Hardwicke tread fine lines—as he feared, it had all been too long ago.

By the end of January 1994, Hardwicke was desperate enough to throw ethical caution to the wind, figuring he had nothing to lose. The classified advertisement he placed in the *Manchester Evening News* indicated that the executors of a deceased estate were seeking to locate a Miss Sara Lnu. The use of the acronym for *last name unknown*, Lnu, Sara's bestowed surname, was designed to tell her the enquiry related to Adrian Ashton and the hook was the implication of a bequest in the offing.

Waiting anxiously in a Manchester hotel room, Hardwicke was as relieved as he was elated to take a call on the telephone number listed in his public notice. Sara was still in the city, alive but not so well. An hour later Hardwicke was on the fourth floor of a hospice on Oldham Road. The sign on the room's door indicated sponsorship by the Polish Association of Manchester.

Sara Lnu was sixty-one, ravaged by breast cancer and in the final days of her life. 'I am Loda,' she said weakly. 'This is my daughter, Lidia.' A pale young woman in her twenties with black rings around her reddened eyes smiled sadly. Sara's brief glance at her daughter was clearly intended to warn Hardwicke that the younger woman was unaware of her previous profession.

Hardwicke was in his element when in the gutter. 'I wonder if you could give us a moment,' he said, smiling apologetically at Lidia, the daughter. 'Your mother and I need to discuss a sensitive matter,' he explained, as if protecting confidences, but in truth needing to ensure there were no witnesses to his discussions with Sara. 'I hasten to add that none of this reflects poorly on Loda, not in the slightest. It concerns certain historical admissions made by another party that to her great credit your Mum has kept quiet about for many years.'

Only when Lidia was out of earshot did Hardwicke sit close to Sara's bed. 'I'm here concerning the late Adrian Ashton,' he whispered, noting Sara's shock at his lie purporting Adrian to be dead. 'After I leave, tell your daughter you knew Ashton when he worked for Lloyd's of London. Tell her we discussed an insurance fraud that arose in 1963 when you temped for Ashton during a stint he did up here.'

This time Sara's eyes flashed misplaced gratitude, telling Hardwicke his prey was now entrapped.

'After I saw the advert,' Sara gasped, 'I told Lidia you contacted me rather than the other way around. She knows nothing of my past as Sara Lnu. Is Adrian really dead?'

'Yes he is,' Hardwicke fabricated without qualm. 'His will names you as the sole beneficiary. But the bequest is subject to you formally swearing that Ashton was a Soviet spy in MI6. He requested that condition on his deathbed. Guilty conscience, I believe.'

Sara's being in a ward sponsored by a Polish charity told Hardwicke she was destitute. He closed in for the kill. 'The money will provide for your loved ones.'

Sara began to cry. 'I am so worried about Lidia. She is an introverted girl who misses her father terribly. Tomasz was a scaffolder. He was killed three years ago in a fall on a building site. Then I got sick. The stress from my husband's accident, they said. The insurance payout we got for Tomasz has all been spent on my medical bills.'

Sara stared at Hardwicke, defenceless as a newborn.

Hardwicke produced his tape recorder, barely able to contain his glee. 'Tell me all you know, starting from when you first met Ashton. After that I'll draft the statutory declaration for you.'

CHAPTER 7

Adrian checked his watch. Roger Hardwicke's taunting note received three days earlier now loomed large. It was past 2 am on Sunday 27 February 1994 and in less than four hours *The Sunday Exegesis* would publish its damning disclosure. Adrian sat forward staring into the winter dark, elbows on knees and cupped hands supporting his chin. He glanced briefly at Feodor's unopened letter. *Where did it all go wrong?* he wondered. Was his biggest mistake to fall in love with Heidi in 1944 while in Germany? 'Possibly,' he mused out loud. After all, Heidi had introduced him to Marxism, which ultimately led him to become a Soviet spy. 'Even so,' Adrian said, as if speaking to someone in the room, 'I could have gone along with the Russians and found a way to back out later.' He pursed his lips. 'Why didn't I?' he asked dolefully. It was a question directed at his head because his heart already knew the answer. He had spied for the Soviets for over three decades because socialism was Heidi's guiding light, the woman he met only the once, fifty years ago, but for whom unstintingly he still carried a torch.

At the time when Heidi and Adrian first met in the boat shed in Kladow early one morning in February 1944, she was forty-five and he a month short of twenty-two. Heidi's marriage to Klaus, the man who later drove Adrian, then a downed Allied airman, to the couple's Kladow home was an odd affair held together largely by a shared devotion to socialism, Marxism in particular. After Hitler banned the communists in 1933, the party leader, Ernst Thälmann, was arrested and his deputy, Werner Ulreich, forced to flee to Moscow. It was this draconian suppression that brought Klaus and Heidi together in an initially plutonic relationship, an alliance forged by the Nazi denial of their basic political rights.

The years passed and when neither party found a deeper attachment, the couple married in 1939. By then their activities had been driven underground, forcing the two to live behind an ostensibly apolitical facade. Five years later, when Adrian entered their lives, Klaus and Heidi were in a utilitarian marriage that had produced no children.

***

Heidi returned home before noon, carrying a small parcel. Adrian had now been three hours locked in the windowless basement of the Kladow house. Klaus had just taken him down a cup of ersatz coffee.

'There's not much in the markets these days,' Heidi complained. 'But I managed to find some beets. I'll make us borscht for dinner.'

'Fine, thank you, dear,' Klaus replied dutifully. He took a deep breath. 'I suppose I should go and leave a chalk mark on the Hausvogteiplatz U-Bahn stairs,' he said. This was the signal Klaus had been instructed to leave once he'd arranged the pick up of a downed British flyer.

Klaus's meekness irritated Heidi. 'Of course you should,' she retorted. 'If we delay unnecessarily, Thälmann could be executed from under our noses.'

'We don't even know if the Nazis will agree to deal,' Klaus said. 'The order to put Thälmann to death came directly from Hitler.'

'Well, if we don't try we will never know,' Heidi said in abrupt dismissal of Klaus's gloom, ending the discussion.

Klaus stood stiffly. 'I'll stop by the store to help my brother close up after leaving the chalk mark,' he said, donning his coat. Klaus was referring to his tobacconist shop in central Berlin, the business that underpinned his image as a respectable, apolitical Berliner.

'Be sure to keep your face covered and use only your Christian name when you go down to make up the airman's bedding,' Klaus reminded

Heidi. 'I told him we are exploring avenues to return him to England. You should continue that line of talk when you're downstairs.'

Heidi nodded her understanding, whereupon she walked into the house's small galley and began peeling beets preparatory to boiling them. Next she gathered a selection of blankets and a pillow from her closet before wrapping a scarf around her face.

'Hello,' Heidi said in English on opening the basement door. 'I am Heidi. I've come to prepare your bed.' Heidi in fact spoke better English than Klaus. She had studied the language at university in the period immediately after the Great War, which was where she was first introduced to leftist politics.

'How long will I be here for?' Adrian gushed, too tense to acknowledge Heidi's greeting.

Heidi did not respond. She was bent over concentrating on arranging the bed coverings.

Watching in anticipation of an answer, Adrian observed her generous proportions, feeling a stirring in his loins as he did. Although technically still a virgin, Adrian was not completely unversed. In 1942, in the company of fellow RAAF recruits, he had visited a dubious hotel in the Rocks area of Sydney. The young men all had too much to drink. One thing led to another and, after parting with five shillings, Adrian found himself upstairs in a room with a woman comparable in age and build to Heidi.

A sexual encounter of sorts ensued, impeded not because of Adrian's alcoholic intake but because of tormenting thoughts linking the predatory Corps Commander at Hester House in Ballarat to his beloved Chantelle coupling with her dressage partner, the despised Andrew Argyll. Soon Adrian was swamped by the graphic recollection of the Corps Commander's grunts of pleasure and their torturing similarity to those of the thrusting Andrew Argyll. Adrian fought vainly to suppress the inhibiting notion that to have sex with the stout older woman would be to re-experience Chantelle's ruination and, by association, the trauma of his childhood rape. But to no avail—even when he was undressed and the woman touched him, he could not be aroused.

Yet despite the awkwardness, the sexual demand that always accompanied Adrian's recall of Chantelle's desecration at the hands of Andrew Argyll compelled him to ask the woman to lie naked on the bed. With a shrug, she complied. The sight of her huge breasts and fierce dark bush caused Adrian to erect. But rather than try to mate, he took the underside foreskin of his penis between thumb and forefinger and gently rubbed it in a motion akin to reducing a soft pebble to sand. He had adopted the habit at age sixteen, having earlier learned from boys at the Ballarat orphanage that masturbation entailed excitement of the penis shaft within a clenched fist. It was an exercise in self-deception—Adrian's delusion that he wasn't really masturbating, thereby avoiding the blindness and damnation the religious instructors in Ballarat had so ominously warned awaited self-abusers.

The bored woman watched Adrian grapple with himself. 'Come on, love,' she said with unaffectionate impatience, 'can we get on with it?'

By now Adrian's knees were shaking. 'No,' he panted. 'No. I have to keep going.' The instant Adrian's spurt signalled his finish, the woman rose from the bed, dressed quickly and, without saying a word, left the room. Dizzied by the force of his orgasm, Adrian stood clinging to the bedpost. On recovering, he cleaned up and re-clothed. But only reluctantly did Adrian proceed down stairs. The cause of his delay was the realisation that something strange and troubling had occurred. It was in fact a crucial juncture in his life; a pivotal moment where the revulsion and lust bred by the sight of Andrew Argyll sullying Chantelle in the Ballarat stables had combined with the antediluvian beliefs instilled in him in boyhood to spawn an enduring sexual dysfunction. It was a condition that Adrian would later describe as his *oddity*.

'Not sure if that was worth five bob,' he boasted on rejoining his colleagues at the bar, speaking loudly with forced bravado. Adrian then proceeded to drink beer upon beer, desperately trying to block out the incident. But the birth of his *oddity* was a memory that no amount of alcohol could ever erase. On waking the next morning, therefore,

Adrian's first thought was not to wonder how he got to bed or why he was still partially clothed but rather for the previous night's sexual misadventure. Unable to face the dreadful alternative, he willed his mind to think his slip up was no different from those occasionally mentioned by other young airmen. So Adrian continued on, easing his natural frustrations with his deceptive masturbation technique, while all the while choosing to believe that to have proper sex would wash away the shame of his sexual failings.

Adrian's subsequent encounters with females, however, were all too few and far apart, with none ever reaching the sexual phase. Not until after he reached RAF Binbrook in the English summer of 1943 did Adrian next have meaningful contact with the opposite sex. The interaction in question, albeit of modest physical proportions, was nonetheless destined to have profound ramifications, for Adrian's sexual disorder and later spying life alike.

The H for Harry aircrew had been granted their first weekend leave. It was two months since their arrival in the UK. Adrian and the others promptly decamped to the nearby port city of Grimsby. On the Saturday night Adrian met a girl called Millie. The two stayed in touch, exchanging letters. Opportunities for actual meetings were limited, but in November 1943 they did enjoy an evening at the Grimsby cinema after which, in a laneway en route to her home, Millie briefly allowed Adrian to place his hand inside her brassiere. And although Millie's forbearance gave Adrian no particular rush of pleasure, it did raise his hope that she might be the means for ridding himself of his vexing sexual shortcomings.

Adrian had one last chance to visit Grimsby before his squadron began flying sorties in the Battle of Berlin in December 1943. But things did not go to plan. 'She ain't here,' Millie's mother said when Adrian knocked on the door of the family home in West Marsh, smartly attired in his RAAF uniform. It was the first Saturday in December 1943 and he carried with him a bunch of puny roses purchased at the exorbitant cost of three shillings.

'But we agreed in our last letter that I should come by at half-past five tonight,' Adrian protested, 'when I had my last leave pass before commencing operations.' Even as he voiced his objection, however, he sensed it was futile. He'd been stood up.

'Don't know, sweetheart,' Millie's mother replied, a look of sympathy in her eyes, mistaking Adrian's angst for that of a lovelorn young man when in fact the cause of his devastation was the cruel dashing of his hope of overcoming the stubborn problem he was shortly to identify as his *oddity*.

Adrian left, tossing his meagre posy over the fence of the house two down from Millie's as he went. In a pub close to the Grimsby Town railway station he morosely watched the passing parade. The sight of Millie arm-in-arm with a large American soldier dressed in an expensive serge coat, smartly pressed trousers and shiny shoes, laughing and meandering as they headed for the local dance hall, left Adrian irreparably wounded. The instincts he would later sharpen in the dark world of espionage were now telling him what he had subliminally known all along: that his sexual dysfunction in the Sydney hotel room in 1942 was not an isolated incident but rather a lifelong companion. 'It's my eternal *oddity*,' he whispered, using the expression for the first time. In the years that followed, Adrian had little compunction when it came to betraying the Americans.

***

Back in the basement of the house in the wooded Berlin Suburb of Kladow in February 1944, Heidi stretched her stiff back. She had finished preparing Adrian's bed. 'I don't know how long you'll have to stay here before we can begin the process of returning you to England,' she said, belatedly answering Adrian's question. 'A few days, a week maybe, I don't know.'

Adrian's disappointment was obvious.

'Let's see what Klaus says when he gets back,' Heidi said.

It was dark before Klaus arrived. Heidi placed a bowl of borscht before him, along with two slices of coarse brown bread.

'The Allied bombing,' Klaus said wearily, 'has damaged a lot of the rail network. It makes for a slow trip these days.' He was referring to his commute to central Berlin, first by bus to Spandau station and then by train and finally subway to the Hausvogteiplatz U-Bahn.

'Did you make the chalk mark?' Heidi asked.

'Yes,' Klaus replied, 'on leaving the station.' A strained look came to his face. 'I will go in early tomorrow to open the shop. I expect they'll contact me then.' Klaus ran a hand through his hair. 'I really don't know how this is going to work.'

'It doesn't help to worry,' Heidi said with rare gentleness.

On receipt of Klaus's wan smile, Heidi took her face scarf and proceeded to the basement with food for Adrian. 'We may get more news tomorrow on your return to England,' she said, placing the tray on the bed.

Adrian was too distracted to reply coherently—in the room's weak candlelight, he could make out Heidi's large round breasts pushing against her woollen sweater, causing an imagined image of her naked to flood his mind.

An hour later Heidi returned to collect the soiled crockery. 'You should try to sleep,' she told Adrian. 'It will soon get cold down here.'

True to Heidi's word, the chill had already settled over the house when Adrian burrowed under the covers. As if of its own volition, his hand extended to his erect penis, taking its underside foreskin between thumb and forefinger while all the while thinking of the candlelit Heidi. Afterwards Adrian fumbled in the dark to mop up before re-burying in the bed's warmth. His last act before falling asleep, as always, was to tell himself he was safe from the dire fate promised by the proselytisers at the Ballarat orphanage.

Klaus departed for central Berlin first thing the next morning, leaving Heidi and Adrian alone in the house. Mindful of the night before, guilt and lust overcame Adrian when the scarfed Heidi entered his basement bedroom.

'Good morning, Adrian,' she said politely. 'I've brought you a little coffee and bread for breakfast.'

The perceived intimacy of Heidi's use of his Christian name triggered a deep desire inside Adrian. 'Who are you people?' he asked. His attraction for Heidi was causing the pulse to pound inside his head. He wanted to be near to and engage her.

'We are socialists,' Heidi answered simply, 'who oppose Hitler.' Adrian could sense her rising anger. 'We have been persecuted by the Nazis,' Heidi said passionately, 'and many of our people have been put to death or imprisoned. But we shall never bow to the fascists. We would rather die.'

'What's so great about socialism that you'd die for it?' Adrian asked, his natural Australian belligerence shining through but matched with surprise that the topic should interest him.

'Fascism,' Heidi replied, 'thrives only if people of dissenting political views are systematically murdered, tortured and oppressed. This is exactly what Hitler does. The Western capitalist model is less extreme but no less damaging. It oppresses working people by exploiting their labour in order to keep the national wealth in the hands of a privileged few. Look at the damage wrought by the Great Depression and, as a direct result, this current war and all its suffering. Socialism, conversely, promotes peace and wellbeing because the means of production are held in public hands. This creates equality for all, in terms of material wealth, political rights and in key social aspects like education, housing and medical care.'

Heidi's spiel, of course, was refined by many years of practice. But for someone as inexperienced and impacted as Adrian, it was powerfully persuasive. After all, the Nazis had once been an impersonal enemy with whom Britain, and by extension Australia, was at war. But now Adrian hated them because they had killed his friends and were threatening to kill him. And Heidi's depiction of Western capitalism resonated even more forcefully as he began to relate to the concept of oppression. He was one of the oppressed. In capitalism's stark divide between the haves and haves not, Adrian realised he had been born on the wrong side of the equation. Abandoned to an orphanage system where he'd been raped, humiliated and looked down on by the likes of Chantelle's lover Andrew Argyll, Western capitalism had failed him. And now, like a beacon in the dark, socialism offered a viable alternative.

Heidi detected Adrian's mounting interest. Encouraged, she invited him to sit on the bed while she expanded, much like a student in a classroom. Adrian listened, enthralled but also grateful for the distraction from his gnawing sexual need.

And there it began. By the time Klaus returned in the evening Adrian had convinced himself that socialism was his answer. Alone in the basement, a convert's zeal took hold; a want to believe the ideology could fill the gaping emptiness in his life, that which had returned with a vengeance now his de facto family, the H for Harry crew, had perished.

CHAPTER 8

That night a lighter mood prevailed in the Kladow house. Heidi because of Adrian's evident attraction to socialism; Klaus because Christel, the Soviet agent he knew as Ilsa, as expected, had made contact; and Adrian, locked away downstairs in the basement, because he was now in love with Heidi and all she stood for.

The instruction delivered by the so-called Ilsa directed Klaus to take Adrian to the Oberbaum Bridge, the Gothic towered structure spanning Berlin's River Spree. He was to deposit him on the Friedrichshain side where another German communist called Dietrich Knote would be waiting. The handover was set for Friday morning, in around thirty-six hours. To where Knote would take Adrian, Klaus neither knew nor cared. By now the airman had been in his home for two days and thankfully he would soon be rid of him and the constant source of worry that he was.

The relayed instruction to Klaus came, of course, from Werner Ulreich in exile at the Lux Hotel in Moscow. The NKVD communication channel to which Ulreich was selectively granted access was necessarily a complicated one. That the network existed at all underlined the importance the Soviet intelligence service attached to having some sort of reach into Berlin as its thoughts turned westward.

Including Christel Metternich, there were four links in the communications chain. Each in its own way was equally vital. But some links were less hazardous than others, like the compromised

RAF loadmaster who concealed slim packages from the Soviet embassy in London on his person when his RAF duties took him to the British territory of Gibraltar, and the Gibraltar dockworker—a man from nearby Algeciras on the Spanish side of the Bay of Gibraltar—with whom the loadmaster discreetly exchanged his secret cargo for documents destined for Moscow. Christel and her Spanish national cut-out in Berlin, however, were obliged to take far greater risks.

Jaume Ascaso had married into a wealthy Madrid household in 1938, after which he joined the family's mineral exporting company as the executive responsible for tungsten shipments to the Nazis. Tungsten was a key ingredient in the manufacture of heavy armour and essential to the German war effort, ensuring Ascaso a warm welcome whenever in Berlin. It was this embrace by the Nazis and the fact of a hard-nosed father-in-law prepared to take violent retribution against anyone who wronged his only daughter that led the NKVD to suborn the Spaniard.

Key in this was that until Hitler invaded Russia in June 1941, a Soviet embassy was resident in Berlin from where secret contact was maintained with German communists who provided all nature of intelligence to their ideological bedfellows. As such, when Ascaso took a Nazi mistress in 1940 the NKVD soon became aware of the liaison.

For a time Ascaso was effectively a banked asset, which is to say he provided the NKVD with only marginal information on Spanish mineral flows to Germany. But with shrewd foresight, the Soviets had also introduced Ascaso to a Dutch academic resident in Madrid who made regular visits to England on commercial flights from neighbouring Portugal. And although the Soviets judged neutral Portugal as too watchful of its air links with England for the Dutchman to carry material, when the NKVD so directed he was well placed to instruct Ascaso to commence a dual cut-out role. With that, Ascaso began to look for opportunities to travel to Algeciras, home to the Gibraltar dockworker. There he would take possession of the Soviet dispatches carried to Gibraltar by the RAF loadmaster, for later passing to Christel

Metternich in Berlin, while handing over material earlier received from Christel that the loadmaster would transport back to London.

All in Lubyanka knew the Moscow–Berlin communication channel was only as strong as its weakest link; at any time, one link could fail taking the others with them. Nonetheless, the medium's longevity surprised many. It was to remain intact for exactly one year, commencing in June 1943, upon Christel's arrival in Berlin, until fractured by the Allied invasion of German-occupied France in June 1944, the so-called D-Day landings.

***

Back in the house in the Berlin suburb of Kladow on the morning of Thursday 17 February 1944, twenty-four hours before he was to be dropped at the Oberbaum Bridge, Adrian woke to the sound of Klaus and Heidi arguing. First, he heard Klaus's raised voice and, although he didn't understand him, discerned his questioning anger. Then came the muffled sound of Heidi's reply filtering down to his basement quarters, patient yet terse and insistent, followed by an uneasy silence punctured by the slamming of a door.

Next thing Adrian knew Klaus was standing in his basement room, wearing no face covering. 'There's been a change of plan,' Klaus said sombrely. 'You might as well come upstairs and eat breakfast while we tell you about it.'

Klaus began, addressing Adrian, but only after first scowling at Heidi. 'Originally,' he said, 'we were to hand you to others tomorrow who were going to organise your safe passage out of Germany.' He defiantly dipped a chunk of bread into his coffee, knowing that Heidi frowned on such eating habits. 'But now Heidi has decided we should make other arrangements.' Klaus shook his head dejectedly. 'And while I'm very unhappy with this, the upshot is you will stay here much longer than anticipated, making it impractical to keep you locked up downstairs and needing to bring you food and so forth.'

Adrian wasn't sure what to make of the development. He was anxious to get back to England and had repeatedly told Klaus and Heidi so. But equally he was now besotted by Heidi and, provided he didn't look too far ahead, the thought of remaining under the same roof as her was welcome news.

Klaus interrupted his thinking. 'Tomorrow morning, Heidi and I will go into Berlin to finalise these new preparations. You shall remain here alone. Please be quiet at all times and never go near the windows. Should any person come to the door, you must hide to give the impression nobody is home.'

That's why at 11 am on Friday morning Klaus watched from a distance as Heidi walked to the Oberbaum Bridge and stood at a point beneath one of its medieval turrets where she stared out at the River Spree. This was the spot where Adrian had been meant to stand in order that those responsible for negotiating his exchange with the Waffen-SS in return for sparing Ernst Thälmann's life could take him under their control.

Shortly after 11 am, Dietrich Knote approached. He was known to Heidi but not in a fraternal way. Knote was a Stalinist, the ideology drawing inspiration from the Soviet leader, Joseph Stalin. Heidi, conversely, was a Marxist, an adherent of the teachings of Karl Marx. The two groups had frequently butted heads. The difference between them, rather than of practical substance, was largely philosophical, an internal party debate about which elements should and should not make up the socialist model.

But it was not the theoretical differences between the respective factions that convinced Heidi to pursue another plan. Nor was it necessarily Adrian's obvious attraction to socialism and his potential as a future servant of the cause. Rather, Heidi's change of heart stemmed from two evenings ago when Klaus informed her that Dietrich Knote's Stalinist faction was to conduct the exchange negotiations.

Heidi had long decided that Knote and his people were not dedicated communists committed to world peace. They were ill-educated thugs, most of them, opportunists intent on using the system for their own benefit who were not to be trusted to bargain with the Nazis. It was this judgement that first caused Heidi to consider an alternative approach, this and her resentment of Knote and his followers for the credence they gave to the anti-communist disparagement that hidden inside every socialist was a little capitalist.

And the more Heidi thought about it, the more troubled she became. Then suddenly the rude reality hit her—Werner Ulreich's strategy was meant to fail all along.

Clever Werner, the awakening Heidi had thought. The Marxist faction led by Klaus had been entrusted with finding a downed British airman because Ulreich foresaw that she and Klaus were sufficiently competent to make it happen. And the actual securing of an airman would be Ulreich's evidence of sincerity—that ever the loyal deputy, he was not prepared to stand idly by and watch his leader die. But in handing responsibility for the exchange negotiations to Dietrich Knote's Stalinist faction, Ulreich knew that, even were the Waffen-SS prepared to deal, Knote's incompetents would bungle it. Yet at the same time Ulreich could hide behind the fig leaf of an argument that party stability demanded the Stalinists be given a role in the exercise.

In short, Heidi's motivation to replace Werner Ulreich's plan with her own was her realisation that the scheming deputy had not so much as a jot of interest in saving Ernst Thälmann's life.

'Frau Frind,' Knote said on reaching Heidi, addressing her formally by her married name. 'What a surprise to see you here?' His raised eyebrows made clear his greeting was a question.

'Herr Knote,' Heidi replied with equal politeness, distaste for the man rising in her throat, 'good morning.' She was now certain her decision not to proceed with the exchange of Adrian for Ernst Thälmann's life was the correct one. For a time she had felt guilt over manipulating Klaus. But now she did not regret lying the previous morning when saying she had come to accept the exchange could not work, not when the order to execute Thälmann was Hitler's personal directive. Ironically, Klaus had become upset and anxious when told this. He did believe that the exchange of an Allied airman for Ernst Thälmann's life was a pipedream. But more than anything, he wanted to be rid of Adrian and his life-threatening presence in the house. It took all of Heidi's guile and persistence to win Klaus's reluctant agreement.

'I have devised an alternative proposal as regards the British airman,' Heidi told Knote. 'As you are in touch with Ulreich, be sure he sees this.' Heidi handed Knote an envelope. He took it in an involuntary response before opening his mouth to object. 'Please don't argue,' Heidi said, 'not here. It's too dangerous. Hitler has demanded that Thälmann be put to death. No offer of a British flyer to the Waffen-SS is going to change that. Instead, we can put the airman to better use as a servant of a future German communist state, one who is trained in Moscow before his return to England as our agent. This is what my letter proposes.'

As Knote digested Heidi's argument, a knowing smile came to his face. Werner Ulreich was a committed Stalinist, which explained why he had survived Stalin's purges while domiciled in Moscow. Abandoning the exchange of the airman, Knote calculated, would ensure Ernst Thälmann's execution and, once Hitler was defeated and the Soviets in control of Germany, Werner Ulreich's installation as prime minister. And being in Ulreich's Stalinist faction, the egregious Knote came to realise, assured him a ministerial portfolio in that future administration.

The pair stared briefly at one another, their looks conveying mutual contempt. With that, Heidi turned heel and walked away, thinking that even though the self-serving Knote was too dim to understand Ulreich's plan was designed to fail, his smirk did guarantee he would pass on her letter because it signalled he had grasped the personal benefit involved.

Knote watched Heidi go before leaving in the opposite direction, her letter stuffed securely in his trouser pocket. On the Kreuzberg side of the bridge, he tapped on the window of an old van parked by the side of the road. 'Our British flyer is not coming,' Knote told the driver. He held up a hand as the man tried to speak. 'Go home,' Knote ordered. 'We will talk later. Right now I must make a visit to the Hedwig.' Berlin's St. Hedwig Hospital was to where in June 1943 the nurse Christel Metternich had requested a transfer, just as the NKVD's Major Feodor Timofeyevich Kozlovsky told her to do.

Christel had no means of calling a meeting with her cut-out, Jaume Ascaso. All she had was a schedule provided by the NKVD, which specified eight locations around Berlin where she was to meet the Spaniard. The meetings were randomly spaced, commencing from the time Christel took up residence in the German capital in June 1943.

Ascaso, of course, could not risk being seen to engage residents of Berlin unknown to him, and especially not in out of the way locations. The Soviets, therefore, had prescribed signals to be observed for his meetings with Christel, all of which were to take place at prominent Berlin landmarks. If satisfied the signal was correctly set, Christel was to make the contact; if not, a fallback meeting was to occur one day and two hours later.

The next rendezvous was not until noon on the last Sunday in March 1944, when the Madrid-based Ascaso would be in Berlin overseeing his company's shipment of that month's tungsten consignment. The NKVD schedule stipulated he was to carry his headwear in his left hand as the signal for the meeting to proceed.

The elaborate NKVD meeting arrangements and the security surrounding them reflected the high risk of detection facing Christel and Ascaso. So it was that only nervously did Christel enter the Kaiser Wilhelm memorial church on Kurfürstendamm on a chilly Sunday morning in late March 1944. Although damaged by Allied bombing, the church spire remained intact, making the landmark a popular symbol of defiance among Berliners.

Ascaso duly arrived at noon. Taking his hat in his left hand, he stepped through the pockmarked portico, where he stood close to Christel. He had seen her several times over the preceding nine months, albeit security considerations dictated the two should not speak.

Christel turned to leave, noting as she did Ascaso's correctly held hat. An exchange ensued. The plain white envelope Ascaso withdrew from his coat was slipped into Christel's handbag, while hidden inside the newspaper she passed to Ascaso were Heidi's letter to Werner Ulreich as well as the reports Christel had earlier prepared on German casualty rates and unit rotations.

Heidi's letter was now in train, leaving her with nothing more to do but patiently await Werner Ulreich's reaction to her curtailing of his cynical charade to exchange a British airman for Ernst Thälmann's life.

CHAPTER 9

'Got a minute, Adrian?' James Newcombe said, standing in the doorway of Adrian's office. Tall, dark and poisonously polite, Newcombe was a bureaucratic head kicker from MI6's top floor netherworld. People like him did not need to ask Assistant Director Generals if they could spare five minutes, especially Assistant Director Generals who by mid-January 1964 had been at level only for five months.

'Certainly,' Adrian said, understanding that Newcombe's enquiry did not come with options.

'Kevin Carstone,' Newcombe said, ushering forth a large man of about forty with perfectly parted short dark hair. The stranger was dressed in a sober business suit and wore a skinny black tie held in place over his starched white shirt by a silver tie clip. 'Over from Langley for a few months.'

'Pleased to meet you, sir,' Carstone said with distinctive American confidence, extending an outstretched hand to Adrian.

'Likewise, I'm sure,' Adrian replied with adopted British reserve.

Carstone stepped back from Adrian's desk, obviously waiting for Newcombe again to speak. The pause introduced by the American gave Adrian time to ponder why the CIA visitor was being introduced to him.

'Kevin wants to ask you a few questions about the Nicaraguan operation,' Newcombe said finally, addressing Adrian. 'I'll leave him with you to explain the background.' The icy glance flashed by

Newcombe as he departed was a warning to Adrian that something serious was afoot. It also dashed Adrian's hope that Carstone was dropping in to dispense more praise for his work in Nicaragua on behalf of the CIA.

Watching Carstone brush imaginary dust from the chair on which he was to sit, Adrian thought about the networks he had established to channel money and military supplies to the president's younger brother, then head of the Nicaraguan National Guard. The set up he'd implemented was a standard subversion model. Unbeknown, though, to MI6 and the CIA the networks were always going to flourish—the Soviets made sure of that. For better or for worse, the US believed that as president the younger brother would be more successful— read hard line—in dealing with Nicaragua's communists. As such, when regime change occurred in May 1963 the CIA feted Adrian, prompting MI6 to promote him to Assistant Director General in August of that year.

The two cheap, steel-framed chairs in front of Adrian's desk were more suited to a rented flat than an office: Adrian was far too junior for designer furniture. He waited as Carstone fastidiously folded his fawn trench coat, placing it on the companion chair before carefully positioning his grey hat on top. Seated in his Notting Hill flat in the small hours of Sunday 27 February 1994, Adrian remembered thinking at the time how Carstone's dress and precise manner suggested an evangelical conservative, someone who fought the Cold War firmly convinced that God was on his side. Adrian smiled wryly; it had been a surprise to later learn of the dark secret of Carstone's youth.

'As you know,' Carstone began, his voice rich with a Southern accent, 'the Agency remains active in recruiting field assets in Nicaragua.' Adrian nodded. 'One of our recent successes was in charge of security for a time in the office of Luis Somoza.' Luis was the eldest son of the ruling Somoza dynasty and had inherited the presidency from his father in 1956. He was also the elder brother whom Adrian had deposed as president in 1963 in favour of his younger sibling, Anastasio.

Carstone grimaced before continuing. 'To be perfectly honest,' he said, aware of Adrian's familiarity with the players, 'Anastasio has been a disappointment to us. He consults Luis so much that, frankly, we could have left Luis in place and saved ourselves a lot of time, money and problems.'

'Picking winners is always fraught,' Adrian commiserated.

To Adrian's surprise, Carstone took affront at this innocently offered observation. Despite the disappointing Nicaraguan outcome, the CIA was actively engaged in similar exercises in Africa and elsewhere. Carstone, it seemed, was hypersensitive to perceived criticism of his agency's activities. It was an odd vulnerability for someone so outwardly self-assured.

'Well, better than sitting on your butt drinking tea,' the American retorted heatedly. In this simple way relations between Adrian and Carstone got off on the wrong foot at the outset, from where they never recovered.

'OK, to cut to the chase,' Carstone said abruptly, once he was composed, 'our recent Nicaraguan success told us that he and some others in Luis's inner circle became aware of the networks you set up to direct support to Anastasio. He also said this same group of advisers later heard that the Soviets allowed the networks to prosper because it benefitted a source they had in MI6. Luis apparently dismissed the rumours as poppycock and despite everything has remained close to Anastasio. But we're told the rumblings persisted of Soviet involvement in Luis's removal. So, we arranged for this former head of security to visit the States on a study tour arranged by our embassy in Managua, to facilitate us having a decent chat with him. An IntVest team interviewed him in New York last month, immediately after Christmas.'

Adrian knew the jargon. *IntVest* was shorthand for the CIA's Internal Investigations section. The unit was charged with identifying traitors within the CIA's own ranks and that of the foreign spy agencies with whom the CIA partnered. 'Luis's ex-security man,' Carstone continued, 'told us the word on the street was that the Soviets weren't sponsoring a minion but rather someone in MI6 involved in the actual organisation of the operation, someone who had decision-making responsibility.' With that, Carstone stopped and stared at Adrian, inviting a response.

'Well, all the big calls had to be cleared by the top floor,' Adrian said, rubbing his chin as if in thought, while all the while feeling a chill of fear tingle down his spine and kicking himself for briefly failing to hold the American's gaze. 'The number of people who would have had input could be as many as four or five.'

Carstone smiled in a particularly unfriendly way. He had detected the brief flutter in Adrian's eyes. And although he couldn't be sure, the fact that he now disliked Adrian left him prepared to think the worst. 'When I say making decisions,' Carstone said slowly, his eyes sharp and narrowed, 'I should have said making decisions on the ground.' Carstone allowed the tension to mount, prompted by a deeply embedded intuition telling him he now had a sniff of blood. 'Since interviewing the security guy, we have determined there were three people at the coalface over the duration of the operation with decision-making powers. One was the person who set up the MI6 station in Managua, another was the person who replaced him midway through the operation, and the third person, Mr Ashton, was you who had hands-on oversight of the exercise.'

Adrian decided attack was the best form of defence. 'I'm not at all sure, Mr Carstone, what you're insinuating with these theatrical looks you're giving me. But I don't appreciate it. All you have at best is circumstantial evidence. How do you know if your Nicaraguan security man is telling the truth? By your own admission, he was effectively bribed to come to the US. Little wonder that when asked about the matter he started big-noting himself in order to earn his keep.'

Adrian watched Carstone as the American considered his response. While doing so, his thoughts returned to the war and training with the H for Harry crew in England before flying sorties in the Battle of Berlin. Specifically, he recalled his last leave in Grimsby on the first Saturday in December 1943, when the local girl Millie stood him up in favour of an American serviceman. 'And in any event,' Adrian continued, now in his mind talking as much to the American GI in Grimsby as he was to his CIA questioner, 'Billy Swanson who set up the MI6 station is dead. He got ill midway through the op and was replaced. How were you planning to interrogate him, I wonder?'

Adrian did not know his response closely paralleled that of the MI6 hierarchy when the CIA had first raised the matter. The truth be known, MI6 was still reeling from a succession of disasters in the 1950s and early 1960s, when every second week it seemed some traitor or other was popping up in Moscow and cheerily admitting to being a long-time KGB asset. And if that wasn't quite enough, now there was the fallout from Profumo. John Profumo had been the Secretary of State for War in the Conservative government of the day. In March 1963, the opposition Labour Party disclosed he had been sleeping with a call girl. But when Profumo finally admitted to his indiscretion the following June and resigned, the matter was not resolved as most conservatives had hoped. Salacious details continued to emerge with none more damaging to the British intelligence establishment than the revelation that concurrent with Profumo, the escort in question had also been bedding the naval attache from the Soviet embassy in London. The press was having a field day and public indignation was rife. The security services, MI6 to the fore, were being asked to explain this bizarre circumstance and how it had been allowed to happen.

In this toxic environment, the last thing MI6 needed was another scandal. So, when the CIA called to advise it had information suggesting that one of a trio consisting of Adrian and two MI6 others was a Soviet spy, the British service prevaricated. Like Adrian, the MI6 management pointed out the Nicaraguan security source was shaky, his information speculative, and that one of the three suspects identified by the CIA was dead, namely the man called William Swanson who established the MI6 station in the British embassy in Managua in order to kick-start Adrian's operation.

But for all that, MI6 was in no position to tell the CIA to get lost.

Its compromise was to accept the Agency's demand that one of its investigators, Kevin Carstone, should come to London and have a poke around. 'Certainly,' the MI6 heavies on the top floor had said, feigning a lack of concern. 'For however long he likes.' Left unspoken, however, was their fervent hope that Carstone's delving would unearth nothing, leaving the matter quietly to recede.

***

That night, some hours after Carstone had completed his interrogation and gone off bristling with suspicion and ill grace, Adrian was anxious and badly needed to share his burden. He contemplated setting the signal for a crash meeting with his Soviet controller. But worried he might be under surveillance, he mustered just enough nerve to resist the temptation. The merest sign of panic—a light left on overnight in his flat or any of the other come hither signals to controllers that were the spy's meat and drink—would be as good as a confession. So Adrian endured the strain aided by the copious quantities of sherry he drank on each of the next three nights, unaware that up on the top floor his MI6 masters were steadfastly resisting the discovery of yet another traitor within their organisation.

Come the weekend, Adrian had more freedom to move about without arousing suspicion. He spent Saturday afternoon at the Portobello Road markets looking for tails. In truth, he was hoping to find none. It was deflating, therefore, to detect a man and a woman, Americans judging by their loud clothing, constantly within watching distance of him. But he also wondered if he was imagining things, if all the sherry he'd been drinking was making him paranoid. That night he put the decanter in the cupboard and went to bed early, hoping to be steadier in the morning.

But no sooner had Adrian arrived at St. John's Church in leafy Notting Hill for the 10 am Sunday service than he spotted the same couple again. Adrian was not a religious man but long ago the Soviets had advised him to attend church now and again because of the respectability it afforded, and currently Adrian was feeling a keen need for respectability.

Mouthing the words to the hymn the congregation was singing, Adrian thought about the repeat sighting. By the time the parishioners were invited to sit, he had decided the couple weren't professional watchers but rather amateurs working on the cheap. Were MI6 surveilling him, a different team from the office's well resourced watcher pool would have been allocated the task. The same, Adrian was sure, applied to the CIA: if those shadowing him were official, there was no way the same team would have been assigned to him on successive days.

Walking home Adrian considered the possibility that the couple monitoring him were a husband and wife duo from the US embassy known to Carstone, friends prepared to freelance for him. It didn't really matter. Carstone was now sufficiently suspicious to be watching him, hoping to discover something that would convince the CIA and MI6 to become formally engaged. And for Adrian this raised the spectre of Sara, with whom he had been terribly indiscreet, and the now heightened risk of Carstone finding out about her.

***

Where else but in the gentlemen's lavatory in Harrods on a busy Friday lunch time on 31 January 1964? It was Adrian's scheduled end of month meeting with his Soviet controller. Anatoly, as Adrian knew him, had been his handler since his return from Nicaragua in May 1963. From Adrian's perspective, he was a vast improvement on his previous controller, the testy decorated war hero whom Adrian failed to impress during the Nicaraguan preliminaries in October 1962.

Anatoly was standing at the giant porcelain urinal, tall as a man, on the far left of the bank. Adrian had spent the last hour wandering Harrods' crowded pathways looking for the pair engaged by Carstone to tail him. On finding no trace, he proceeded to the men's toilets where he stood washing his hands at a sink adjacent to the burly Russian.

Anatoly was confused. He was expecting Adrian to place a Harrods shopping bag on the floor and depart, permitting him to turn and in the one motion scoop up the drop. But Adrian had no such bag with him, and nor did he leave; instead, he remained standing at Anatoly's back.

'What?' Anatoly whispered anxiously, still staring ahead.

'In front of Big Ben,' Adrian replied with equal terseness. 'On the bridge. In one hour.'

Fifty-five minutes later, Adrian exited Westminster tube station, confident he wasn't being followed. From Knightsbridge he'd taken the Circle Line as if intent on returning to MI6 headquarters. But after one last back check, he did not alight at his usual stop but the one after, at Westminster. Anatoly was waiting. The two fell in without greeting and headed south across Westminster Bridge.

'I'm in trouble,' Adrian whispered, leaning into Anatoly and explaining his predicament as they went.

Anatoly was not a young man. And having long ago reached the zenith of his career, he was on his last assignment and concentrated on securing a comfortable retirement at his dacha near the Black Sea.

'What have you got to worry about?' he said, downplaying Adrian's concerns. 'If this CIA fellow can't find independent validation for his Nicaraguan source, he won't get past first base.' Anatoly smirked, seeming to find enjoyment in his use of an American idiom. 'And even if the CIA finds someone in Nicaragua who can vouch for the allegations, how could they sheet it home to you? The success of the Nicaraguan operation relied on us withholding information from our communist friends, particularly that we wanted the networks to succeed for your benefit. It's possible that some perceptive people close to the deposed president suspected things went a little too smoothly for the younger brother. Those same people might even have speculated it was the USSR who wanted the MI6 networks to prosper. But it would have been a long bow to link you to any Soviet wish for the operation to succeed, principally because there is no factual evidence of this. MI6 is not going to shoot you on the basis of rumours.' Anatoly chuckled. 'You're not living in socialist Russia, you know.'

Adrian was dismayed. He knew Anatoly was ducking the issue, wanting it to go away. And while he accepted that under no circumstances could he tell Anatoly about Sara—especially that she knew it all and the unmitigated disaster it would be if Carstone spoke to her—he was expecting a level of concern.

Suddenly Adrian was angry and, as usual when he had a rush of blood, his decorum deserted him. 'You don't care, do you?' he spat accusatively. 'All you want to do is finish your tour and get home.' Adrian took a deep breath; he was incensed now. 'You're not getting another fucking thing out of me until I have Lubyanka's assurance it will extract me if things go bad. In fact, tell them I want to defect, right now. I mean it. It's all very well for you to tell me not to worry, but you're not the one in the firing line with CIA bloodhounds on your back.'

Anatoly could see his Black Sea dream evaporating before his eyes. 'All right, all right,' he said, this time resorting to the British vernacular. 'Keep your shirt on.'

'So you'll make Lubyanka aware of the pressure I'm under and pass on my request to defect?'

'I will, I assure you,' Anatoly said. 'I will even head my report: *Weather over Mendoza*,' he added, knowing Adrian understood this was the emergency code to be used if he was at risk of imminent discovery.

'Good,' Adrian said, exhaling forcefully, Anatoly gratefully interpreting this rush of breath as a sign of relief.

Mendoza is under constant CIA surveillance, Anatoly would later add to his report in order to justify his use of the code red, *and drinking to excess. He says he wants to defect. I calmed him down by telling him to avoid contact for the time being. But action needs to be taken or else he is guaranteed to make a mistake.*

CHAPTER 10

In the dark and quiet of the Notting Hill early morning in February 1994, Adrian's gaze shifted into the street and to the fine flakes of snow gently floating to ground in the pale street lighting. In an odd way he found affinity with the icy wisps, mainly because he related to their fragility. Adrian winced, as he always did when prompted to think of the brittle moments in his life, with no instance more bothersome and cringeworthy than his appalling indiscretion with Heidi Frind fifty years ago in the period after her meeting with Dietrich Knote on the Oberbaum Bridge. It was on the bridge where Heidi passed Knote her letter to Werner Ulreich proposing that, rather than as a bargaining chip, Adrian's worth was in England as a deep cover agent for a future German communist government.

Heidi's plan, of course, envisaged Adrian first going to Moscow to be trained as an intelligence operative. Only then would he be returned to England. To this end, she suggested that Russian troops advancing on Berlin should purport to discover him in a labour camp in the east before passing him to the British authorities armed with a suitably credible story as to why he, a captured Allied airman, had been found there. In making her case to Ulreich, Heidi was at pains to emphasise Adrian's wholehearted adoption of socialism, twice reiterating it in order to imply his full commitment to her proposal.

But although Heidi's letter had effectively vouched for Adrian's cooperation, privately she knew there was still a sizeable margin for error. At the forefront of her mind was Adrian's keen wish to return to England, raising the distinct possibility he might not be receptive to spending time in Moscow beforehand learning the necessary spy skills or indeed of becoming a German agent in the first place. But knowing it would be some months before Adrian was able to leave her home, when writing to Ulreich the ever optimistic Heidi had judged that time was on her side.

Heidi understood that Werner Ulreich's Machiavellian plan to become the leader of post-war Germany had sealed Ernst Thälmann's fate—regardless of whether Adrian stayed or went. Yet she was also aware Ulreich could order that the pretence of saving Thälmann's life be continued. But now Heidi had disrupted the deception she hoped not, banking on Ulreich accepting the moment had passed and appreciating her proposal's practical benefit. Until Ulreich adjudicated, however, nothing was certain. All she could do was ready Adrian for the journey to Moscow, in the event, through Nazi-occupied France into Spain and thence to Russia, most likely on a Soviet freighter sailing under a neutral country flag.

Thinking of Adrian's passage to Moscow also caused Heidi to reflect on her related concern that once in Spain, Adrian could be tempted to abandon her plan and make for Gibraltar and the British forces there. The imperative, she decided, was to extract from him before he left the house his ironclad guarantee to go to Moscow. If not, her plan would fall apart were he to waver at any point between Berlin and Moscow. Heidi wrestled with her dilemma, endlessly debating how best to secure this outcome. She could not have known that Adrian would eventually play into her hands.

Spring had arrived in Kladow as Klaus, ever worried, and Heidi, diligently ideological, settled in to wait for Werner Ulreich's response. Time passed slowly. Adrian had been told that plans were firming up to return him to Britain via a new escape route but how the establishment of this pathway was still some weeks off. In the meantime, Klaus commuted to his tobacconist shop in central Berlin while Heidi remained at home with Adrian where she extolled socialism's virtues and urged his unquestioning embrace of them.

By the end of March, however, it was clear to Heidi that, notwithstanding Adrian's unflagging enthusiasm for communist ideals, he remained fixated on returning to England. She concluded that resort to another tactic was necessary, something more creative than dogma.

The lull also began to present problems for Adrian. Cooped up in the Kladow house in close proximity to Heidi—day in, day out—his abnormal sexual personality began to agitate. Soon he was struggling to suppress the irritation. The fact that Adrian could not so much as look out a window, let alone leave the house, only compounded the situation.

The nights were especially problematic. Adrian was increasingly deluged with images of Chantelle heaving under her lover Andrew Argyll in the Ballarat stables. He fought the seemingly limitless lust with his *oddity*, drawing on memories of the hotel room in Sydney in 1942 and the stout older woman whose lewd nakedness had honed his peculiar self-satisfaction technique when he was unable to have sex with her.

But although it was barely two years since the Sydney event, Adrian's recall of the woman's physical specifics had faded. The thought of Heidi lying naked before him began to take hold, such that it became a throbbing need.

The dam wall broke on a cool Monday afternoon in the first week of April. Adrian had come up from his basement quarters, intending to sit in the house's enclosed rear room. He reached the top of the stairs just as Heidi walked towards the galley. Each tried to avoid the other only to move in the same direction and collide in a clumsy embrace.

The brief feel of Heidi's body against his caused an electric impulse to course through Adrian. He fought the erratically racing surge but, try as he might, it rapidly overpowered him. Adrian lumbered into the galley. Heidi turned, wondering why he was shuffling and noticing the dazed look in his eyes. Adrian moved closer and, without warning, robotically placed a hand on each of her ample breasts.

Although shocked, Heidi was sufficiently robust as to push Adrian from her. 'What do you think you're doing?' she screeched.

'I love you, Heidi,' Adrian said, the sexual tension causing his words to slur.

Heidi was thunderstruck. 'You what?' she retorted. 'I am old enough to be your mother.'

Adrian made no response and continued to stare with a stupefied look on his face.

Heidi took a knife from the sideboard. 'Keep away from me, you filthy pest,' she warned, waving the implement about. 'Touch me again and I will cut you to pieces.'

The threat in Heidi's voice permeated Adrian's consciousness, snapping him from his stupor. He could scarcely believe what he had done. Tears began to course down Adrian's face. 'Heidi, Heidi, I'm sorry,' he pleaded, 'I don't know what overcame me. I didn't mean to scare you.' Adrian slumped to his knees, devastated. 'Please forgive me, Heidi. I meant you no harm.'

Heidi stared at the whimpering Adrian, beginning to think. 'Go to your room,' she ordered in a tone of voice that reminded Adrian of the matron at his Ballarat orphanage. 'And don't come out until I say so.'

Adrian meekly did as directed, flopping face down on his bed and covering his head with his pillow. An hour later Heidi opened the door. 'Come upstairs to the back room,' she said coldly. Heidi closely watched the miserable Adrian, confident she now held a commanding leverage over him.

'Klaus and I,' she began, 'have kept you safe in our home, fed you and looked after you. And your response to our generosity is to try and take advantage of me. If Klaus knew this he would shoot you.' She sought to control her rising anger, only half succeeding. 'The socialist calling,' Heidi spat at Adrian, 'is my life mission and I will not be pawed by the likes of you.'

Adrian nodded. He was beyond mortification. His obviously profound regret convinced Heidi to press home her advantage. 'And while I will never forgive your inappropriate behaviour,' she said, 'I will keep quiet about it provided you do exactly as I ask.'

'Anything,' Adrian whispered hoarsely.

Heidi remained po-faced but privately she was delighted—Adrian's cowed obedience had gifted her the means to ready him for removal to Moscow. 'When eventually you leave here,' she said, determined to proceed as if she already had Werner Ulreich's approval, 'you will be sent not to England but to Moscow. There, you will be trained in the art of espionage. You are to immerse yourself in this learning such that you will be fully prepared to become a servant of the Marxist government that will preside over Germany after the war.'

Adrian stared, his eyes wide in disbelief. 'You're not sending me back to England?' he asked in timid astonishment.

'Not initially,' Heidi confirmed. 'After training in Moscow, you will be taken to a Red Army unit which will claim to have found you in a concentration camp in the east while on its march to Berlin. Only then will you be handed to the British authorities.'

'A concentration camp?'

'Yes.' Heidi paused. 'You will need to be treated badly in the weeks preceding your supposed discovery. It is important you are in sufficiently poor condition as not to arouse British suspicions.'

Adrian opened his mouth to speak but although his lips moved he could utter no words. Not that Heidi would have brooked any argument. 'Never forget,' she said, 'that your suffering will be for the greater good. You must always focus on the prize of a socialist-ruled world where all are equal and live in peace and harmony.'

In the chill Notting Hill dark in February 1994 Adrian laughed humourlessly, remembering his pledge of unconditional loyalty to Heidi's plan that he become an agent for post-war Germany. In the years following, he preferred to believe that remorse over his assault on Heidi was behind his response. But now, with the shame of his life about to confront him courtesy of Roger Hardwicke's *Sunday Exegesis* article, Adrian could no longer deny the truth. 'I agreed only because Heidi had so comprehensively rejected me,' he whispered. 'Only that— only because of my intense longing for her to love me.'

***

Heidi Frind's letter did not reach Werner Ulreich at the Lux Hotel in Moscow until 10 July 1944, over three months since Christel Metternich had passed it to Jaume Ascaso at the Kaiser Wilhelm memorial church. Hostage to circumstance, the Moscow–Berlin communication channel could be as slow as it was fragile. Ascaso had promptly handed Heidi's letter to his contact from Algeciras, who worked at the Gibraltar docks. But then followed an unexpectedly lengthy delay when the London-based RAF loadmaster co-opted by the Soviets was diverted to other duties and temporarily unable to visit the British territory.

Werner Ulreich's first thought was for his sham plan to save Ernst Thälmann's life. But he soon decided he could tolerate its lapsing because Heidi's intervention permitted him to point to underlings disregarding his instructions and thwarting his sincere intention. Confident that his ambition to lead the German communists remained unimpaired, Ulreich next considered Heidi's proposal. He saw its merit but also recognised that developments in the war since the letter's dispatch had overtaken the idea.

On 6 June 1944, while Heidi's letter was in transit, Allied troops had landed in France, at Normandy. The fighting was ongoing, but Ulreich understood the D-Day landings ruled out transporting Adrian through formerly German-occupied France and into Spain. A shame, Ulreich thought, because before the Allied invasion there was regular movement of any number of non-German speakers from Germany to Spain via France, not least the Spain to Germany link in the Moscow–Berlin communication channel, the Spaniard Jaume Ascaso.

Three days after receiving Heidi's letter, the Soviet press

triumphantly reported the Red Army was in control of the Lithuanian capital Vilnius and advancing on Lithuania's land border with East Prussia. The Soviet gains caused Ulreich to reflect on Heidi's proposal.

East Prussia was an island of territory within Poland ceded to Germany after the Great War. Since Germany's occupation of Poland in 1939, however, the normally isolated East Prussia had effectively been joined with Weimar Germany to the west, Germany proper as it were. If the Australian flyer could link up with the encroaching Soviet forces he would be as good as in Moscow.

But no sooner had the thought entered Ulreich's head than he dismissed it. Even if it could be arranged, the risks were insurmountable in transporting the non-German speaking Adrian from Berlin into occupied Poland, where foreigners travelling privately were non-existent, and across East Prussia, nearly 800 kilometres in all to the Lithuanian border. And then there was the question of whom in their right mind and without good reason would voluntarily travel towards the advancing Red Army.

Werner Ulreich did not bother with a reply to Heidi—with the advent of the D-Day landings, there was no longer a communication channel to Berlin through which to send it. But a week later, on 20 July 1944, fate intervened in a momentous way, not that Ulreich initially appreciated this. Rather, he viewed the 20 July event purely in terms of the volatility it created in East Prussia.

The issue in question was an assassination attempt on Adolf Hitler at the Wolf's Lair, a heavily fortified compound just 150 kilometres from the Lithuanian border that was Hitler's Eastern Front headquarters. The high-ranking German military officers who perpetrated the coup, and failed, paid the ultimate price. But not satisfied, Hitler wanted more. With that, Waffen-SS and Gestapo units dispersed across Germany relentlessly searching for culprits, any possible culprit.

As Hitler engaged in his fearsome retribution, German state radio, also broadcasting internationally, denounced the traitors while reporting that the Führer had personally ordered the criminals be treated fairly in accordance with German law. Listening to short wave broadcasts in Moscow, Werner Ulreich knew full well what was happening. He also came to realise that across East Prussia there would be considerable fluidity as the Nazi security services scoured the territory looking for signs of further insurrection. This would mobilise all sorts of sinister people. And in so tense and dangerous an environment, few German soldiers would dare to ask questions of official-looking civilians. In theory, Ulreich reasoned, the prevailing fear and confusion in East Prussia would be an ideal smokescreen for any person seeking to sneak across the Lithuanian border—but only in theory and then only if such persons were able to reach the territory in the first place.

CHAPTER 11

On the stroke of 3 am Adrian had another of his rushes of blood. Not that there was anything unique to the hour warranting the flurry. Rather, he had been mulling, thinking of his critics in MI6, those who routinely derided him over the years, and how he usually managed to ignore them. But by 3 am Adrian was distressed by the visualisation of his detractors' smug delight and all-knowing telephone calls when in three short hours Roger Hardwicke's *Sunday Exegesis* article uncloaked him. Fierce anger gripped Adrian and, as usual when upset, impulsiveness set in. He ripped at Feodor's unopened letter as if hoping for better than expected news. The impetus, however, was short-lived, arrested by the re-assertion of the sobering reality that Feodor had betrayed him. Dropping the torn envelope, Adrian despondently rubbed his forehead with all eight fingers. Rashness had become sentimentality. Right now, like a quitting smoker having a final cigarette, he wanted to think fondly of Feodor one last time, to remember how the Russian had come to his rescue in times of crisis. Adrian's thoughts turned to mid-1944.

Two weeks after receiving Heidi Frind's letter, the German communist Werner Ulreich attended a meeting with an aide to the Central Committee of the Soviet Communist Party. The man's job was to screen requests made by Ulreich and where necessary arrange meetings with Politburo ministers, including occasionally with Joseph Stalin himself.

It was towards the end of the pair's conversation that Ulreich casually mentioned Heidi's proposal. He did so not in an attempt to win the aide's support for the idea—Ulreich was more convinced than ever that it was far too difficult to bring Adrian to Moscow. Rather, Ulreich's aim in raising the letter was to convey that, despite their precarious circumstances, his people in Germany were still active in support of the socialist cause, knowing this would reflect well on him.

But to Ulreich's surprise, the aide's interest immediately piqued. 'Comrade Ulreich,' he said. 'I think a meeting with Deputy Commissar Gorsky is required. Please present yourself here on Wednesday afternoon at 2 pm in order to discuss this British airman held by our brave and admirable comrades in Berlin.'

Pavel Gorsky was a brute of a man who in 1941 had risen to be second in charge of the NKVD. He had much blood on his hands. And now that the Soviets, confident of winning the war, were making plans to win the peace, Gorsky had been entrusted with expanding the stable of Soviet agents in the West. 'Tell me about this proposal to transport an Allied airman here to Moscow,' Gorsky instructed Ulreich. It was Wednesday 26 July 1944, just six days since the unsuccessful attempt to assassinate Hitler at the Wolf's Lair in East Prussia.

Ulreich did as bid, showing Gorsky Heidi's letter. 'The proposal envisages the airman going to Spain via France,' Ulreich explained. 'As that's now out of the question the Lithuanian border is the only possible route. But given the flyer doesn't speak German, moving him from Berlin across Poland would be fraught even with passable identity documents. And then there's the fact that he'd be travelling east.' Ulreich smiled, trying to make light of the situation. 'Nobody in Germany willingly goes to the east these days. Together, these are overwhelming difficulties.'

Gorsky made no response other than to stare coldly at Ulreich, having long mastered the art of giving his interlocutors enough rope to hang themselves, sometimes literally. 'Mind you,' Ulreich continued, no match for Gorsky's icy silence and forced into saying more than he would have liked, 'if we could get him to East Prussia, the confusion and disruption going on there at the moment means he could conceivably cross into Lithuania.'

'Where?'

'Lithuania,' Ulreich replied, only understanding Gorsky's question once the Russian had exhaled exasperatedly. 'Sorry, I didn't realise you were asking at which point he would make the crossing. At Tilsit I should think. It's right on the border and the logical location.' Ulreich smiled, failing yet again to inject some warmth into the conversation.

'In what timeframe?'

Ulreich hid his frustration. *Didn't Gorsky understand that getting this Adrian Ashton fellow to East Prussia was impossible?* 'It would be very, very difficult to get instructions back to my people in Berlin,' he replied cautiously, 'now that the Germans are no longer in control of France.' Ulreich paused for effect. 'And even if an instruction could be sent, there would be considerable lead time in making the necessary arrangements: papers for the airman, finding a suitable escort and so forth.'

'But by then this ruckus over the Wolf's Lair incident could have died down?'

'Yes, I agree, Comrade Gorsky.' Ulreich took a deep breath, now wishing he had never broached Heidi's letter in his earlier meeting with the aide. 'And to reiterate, there are huge barriers to moving the airman to East Prussia. One, he can't speak German and, two, inevitably someone would interrogate him and demand to know why he, a non-German speaker, a foreigner, is travelling east.'

Gorsky did not reply. The man was a thug and a murderer but had a keen sense of intuition with it. 'Wait outside,' he said abruptly dismissing Ulreich. The German did as directed, humiliated by Gorsky's offhanded treatment. Gorsky waited for him to go before pressing a buzzer under his desk.

'Go and find Major Kozlovsky in the Foreign Directorate,' he ordered his young assistant. 'Tell him to come here immediately. Major Feodor Timofeyevich Kozlovsky.'

***

Feodor Kozlovsky had been born in 1911 in Kursk in western Russia. A gifted student, he had graduated in behavioural science at Kursk State University before winning a scholarship to The Institute for Social Research in Frankfurt. Feodor's postgraduate course had included a year of German language tuition commencing in 1932, coincident with the Institute's renaming as the Goethe University.

Young, handsome and blond, thanks to an ancient gene on his mother's side traceable back to Germany, Feodor embraced life in Frankfurt. In this new and exciting environment he came across Adelaida, a fellow student who hailed from Berlin. Adelaida had been born in the western Argentine city of Mendoza. Her parents had come to Germany in 1925 when her father, a philosophy professor, was offered tenure at the Friedrich Wilhelm University in Berlin. Enjoying the lifestyle and prestige of her father's work, the family stayed on, later taking German citizenship in order to avoid running afoul of the sweeping changes to employment law instituted by the Nazis as it related to foreigners working in Germany.

Yet despite their carefree existence and the inclusiveness of university life, Feodor and Adelaida's foreign backgrounds set them apart from the majority of the student cohort. They gravitated to each other. A love affair ensued, with Feodor and Adelaida taking frequent trips to Berlin to visit her family. It was in Berlin in 1933 that Feodor first witnessed the ruthless rise of the Nazis. Unsettled by the experience, the young ones privately pledged to keep a distance from the politics of the day. A permanent move to Berlin took place in 1936, once Feodor and Adelaida had completed their high-level studies. Three months later they married. For all the Nazi excesses, it was an idyllic time. Adelaida taught school and Feodor, as a foreigner with limited employment options, found a job as a porter at the Adlon Hotel near the Brandenburg Gate.

But by 1938 Germany was an extra-dangerous place. Adelaida found this out to her great cost in November that year when one morning she attended a meeting of fellow teachers to discuss a mundane school matter. It was an opportunity too good to miss for the Nazi functionary installed as the school principal.

'Frau *Kozlovsky*,' the principal said on later summoning Adelaida to his office, his spitting emphasis on her married name startling Adelaida. 'I'm hearing that you are inciting unrest by trying to form a teachers' trade union.'

'No, no not at all, Herr headmaster,' Adelaida replied courteously. 'I assure you I have no interest in politics.'

'But are you not married to a communist?'

Adelaida smiled pleasantly, while all the while her heart was pounding. 'My husband is Russian, certainly, but like me he takes no interest in politics.'

Without more, the principal told Adelaida to return to her classroom. This she did, nervously wondering what had precipitated the man's unsettling allegation. She didn't have long to wait to find out. That afternoon Adelaida was again called to the headmaster's office, where a Nazi Party bureaucrat summarily terminated her employment. The principal, it transpires, had denounced Adelaida as a communist, resentful that this pretty immigrant girl should thumb her nose at Germany by marrying a Russian in preference to a good local boy. Two hours later Nazi officials called at the Adlon Hotel to remove Feodor from his porter's position.

Had the matter rested there, Feodor and Adelaida would likely have coped. But there was Nazi vindictiveness in the air. That night the young couple's apartment was raided. Adelaida was arrested and taken away. Two days later, her family's German citizenship was revoked ahead of deportation to Argentina.

Feodor neither saw nor heard of Adelaida again. But he was spared the same grim fate as his wife by the fact that Hitler wanted to invade Poland and defeat the West before addressing the Slavic menace in the east. Accordingly, in the lead up to the outbreak of the war, Hitler had sought to keep relations with Soviet Russia on an even keel. As a Soviet citizen, therefore, Feodor was well treated. After a week in not uncomfortable detention, where he agonised over Adelaida's disappearance and the utter callousness of the Nazi injustice, he was also deported.

Feodor returned to Kursk in late 1938. At just twenty-seven, he was an irreversibly changed man, heartbroken and full of hate for the Nazis. But as grief turned to longing so inexorably did Feodor's conviction grow that Adelaida would live on in his heart were he to devote his life to fighting Nazism. With that, he began to think of his seven years in Germany as fate equipping him for this crusade, his ability to speak the language flawlessly and his many German mannerisms.

When the NKVD came knocking, predictably attracted to these very same qualities, the resolute Feodor had no hesitation in joining up. He could not have known how this twist of destiny would bind him so profoundly to Adrian Ashton.

***

'Comrade Gorsky will see you now,' the assistant said. Werner Ulreich nodded grimly. He resented being made to sit for two hours in a drafty corridor. But he also knew he had no choice other than to swallow his pride. On entering Gorsky's office, Ulreich was surprised to see a handsome, Germanic-looking young man in the uniform of an NKVD major seated in front of the Deputy Commissar's desk.

Gorsky made no effort to introduce Ulreich to the newcomer. Feodor broke the ice. 'Kozlovsky,' he said, rising with his hand extended.

'Ulreich.'

Gorsky broke in impatiently. 'I've just discussed the matter of your British airman with Major Kozlovsky,' he said. 'The major speaks excellent German and knows Germany well. With our advances in Lithuania we agree it would be possible to insert Kozlovsky here into Germany. I am proposing that he go to Berlin, pick up your British airman and escort him back to Lithuania.'

Ulreich stared at Gorsky, wondering if the man had gone mad. His gaze switched briefly to Feodor as he sought to find the right words, and courage, to address Gorsky. 'But comrade Deputy Commissar,

Berlin is 800 kilometres from the Lithuanian border. That's a 1,600 kilometre round trip. Even if Major…'

'Kozlovsky,' Feodor offered helpfully.

'Even if Major Kozlovsky speaks German, it's unlikely he could make such a trip without being discovered. And then there's the matter I raised previously about this British, Australian actually, airman not speaking German.' Now despairing, Ulreich clutched at his forehead. 'They'll both be killed,' he blurted, 'and probably expose my people in Berlin in the process.' Ulreich looked into Gorsky's cold eyes and a chill ran down his spine. 'Under torture,' he added lamely, desperate to convey he was casting no aspersions.

Pavel Gorsky did not like his decisions to be questioned and offered Werner Ulreich no explanation. Rather, he ordered Ulreich to provide a description of Klaus and Heidi Frind as he remembered them, after which Ulreich precisely marked the location of their Kladow home on a Berlin street map, knowing that Klaus and Heidi lived in the house once owned by Klaus's father. With that, Ulreich was dismissed, leaving in a blur of anxious bewilderment.

'He's a fool,' Gorsky said contemptuously to Ulreich's back. 'But we'll install him as the German leader after the war. He'll be a useful idiot, putty in our hands.'

Feodor Kozlovsky gave no reaction beyond a wry smile. He had noted Gorsky's emphatic gesture in slapping shut his notebook and knew this signalled the end of the discussion. It was time to look forward. Even so, Feodor proceeded with care, aware of Gorsky's sensitivity even to the slightest hint of dissent. 'The Australian flyer,' he said, couching his words so as to signal support for the plan to move Adrian from Berlin to Moscow, 'I assume we're going to use him as our own asset after the war rather than gift him to Ulreich's government?'

Although Gorsky was a psychopath, like all Russians he had an appreciation of the arts. It was this sentience that caused him to detect Feodor's deftness. 'Major Kozlovsky,' he said formally, but without rancour, 'the operation I propose entails many risks I would not usually take. But it is extremely vital that the NKVD prepare for the not too distant day when this war ends and the new conflict begins. Events are moving quickly and, now they've landed in Normandy, the Allies will soon liberate Paris and invade Germany from the west, just as we invade from the east. In readiness for the new post-war era, the NKVD must make a concerted effort to increase the number of agents we have within the Western security services.'

'Yet,' Feodor pressed gently, keen to hear what Gorsky had in mind now it was clear he had decided to hijack Heidi Frind's plan, 'we know virtually nothing about the Australian airman, this Adrian Ashton.'

Gorsky briefly bared his teeth in what passed for a smile. 'Yes,' he said, speaking with rare restraint, 'that is true, which justifies you thinking I have little to go on other than instinct. But the letter from Berlin indicates the airman is thoroughly devoted to socialist ideals. And in my long experience the ideologically committed always make the best spies. Such individuals, however, do not come along every day. This convinces me that Ashton is a rare opportunity we should not pass up, which is why I need to send you to Berlin to escort him back to our front line in Lithuania.'

Feodor nodded, eyes now sharp and alert and arms folded across his chest, watching Gorsky intently. 'If we can return Ashton to the British forces,' Gorsky elaborated, 'as someone supposedly who has survived time in a German concentration camp reserved for civilians, those whom the British entrust after the war to investigate the Nazis' criminality will surely court him. With that grounding behind him, should he prove to have half a brain, he would likely attract MI6's interest. We must ensure, therefore, he returns to civilian life as soon as possible when back in England, to be free of military commitments and able to join MI6 at the first opportunity. Be under no illusions, Major Kozlovsky. Once Germany is defeated and the post-war tidying up complete, the Soviet Union's next war will be against the West. However it might be achieved, my ultimate aim is for our socialist convert to become a Soviet source in MI6.'

CHAPTER 12

Fifteen days on from his meeting with the NKVD Deputy Commissar Pavel Gorsky, Feodor Kozlovsky was in a leaky wooden dinghy in the Curonian Lagoon, a freshwater body bordered to the east by the Lithuanian coast and to the west by the Curonian Spit, a narrow splinter of land running from Lithuania to East Prussia separating the lagoon from the Baltic Sea. It was the small hours of 10 August 1944 and a Russian motor vessel was in the process of attaching a towline to the dinghy.

Two others accompanied Feodor in the boat. Both wore bloodied and tattered Waffen-SS uniforms, indicating they had recently engaged in conflict, and were emaciated by a lack of food and water and burned red by the sun. And both were dead. The two SS soldiers had been starved by the Soviets in preparation for the operation and given poisonous berries to eat the day before.

For his part, Feodor was fit and healthy. But that would change in under an hour when the black pill he was about to swallow induced severe diarrhoea accompanied by vomiting and dehydration.

The dinghy would be towed into the deeper and wider expanses of the lagoon from where it would be cut loose. It would then drift south on the current towards the Sambia Peninsula and beach close to the East Prussian capital of Königsberg.

Feodor wore the uniform of a German pioneer detachment, specialist engineers who, among other things, set booby-traps as the

German forces retreated. He carried dog tags and a military paybook identifying him as Captain Hans Rehhagel. As well he might. Hans Rehhagel was a member of a company-strength pioneer unit and the only one of its seven survivors captured by the Soviets who was from Frankfurt, Feodor's old student stamping ground.

And although Rehhagel's background made it logical for Feodor to adopt his identity, there was also another factor in the Russian assuming the Rehhagel persona, once the real Rehhagel and his six comrades were put to death. It was the German's Iron Cross First Class awarded for conspicuous bravery during Operation Barbarossa, the code name given to Hitler's invasion of the Soviet Union. Once Feodor reached Berlin, the medal would play a key role in his plan.

Feodor of course knew Berlin well, having lived there with his wife Adelaida from 1936 up until the time of her disappearance in November 1938 and assured murder at the hands of the Gestapo. It was her memory that motivated and drove Feodor every single day of his life.

***

'After the Reds overran us in Vilnius,' Feodor told the Wehrmacht intelligence officer whose job it was to interrogate German soldiers who had escaped into East Prussia ahead of the advancing Soviets, 'six others from my unit and I commandeered a lorry and headed towards the Lithuanian coast. It was bedlam—soldiers, civilians and animals everywhere and a constant threat of being seen from the air. Somewhere along the way we picked up four Waffen-SS.' Feodor watched the intelligence officer closely as the man absorbed his explanation, detecting no body language to suggest the German's suspicions had been aroused. 'But near a place called Derceklial,' Feodor continued, 'two MiG fighters spotted us and began to strafe the lorry. We abandoned the vehicle and ran for our lives. Two of the Waffen-SS and I ended up hiding in the same gully. I never saw the others again.'

'Show me on the map,' the intelligence officer demanded. Feodor raised himself from the cot on which he lay. He had been in the field hospital in Königsberg for two days now, attached to saline and glucose drips. With a shaking hand, he pointed to the Lithuanian village near the coast.

The intelligence officer wrote in his notebook. 'And then, Captain Rehhagel?' he asked.

Feodor was exhausted from the effort of pointing to the map. He fell back in his bed, spent. 'We continued towards the coast on foot,' he said after a time, 'using the western sun as our compass.'

'Yes?'

'It was hot. We were dehydrated and starving. The SS pair started eating berries.'

'Yet you didn't?'

'I had a chocolate bar I hid from the others,' Feodor replied. 'I rested under a tree while they went into the field to harvest berries and ate my chocolate then.' Feodor looked into the intelligence officer's eyes, searching for danger signs. On seeing none, he continued. 'It was every man for himself by this stage. If I had shared my chocolate with the other two, they would still have eaten berries I'm sure. We all would of, probably. A third of a bar would not have satisfied any of us.'

The chocolate bar story was one of a number of delicate fabrications Feodor had to make. But as a behavioural science expert, he knew better than most his story would not ring true if he came over as too considerate of his supposed comrades. After all, they were in an extreme situation where most human beings would normally act selfishly towards strangers.

Watching the intelligence officer, Feodor judged he had got the balance about right. His interrogator confirmed this shortly after. 'Yes, I understand,' the man said sympathetically. 'You faced a very difficult choice.'

Forty-five minutes later the interview drew to a close. Feodor had explained how he and the others came across an old dinghy on the beach and, under cover of dark, set off using the boat's single paddle to propel it, navigating by the stars as they went. At some point on the first night one of the two Waffen-SS soldiers became violently ill and died. By morning the other Waffen-SS soldier was also dead. Feodor told how he pressed on only to lose his paddle over the side when he fell asleep. It was then he accepted he too was going to die. That's why he elected to eat some of the berries still on the Waffen-SS duo, in order to ease his crippling hunger pains. He had passed out at some point, after fortuitously throwing up and purging himself of the bulk of the berries. Next thing he knew, a German patrol had found him beached on the shore.

The intelligence officer stood and extended his hand. 'Thank you for your time, Captain Rehhagel,' he said. 'I hope with some rest you will get well soon.' Feodor was desperately fatigued. He smiled in tepid acknowledgement of the German's good wishes, all the while knowing that the effects of the pill he had swallowed would begin to wear off after ten days—unlike the European yew berries force-fed to the two Waffen-SS soldiers, the toxic seeds of which attacked the heart function.

Feodor closed his eyes, intending to doze, only for a familiar voice to disturb him minutes later. It was the intelligence officer who had returned unannounced. 'Tell me, Captain Rehhagel,' he said, watching Feodor intently, 'what did you do with the wrapper from the chocolate bar you ate? You would not have wanted the others to see it.'

The behavioural scientist and intelligence officer combined in Feodor to generate a newfound respect for the German. 'It was the standard Wehrmacht ration pack plain chocolate bar,' Feodor answered. 'I hid the wrapping inside my trouser back pocket.'

And when the intelligence officer took Feodor's stained trousers from the pile of dirty clothes destined for laundry on completion of the interview, the brown packaging Feodor had carefully placed in the garment was there to be found. The intelligence officer nodded in satisfaction and left. Feodor was more relieved than ever to have survived his interrogation. The German was shrewder than he appeared and had craftily combined his question with an element of surprise, at a moment when the debriefing exercise appeared to be over.

That said, Feodor was pleased the intelligence officer chose the chocolate bar aspect of his story around which to spring a surprise test. The reason being that this diverted attention from his footwear, since sown into the inner sole of Feodor's right boot were his identification as Dr Franz Schick, a special duties Gestapo investigator, and forged orders authorising his urgent travel from Berlin to Tilsit in East Prussia. The bulk of this journey, from Berlin to the East Prussian capital Königsberg, Feodor planned to undertake by train. The remaining 120 kilometres further east to Tilsit on the Lithuanian border he envisaged bridging by road.

While in transit from Berlin to Tilsit as the Gestapo investigator Franz Schick, Feodor would tell anybody important enough who asked that his task was to locate a member of a Spanish Blue Division, a man believed to be the cousin of the Spanish leader, General Franco. Blue Divisions comprised units of Spanish fascists who had fought alongside the Germans in Russia, with some units still engaged on East Prussia's eastern flank.

Franco's supposed cousin, however, was an invention as it follows was the scripted-for-use-as-necessary claim of his suspected involvement in the Hitler assassination attempt. But however fanciful the story, it made for good cover. Spain was one of Nazi Germany's few remaining friends; the interrogation of a close Franco relative on a matter so serious as the Wolf's Lair attack was hugely sensitive and not something that could be left to the Gestapo office in Königsberg.

Feodor's travelling companion on the trek east was to be an unarmed civilian interpreter, a Spaniard by the name of Antonio Navarro. Navarro, of course, was to be Adrian Ashton. Sown into the inner sole of Feodor's left boot, therefore, was the so-called Navarro's identity document. If pressed, Feodor would explain that relationship considerations obliged the Gestapo to involve its Spanish counterpart in the Tilsit exercise, the Germans opting to ask Francoist intelligence for an interpreter. The Spanish security agency, however, faced its own domestic political concerns, those demanding distance between it and the interrogation of the dictator Franco's family member. That's why Francoist intelligence chose a non-German-speaking civilian translator, simply because no worthy government security bureau would make such an odd appointment. Navarro was a Spanish–English interpreter who fitted the bill. And capping it all, Feodor would further explain as required that since he, Franz Schick, spoke no Spanish and Navarro no German, the pair was reduced to conversing in English.

Posing as Captain Hans Rehhagel of the Wehrmacht Third Pioneer Battalion, Feodor was unable to carry all the trappings peculiar to Gestapo investigators, items such as the Czech-made Browning pistol typically issued to Gestapo agents. In this regard, as in many others, Feodor was expected to improvise as best he could when in the Gestapo guise. The risks were significant. But the NKVD judged that Feodor and Adrian's cover on the return leg to the Lithuanian border was capable of holding for twenty-four hours—the Gestapo's pitiless pursuit of those thought to be linked to the Hitler assassination attempt the ace up their sleeve protecting them from random questioning. After twenty-four hours, however, all bets were off.

***

The days passed and Feodor became stronger, joining with fellow patients at a similar stage of recovery to play chess or Skat, a popular German card game of which his wife Adelaida had been especially fond. He had successfully breached the German anti-infiltration defences and with his health on the mend was now ready to tackle the Adrian Ashton assignment.

After ten days in the Königsberg infirmary, Feodor and others were readied for removal to Weimar Germany. The repatriation of wounded soldiers was a regular occurrence and, all along, the hospital train had been Feodor's preferred option for reaching Berlin. He was pleased to be leaving Königsberg, knowing if he stayed much longer he would inevitably encounter a Hans Rehhagel acquaintance, notwithstanding that all in Rehhagel's unit were dead.

A day later Feodor's journey was over. The trip had gone as smoothly as possible. The soldiers were happy to be returning home and in that environment jokes and good humour had taken precedence over suspicions and questioning.

There was, however, one major hiccup in that Feodor's train went not to Berlin as hoped but to a German military hospital in Egendorf. This was highly problematic. Egendorf was 230 kilometres south of Berlin and much closer to Hans Rehhagel's home city of Frankfurt than the capital. This left Feodor with considerably less time at his disposal before Rehhagel would be expected to reunite with his family. Feodor had to act quickly and boldly. Prepared in the circumstances to risk scrutiny, he stepped forward from the mass of new arrivals to request an early discharge.

This perplexed the medical staff—the longer able-bodied soldiers could stay in the hospital, the longer it would be before they were returned to the misery of the Eastern Front. But fortunately for Feodor beds were scarce at Egendorf and, after the doctors dithered for a whole three days, his unusual request was approved.

In a moment of fantastic irony, a paymaster arrived on the day of Feodor's discharge to give him three months of back pay owed to Hans Rehhagel. Feodor had earlier folded a small amount of German currency into his paybook. It was the habit of most German soldiers on the Eastern Front to carry some cash for use on return home—if they were lucky enough to survive. But now, thanks to German administrative efficiency, Feodor was flush with funds, money he would later put to good use.

Feodor left the hospital in the company of other discharged soldiers, heading for the nearby railway station from where they would catch trains to their respective destinations. The officers among them, Feodor included, toted military-issue leather carry bags, parting gifts from the hospital in which they stowed their personal items. Feodor was grateful for this. The bag would provide another layer of authenticity, however minor, both now as Rehhagel and later as the Gestapo investigator Franz Schick when, like many other Gestapo agents, he could point to a background as a former army officer.

Feodor's leave pass was good for a week. But the train ticket issued to him was for travel to Frankfurt, where Hans Rehhagel's family would be expectantly waiting. Yet Feodor's imperative was to get to Berlin and switch identities, something made more urgent by the fact that he had only around twenty-four hours, half his originally estimated time, before Hans's no show raised the alarm.

While in the German military's medical care, Feodor had kept a low profile to avoid unwanted attention, especially from Gestapo informants. Indeed, upon arriving in Egendorf it was his emergence from the ruck that made so fraught his request for an early discharge. But having jumped that hurdle unscathed, and now no longer a hospital inpatient, a change of personality was necessary.

'Klinsmann,' Feodor said, deliberately speaking within earshot of the soldiers sauntering towards the railway station, 'are you married?' The young Wehrmacht lieutenant was someone on whom Feodor had focused in the preceding days as a plan formed in his mind.

'No,' Klinsmann replied. 'And I'm unlikely ever to be,' he added glumly, holding up a hand missing three fingers. 'Who would want to marry a cripple?'

Feodor and the others laughed. The culture of soldiering was such that the men were unable to show empathy. 'Cheer up,' Feodor said to the young man. 'Let me tell you that being married is not all it's cracked up to be.' Feodor leant into Klinsmann, speaking softly but still loud enough for the group to hear. 'Do you know why I badgered the doctors for a discharge?' Klinsmann shook his head as the others eavesdropped attentively. 'Because I'm not going straight home to Frankfurt.' Feodor smiled. 'No. Once I get there, it'll be nag, nag, nag—fix the leaking roof, cut the grass, mend the fence. That's not for little Hansie, not after the deployment east nearly killed me. I'm going to Berlin first, paying my own way.'

'Why?' Klinsmann asked innocently.

Feodor directed a licentious wink at the young man, one the others could not fail to see. 'To fuck my girlfriend,' he stage whispered, laughing crudely. 'I haven't seen her in months. The hausfrau can wait a little longer for my salami.' With that, Feodor slapped Klinsmann on the back and waved farewell to the others, making for the north-departing platform and the train to Berlin.

'He's a dark horse, that Rehhagel,' one of the soldiers said, slowly shaking his head, while all the while the gaping Klinsmann stared at Feodor's disappearing back.

CHAPTER 13

Sara, of whom Adrian did not want the Soviets to know, lived in Manchester. It so happened in April 1962 that Adrian had a need to visit Iceland, and to fly there from England it was necessary to depart from Sara's hometown. The trip came about because of a UK–Iceland fishing dispute dubbed the *Cod Wars*. MI6 became involved when the Foreign Office was unable to resolve the disagreement. Upping the ante, Number 10 ordered its spies to warn their Icelandic counterparts that the UK was prepared to use naval forces to have its fishing fleets regain access to the waters Iceland now claimed as its own. But MI6 was far more interested in Cold War geopolitical issues and not pleased to be handed the task, believing that by rights UK trade officials should have been asked to step up now that diplomacy had failed.

At the start of 1962 Adrian was made a supernumerary, which was a polite bureaucratic way of saying that MI6 had found him surplus to requirements. In early the previous year, 1961, he had been promoted to section head level and given responsibility for a group of East African countries. Adrian's had been a fortuitous elevation brought about by MI6 receiving a glut of government money in support of a pressing political imperative. But by the end of 1961, it was clear to the MI6 management that someone more dynamic than Adrian should have oversight for East African affairs.

'We're going to build a surge capacity,' the administrators told Adrian before shuffling him off to a cold and dank office, a halfway house from where he was to begin life as a supernumerary. 'It's a pool of resources,' they said, 'designed to give us the flexibility to meet peaks in demand as they occur.'

The supernumerary experiment was short-lived. By mid-1962 the MI6 managers had worked out that the surplus officers were of more use if placed in low priority areas, thereby releasing better performing staff for the more important work. Hence, by August 1962 Adrian was heading the Central America section from where the following year he conducted the Nicaraguan operation demanded by the Americans.

But in April 1962, when the supernumerary concept was still a going concern, Adrian was at a loose end. The combination of his availability and MI6's general reluctance to deal with a matter it viewed as none of its business made Adrian the ideal choice to go to Reykjavik and threaten the Icelanders that the UK was about ready to send a gunboat to resolve the fishing standoff.

In due course the Icelandic authorities listened politely to Adrian's stumbling representations, and then ignored them. Later that afternoon, accompanied by a junior officer from the British embassy, Adrian travelled to the airport looking forward to returning to London. It had been a futile couple of days. The flight to Manchester, however, was delayed whereupon Adrian and the embassy officer adjourned to the bar where they drank high-strength Carlsberg beer, somewhat too much in Adrian's case.

Emboldened by the beer, Adrian unwisely accepted a complimentary whisky when finally on the plane, and then another. Arriving in Manchester too late for the last flight to London, Adrian was still affected by the alcohol as he taxied into the Manchester city centre in search of a hotel room, eventually finding lodgings at the Dumbrille Hotel, a seedy establishment close to Deansgate train station. As his taxi departed, Adrian stood on the footpath next to his suitcase, fumbling awkwardly while trying to stuff the fare change into his wallet.

From out of a gloom a woman of about thirty appeared. Her sweep of dark hair was parted on one side while high cheekbones gave her face an air of resigned amusement. But her eyes were a contradiction, deep and dark and telling of less joyous things.

'You're out late, handsome,' she said, tottering on high heels as she approached, her short skirt and fishnet stockings garishly finished by a fake fur stole wrapped around her shoulders.

Adrian swayed a little, grinning stupidly. 'I could say the same about you,' he offered.

'Feel like a little fun?' she asked, nodding at Adrian's wallet as if making some sort of commercial disclosure she wasn't suggesting no-cost fun.

At another time Adrian would have run a mile. But his free spirit had temporarily escaped the prison of his unadventurous sober personality. 'What's on offer?'

The woman turned and in an exaggerated action extended her right buttock in Adrian's direction, slapping it as she did. 'This,' she giggled.

Sara, as Adrian came to know her, had ample flanks. Her gesture transported Adrian back in time, simultaneously in two separate directions. One was to the Rocks area in Sydney, Australia, to the hotel where he first discovered his *oddity*, the curious means by which he satisfied his sexual need. The other was to Kladow in Berlin and the voluptuous Heidi Frind who had rejected his clumsy advance but whom Adrian still loved and could picture as clear as day despite the passage of nearly twenty years.

'I'm in room 309 on the third floor,' Adrian said, his voice husky in the way it was in Sydney that night when his *oddity* first emerged. 'Can you get into the hotel if I go in ahead of you?'

Sara was smart as a whip. 'This is my patch,' she said. 'The night staff will let me in for a quid.' This was only partially true; the levy was in fact half of that, ten shillings. And if the basement door leading to the internal stairs had been left open by careless staff, which often it was, the cost was zero.

'You'll need to give me the quid now,' Sara said. 'Once I'm in the room we can talk about other costs.' She looked questioningly at

Adrian, as if to say: *Deal*?

Adrian felt like he was dreaming. 'Here,' he said, giving Sara a pound note, furtively looking up and down the deserted street.

Sara did contemplate disappearing with the money. But it had been a slow night and being a good judge of character calculated she could comfortably relieve Adrian of a little more cash. Less than ten minutes later she knocked on the door of room 309, panting slightly from her walk up three flights of stairs.

At first Sara put Adrian's odd behaviour down to nerves. The business preliminaries had gone smoothly, better than hoped, and she gratefully pocketed the five pounds that Adrian coughed up without so much as an argument. With that, Sara disappeared into the bathroom, inviting Adrian to *get comfortable* as she left.

After peeing, Sara emerged wearing only her briefs. Adrian had undressed and was lying naked in the bed, covered by a sheet. Sara removed her underpants and slipped in beside him. The appointment was for thirty minutes but if things were going OK she was prepared to give him another ten. 'The clock's running, sweetheart,' she said. 'Do your best.'

Adrian, however, didn't move. Instead, he lay stiff as a board, staring at the ceiling.

Sara reached down to encourage him only to feel his flaccid member. *Come on*, she thought, *I haven't got all night*. It turns out she had, in fact.

'I can't.'

'What?'

'I can't do it the usual way,' Adrian repeated. He was now fully sober and regretting the terrible bind he was in.

Sara wasn't easily fazed. She'd dealt with her fair share of oddballs since becoming a *Tom* three years ago. She wondered if Adrian was suggesting something exotic that people on the Continent might do.

'So, what works for you?' she asked cautiously.

'Looking.'

'Looking?'

'Yes,' Adrian said sheepishly. 'I like to see a woman naked and…' He was too embarrassed to finish the sentence.

'Wank?' Sara suggested.

'No, not at all,' Adrian said indignantly, the denial born of his orphanage days in Ballarat as steadfast as ever. 'More like stimulate,' he added, offering his defence softly as if fearful the God he didn't believe in was listening.

Sara shrugged. She wasn't about to get into a debate about the differences between stimulation and masturbation. Throwing back the sheet, she parted her legs and placed her hands behind her head. 'There you go,' she said like a waitress in a motorway café delivering Adrian a meal. 'You have a proper nosey while you polish your knob or whatever it is you do.'

'You must think I'm strange?' Adrian said morosely, still not moving.

Sara was a graduate of the university of life. 'We're all strange, darling,' she assured Adrian.

Something in Sara's equanimity stirred Adrian. He rose from his supine position and moved to the end of the bed where he knelt on all fours. Adrian began to masturbate, or stimulate, as he would have it. Sara disinterestedly noted his unusual thumb and forefinger technique before closing her eyes. She had decided to rest while waiting for him to finish.

But Sara had barely relaxed when Adrian's voice—now firmer—broke the quiet of the room. 'Can I kiss you?' he asked. Sara opened her eyes. She could see Adrian was enlivened and understood this had freed him of inhibition.

Sara would usually have rejected the request outright because it was a firm rule of tomming never to kiss clients. But Adrian's bumbling ineptness had endeared him to her, prompting her to relent and kiss him fully on the lips as he wanted. And later, when his *oddity* was over, she allowed Adrian to kiss her again, after which he nestled his head against her chest, much like the snuggling child of which Sara often dreamt having, a daughter especially given she was closer to her mother than her father. Contentment was a rare commodity in Sara's life. In further breach of her rules, she gave in to the urge to sleep.

Adrian and Sara were still intertwined when they woke six hours later. Hints of the morning light were visible through gaps in the cheap window curtains. 'Cup of tea?' Adrian enquired politely, reflexively asking the question.

'If you're making,' Sara replied groggily.

But having made the offer Adrian was now in a fix. His clothes were on a divan a good three paces from where he lay. And in the literally cold light of morning, the thought of parading naked before Sara bothered him enormously.

'What's your name?' Adrian said, trying to deflect his offer to make tea, protectively pulling up the covering sheet to his neck as he did.

'Sara. I told you last night.'

'I meant your family name.'

With that, Sara placed a foot against Adrian's buttocks and playfully pushed him from the bed. He scrambled to the divan and quickly donned his Y-front underpants. Thereupon they began to laugh with wholehearted humour, both appreciating the high farce of the situation. And in that moment of shared levity their relationship was forged, even if neither Adrian nor Sara appreciated it at the time.

'Get me a cuppa, sweetie,' Sara said, still laughing. 'There's a pet.'

Adrian had never felt so happy in all his life. He had to stop himself from whistling as he prepared the beverage. For all the good cheer, however, Adrian never did find out Sara's family name. She was, in fact, the daughter of Polish settlement immigrants from Krakow named Lichocki who had come to England before the war when Sara, whose real Christian name was Loda, was a babe in arms. But caught in a classic pincer movement between the contemporary English culture of her schools and traditionally religious parents, by her teens Sara's relationship with her father was sufficiently damaged for him to disown her. 'Don't have a family name,' she said bluntly, after the beaming

Adrian repeated the question on rejoining her in bed with their cups of tea.

'Last name unknown,' Adrian said, smiling at Sara, content not to press her and destroy the happy mood. The phrase Adrian used, of course, was from the intelligence world, a reference to persons of interest with an unknown surname. Thereafter, the letters Adrian wrote to Sara care of the Dumbrille Hotel were always addressed to Miss Sara Lnu.

***

Had Adrian left it at a single encounter with Sara, his current problem would have been avoided. But as he strolled over Westminster Bridge with his Russian controller on the last day in January 1964, worried sick about Kevin Carstone, he could not muster the outrage to castigate himself, even with the benefit of hindsight. Sara had become a combination of wife and lover, satisfying his personal needs in whichever role she adopted, not least when she would parade her large backside before Adrian while he fantasised about Heidi.

Adrian had even accepted without complaint that Sara needed to continue to ply her trade—'A girl's got to eat,' she was forever telling him. But now on Westminster Bridge, he did regret his foolish bragging to Sara once the Nicaraguan operation reached its triumphal conclusion and he had been promoted.

In the period before his Nicaraguan success, Adrian had represented himself to Sara as a claims clerk with Lloyd's of London. This was his spying tradecraft at work, the need for caution ingrained in him over the years, even if the cover was an obvious choice in keeping with his grey man persona. But it was a deception that totally fooled Sara and, thereafter, Adrian had cheerfully tolerated her teasing of him for his blandness.

The day Adrian's promotion was announced in August 1963, his reward for his sterling efforts in Nicaragua, he had after-work drinks with a handful of well-meaning colleagues and a couple of ambitious parasites who wanted to be in a position to benefit from his advancement should the chance ever arise. But the occasion Adrian enjoyed most was at the end of the week, on Friday lunchtime, when he met his Soviet controller, old Anatoly.

Anatoly pushed out the boat, buying Adrian fish and chips at a café on Brixton Road. 'You, Mendoza,' Anatoly said, knowing how well news of his agent's promotion would be received in Lubyanka, 'are now a prospective candidate for the Order of Lenin for meritorious service.' And while Adrian had earlier fended off Anatoly's bear hugging, cheek-kissing greeting, he did lap up his handler's outrageous praise, conveniently ignoring the fact that his achievement was artificially contrived by the Soviets.

Up early on the warm Saturday morning, Adrian caught the first train to Manchester. It had been a heady week, dangerously inflating his self-esteem. And when Sara began to make cheery fun of the uncharacteristic spring in his step, Adrian's rarely uplifted ego was bruised. Next thing he knew, he had blurted it all out—lock, stock and barrel, images of Heidi cluttering his mind as he did.

'You're a Soviet spy inside British intelligence,' Sara squawked, 'who single-handedly brought down some foreign government? Fat chance. I don't believe it for a second.'

'My work is not like *Dr. No,* I assure you,' Adrian replied primly, smugly pleased at the impact of his revelation on Sara. *Dr. No* was the first of the James Bond movies and had proven to be very popular. As a Christmas present in 1962, Adrian had taken Sara to see it. 'No, no, it's far more cerebral than that.'

Sara didn't know what cerebral meant and this only made Adrian's claim harder to fathom. 'When did you become a spy?' she asked, unconvinced but perversely intrigued nonetheless.

CHAPTER 14

The question posed by Sara over thirty years earlier, as to when he became a spy, rang in Adrian's ears. It was after 4 am on Sunday 27 February 1994 and his last vestige of resilience had evaporated, primarily because he believed it would. 'Drag 'em out of bed at 4 am,' the Special Branch people used to say on those rare occasions when Adrian sat in on planning meetings to discuss lifting someone or other. 'It's a psychological fact that at 4 am, when they've got no knickers on, they're at their low point of resistance.'

So it was on crossing the dreaded time threshold that Sara's question came to mind—after all, becoming a spy was the wellspring of Adrian's current problems with Roger Hardwicke, *The Sunday Exegesis* and, relatedly, the letter from Feodor in the now torn envelope he would not fully open. But identifying precisely when he passed the point of no return proved harder to pinpoint than he imagined. Certainly though, Adrian decided, the process began in earnest when earlier than usual one workday afternoon Klaus returned to the Kladow house in Berlin. By now it was August 1944 and Adrian had been hidden in the Frinds' home for six months.

'Ilsa contacted me this morning,' Klaus told Heidi in a breathless reference to Christel Metternich, the German nurse and key link in the Soviet Union's Moscow–Berlin communication chain. 'I haven't seen her for ages and then, pop, there she was.' He giggled animatedly, his careworn expression of the last six months now gone.

Although Klaus spoke German, Adrian apprehended that his host's glee had something to do with him leaving the house. All the while, Klaus eagerly continued to share his news with Heidi. 'Tonight at 5 pm,' he gushed, 'a visitor is coming to dine with us. It is your nephew, Franz Schick, who is a member of the Gestapo.'

Heidi wasn't easily flustered. But Klaus's garbled mention of the Gestapo and a nephew she didn't have had caught her off-guard. 'Why?' she asked involuntarily.

'Why what?' Klaus responded impatiently.

'Why is the man coming here?'

'For him, obviously,' Klaus snorted, pointing at Adrian. '"He has come from Moscow to pick up the Australian airman and escort him back there." That's what Ilsa said.' With that, Klaus clasped his hands to his chest in an act of pure Teutonic delight, his sheer want to see his houseguest gone leaving him temporarily immune to the endless difficulties involved in moving Adrian such a vast distance.

***

The day before Christel contacted Klaus, the train from Egendorf carrying the NKVD's Major Feodor Kozlovsky docked at Berlin's intercity train terminus in the late afternoon.

Dispensing with his current identity as Captain Hans Rehhagel was Feodor's immediate priority. But this was no simple matter; booking into a hotel or the like in Hans Rehhagel's uniform and emerging the next morning as the Gestapo investigator Dr Franz Schick entailed many unacceptable risks, not least from alert hotel staff who had witnessed his arrival.

Feodor also needed ahead of time to procure appropriately smart civilian outfits for he and Adrian, something he had no option to do but while still in Rehhagel's uniform. His pressing demand, therefore, was to find a safe place where overnight he could transform into Schick and make the arrangements necessary for escorting the Australian airman back to the Lithuanian border.

It was Feodor's advance planning for this requirement that took him to Potsdamer Platz, travelling there by subway. Twenty minutes later he was standing in a hotel foyer close to the Bendlerblock complex housing the headquarters of the German army, the Wehrmacht. And once the elderly lift operator had accepted Feodor's reichsmark note and taken temporary custody of his Wehrmacht officer's carry bag, the Russian was soon on the hotel's fifth floor. From there he made his way to a heavy timber door upholstered in tufted leather and rang the doorbell.

The door opened offering Feodor a glimpse of a tasteful, wood-panelled room. This was the so-called Reich Room he'd been looking for. But Feodor could not enter immediately.

'Membership number?' barked an officious man in civilian garb blocking the entrance.

Feodor felt his adrenalin begin to pump. In the days before embarking on his mission he had interrogated several captured German officers seeking information about exclusive military clubs in Berlin. It was the former staff officer at the Bendlerblock complex who alerted Feodor to the Reich Room and the fact that admission was usually granted to non-member officers about to deploy to the Eastern Front. Feodor was now to put this intelligence to the test.

'Just back from the steppe,' Feodor said deadpan. 'Arrived only this afternoon and next week I'll be going back.'

'Documents.'

Feodor produced papers identifying him as Captain Hans Rehhagel, along with his one-week leave pass in the same name. 'There's nothing here indicating you're redeploying east next week,' the doorman objected.

'I don't need to be ordered to go back,' Feodor retorted, breathing in to expand his chest so that the medal he had taken from Hans Rehhagel and wore on the breast pocket of his tunic was fully in the man's field of vision. 'It's both a duty and a pleasure to return to finish the task the Führer has given us. I haven't been issued orders because I've volunteered.'

The man looked hard at Feodor, knowing he could not question the veracity of someone sporting an Iron Cross First Class, not when the room was full of high-ranking Nazis and especially not when to so much as hint that the war in the east was lost was effectively a death sentence. Best not to make a scene.

'Of course,' the man said, stepping aside. 'I envy you the opportunity.'

The room was decorated in the style of a Bavarian hunting lodge and authenticated with big game trophies stuffed and mounted on the walls. At the room's far end, beneath a portrait of Bismarck, bottles of alcohol and an array of cut crystal drinking glasses sat on a sturdy old European beech table. A white-coated steward hovered nearby ready to offer assistance. Three huge round chandeliers, each holding a score of candles, were suspended at evenly spaced intervals from the room's massive ceiling beams. And under the span of the chandeliers, plush sofas augmented by cast iron tables with glass tops were dotted about.

Feodor strolled nonchalantly to the drinks table, where he ordered a glass of brandy from the steward. The behavioural scientist in him knew that so long as he could act relaxed and confident he would not attract adverse attention. But were he to become awkward and discomforted, his body language would undo him in a trice.

Although still early evening, the room was thronging with patrons. Feodor sipped his drink and looked about him. On weighing several possibilities, he strolled across the polished timber floor to a group of five men seated in the middle of the club. With one exception, all were Wehrmacht officers attired in regulation field grey battledress. The outlier was a blond man in his mid-thirties with a sharp face. He wore the collar and shoulder insignia of the feared Waffen-SS, his immaculately turned out uniform fitting snugly about his trim, angular body. It was the SS man's fastidious attention to appearance that had caught Feodor's eye.

'Rehhagel,' Feodor said on joining the group. The four Wehrmacht officers looked Feodor up and down. They were all senior men and resented the intrusion by the more junior captain. But they also considered themselves cultured individuals given over to good manners and, on noting Feodor's Iron Cross, were prepared to give him the benefit of the doubt.

Introductions were made. 'Major Hoffman,' the SS man said with a smile. 'Lothar Hoffman,' he added, smoothing back his blond hair as he did. The signal did not escape Feodor.

Feodor's plan was specific in intent but open-minded as to execution. Put simply, he needed to find a private place where he could access civilian clothes and lie low until the morning when he would emerge as Franz Schick. Knowing the club was a men's only venue, the Russian's inclination was to engage in a drinking session with one of the patrons. Unlike enlisted men who lived in barracks, the officers who frequented the Reich Room were generally accommodated in private homes around Berlin. Feodor's aim was to wait until late at night when he would pretend to be too drunk to go in search of accommodation and propose that he sleep on the apartment floor of a German officer he had befriended, ideally one who lived alone. Provided the targeted German was sufficiently inebriated, Feodor was confident he could pull it off. Once inside the apartment with the door securely locked, all he had to do was break the occupant's neck and he would have free run of the place.

But having met Lothar Hoffman, Feodor's plans changed. The Nazis had outlawed homosexuality and imprisoned and murdered tens of thousands of their homosexual citizens. The Third Reich, however, was nothing if not hypocritical. As and when it suited them, the Nazis would overlook transgressions by their own, the rider being that those concerned were not to openly flaunt their activities. Indeed, it was rumoured that Hitler himself had practised homosexuality over a lengthy period before reluctantly embracing heterosexuality for political purposes.

Feodor took a seat next to Lothar Hoffman and began to regale the Germans with stories of the Eastern Front, his obvious knowledge enhancing his credentials. Soon the conversation was free flowing, and decidedly devoid of truth where the military situation in the east was concerned. Three rounds of drinks later, Hoffman told a coarse joke about the rape and torture in custody of a young woman who unwisely had defaced a Nazi swastika flag. Picturing Adelaida in similar circumstances, Feodor roared loudest in appreciation and was rewarded by the SS man's fulsome smile. Little did Hoffman know from that moment on he was a guaranteed dead man walking.

The night wore on and the Reich Room crowd thinned out. In time three of the Wehrmacht officers in Feodor's drinking party departed, leaving behind only Feodor, the SS officer Hoffman and the remaining Wehrmacht officer, a lieutenant colonel. Suddenly, it dawned on Feodor that he had a rival for Hoffman's affections. Feodor assessed the Wehrmacht officer. He was late-thirties, overweight and with a florid face. And as Feodor noted with interest, the man's jet-black hair showed no trace of grey, suggesting his hair was dyed. *Connected too*, Feodor thought. *Someone's got him a nice safe desk job in Wehrmacht headquarters.*

Hoffman left to get in another round of drinks. The two Germans were quite drunk by this point, unlike Feodor who, when he could, had been surreptitiously filling his glass with dark apple cider of similar appearance to brandy. The others, conversely, had been drinking neat brandy all night.

'Where do you live, Gerhard?' Feodor asked the lieutenant colonel, judging the man was too affected to suspect a trap.

Gerhard could not have played into Feodor's hands any better had he tried. 'I have a quiet little place in Wedding,' he said, smiling. 'It suits all my needs, if you understand me.'

'I would love to see it,' Feodor replied, directing his charm at the Wehrmacht officer. 'Why don't we three—you, me and Lothar—go back there for a nightcap?'

Hoffman returned with the drinks before Gerhard could answer. 'Hans has suggested we adjourn to my place for a nightcap,' Gerhard said, raising his eyebrows suggestively at Hoffman. 'I can cook us some Bratwurst in beer.'

Hoffman looked around him. Drunk as he was, he knew the importance of proceeding with discretion. 'Fine,' he said. 'You two wait down by the canal. I will pick you up in my car.' Feodor could sense the sexual tension rise in the two men. Without more, Hoffman downed his brandy in a single gulp and for the benefit of those still in the club loudly bid his drinking companions good night.

Shortly after, Gerhard left the hotel. Feodor followed five minutes behind having been delayed while he recovered his officer's carry bag from the hotel lift operator. At the canal the two men stood some distance apart and waited. Soon a sleek four-door Adler convertible appeared out of the gloom, slits of light protruding from its otherwise blacked-out headlamps. Feodor ran to the car as it pulled up in front of Gerhard.

'Quick,' Hoffman hissed. 'Get in the back and stay low.'

Hoffman drove at speed through the darkened Berlin streets, not once asking Gerhard for directions. Slumped down below the level of the window, Feodor searched for reference points for future use. Just as he glimpsed a sign announcing the entrance to the Leopoldplatz subway, he felt Gerhard's hand on his thigh. Feodor knew he couldn't object and was thankful that the carry bag resting on his lap denied Gerhard further intrusion. But when Gerhard leant over and kissed him, Feodor had no such protection. In any event, he was not about to resist. Feodor was a man driven by personal tragedy—he would act as any given situation demanded.

'Behave yourself,' Feodor giggled, smiling at Gerhard and gently pushing him away. 'We can't risk being seen.'

Gerhard also laughed. 'Five minutes,' he whispered, 'and we'll be there,' stroking Feodor's face before slumping back in his seat.

'That's right,' Lothar Hoffman said from the driver's seat, 'just a few minutes more.' Hoffman, Feodor realised, had been watching his response to Gerhard's overture in the rear-view mirror. Their eyes met in the reflection. Feodor winked at the SS man and in the dull light was relieved to receive Hoffman's wide smile in return.

***

Gerhard's abode in Wedding was not an apartment but a small, freestanding house of bland external appearance. The dwelling was located in a back street behind a three-story brown-brick pension hotel, the front entrance of which, unbeknown to Feodor, was diagonally opposite the Leopoldplatz subway entrance he had glimpsed en route. Hoffman pulled up at an attached garage, alighted to open its door and drove inside. Hoffman and Gerhard began to disrobe the instant they reached the house's living room. It was obviously a well-practised routine.

Feodor knew he should do likewise. He tore off his jacket and shirt before making for his carry bag, which he had strategically dropped next to the telephone in the entrance hallway. 'I've got some Spanish Fly in my bag,' Feodor yelled over his shoulder, rushing from the room in simulated haste. Spanish Fly was an aphrodisiac, the chemical extracted from the crushing of a particular species of beetle.

The house was exquisitely decorated and graphically underlined that Gerhard came from wealth and influence. Standing in the marble hallway, having dropped the key to the locked front door into a Greek urn, Feodor gathered himself for what lay ahead. He decided he should kill Hoffman first. The Nazi was the most physically able of the two and, more to the point, someone whom Feodor badly wanted to kill, unlike the unfortunate Gerhard who was simply in the wrong place at the wrong time.

Feodor returned to the living room but not before ripping the telephone's lead from its junction box. Gerhard was performing oral sex on Hoffman. 'Come here,' Hoffman hoarsely commanded Feodor. Feodor stood bare-chested behind Hoffman and began nuzzling the German's neck, wrapping his arms around the man's shoulders. 'Cradle my balls, for Christ's sake,' Hoffman screamed, agitated by sexual need. But in the instant that he spoke, the SS man's fine-tuned intuition detected Feodor's stalling. He tensed, prompting Feodor to bring up his left forearm under Hoffman's chin while positioning his right at the back of the German's neck. Then in the one sharp motion he snapped Hoffman's spinal cord. The naked Gerhard looked up in stunned amazement as the SS man's deadweight sunk to the floor.

'Take me to your dressing room,' Feodor said calmly. 'I want to inspect your wardrobe.' The terrified Gerhard scrambled to his feet. Knocking over ornaments in his desperation to escape, he scurried away. Feodor walked slowly after him. He found the German in the house's entrance hallway, furiously thumping the cradle of the telephone— unable to open his front door, Gerhard was now dismayed to find that his handset would not work.

Feodor gently took Gerhard's arm and led him to the house's sleeping quarters. 'First thing,' he said, 'could you please show me your three smallest suits?'

'My smallest suits?' Gerhard repeated, baffled by Feodor's instruction. He and his tormentor were roughly the same size, give or take a few kilos; this Hans Rehhagel could not possibly fit into a smaller garment. Gerhard would never know that the small suit was not for Feodor's use but rather for Adrian Ashton's, on becoming the Spanish interpreter Antonio Navarro. The Australian was a downed Lancaster bomber tail gunner, this telling Feodor that Adrian would be small in stature and unable to obtain the outfit he needed from Klaus Frind, the lanky Klaus Frind according to the German communist Werner Ulreich.

'Yes, your smallest suits,' Feodor repeated patiently.

The naked Gerhard sorted through his array of clothing, his fat buttocks wobbling in haste. 'Here,' he said, throwing three suits on the bed, those he had once bought for a lighter, shorter acquaintance and kept when the relationship lapsed. He looked anxiously at Feodor as Feodor studied the garments and was relieved when the so-called Rehhagel placed one aside.

'Now find me something larger,' Feodor said. 'Something my size but not too gaudy.' Gerhard produced a sober, double-breasted dark grey number. 'Yes, perfect,' Feodor said. 'I'll need a shirt, tie and a hat to go with it. Items that will make me look like a senior and respectable civil servant.' Gerhard knew exactly what Feodor wanted; he understood the need to be seen to conform. His skilled eye soon found suitably matching apparel. With that, Feodor directed Gerhard to return the remaining suits to his closet and lie face up on the bed.

For a brief moment, Gerhard thought Feodor was about to engage in some sort of obscure sex act. But when the steel-eyed Russian picked up a pillow from the bed, his hope was dashed. 'Please don't,' Gerhard pleaded as Feodor held the pillow above his face, repeating the entreaty twice over, each utterance more muffled than the last as Feodor pressed harder and harder—until Gerhard was dead.

CHAPTER 15

Eighteen months had elapsed since Major Feodor Timofeyevich Kozlovsky of the NKVD's Foreign Directorate confronted the German nurse Christel Metternich at Rostov-on-Don in February 1943. Accordingly, when the bespectacled man in the homburg hat seated on a bench in the Berlin Tiergarten, the huge inner city park near Christel's apartment, folded his newspaper and approached her that morning in August 1944 she did not recognise him immediately. With good reason—the Russian had been busy in the preceding hours transforming into the Gestapo investigator Dr Franz Schick.

Feodor's first job after killing Lothar Hoffman and Gerhard was to find a sharp knife in the kitchen of Gerhard's Wedding home. Levering open the inner sole of his right boot, he extracted his identification as Franz Schick, along with the so-called Schick's tasking orders, both documents carrying the forged, officially embossed signature of the notorious Gestapo head Heinrich Müller. Müller was a ruthless operator and a feared, loathed and immensely powerful figure. This is why the NKVD had decided that Feodor's urgent travel from Berlin to Tilsit on the East Prussia–Lithuania border, with Adrian Ashton posing as his Spanish interpreter Antonio Navarro, should appear to be undertaken at Müller's personal direction.

Feodor next began to cut Hans Rehhagel's uniform into small pieces, painstakingly flushing each segment individually down the lavatory to avoid clogging the system. This included Rehhagel's Iron

Cross wrapped in a square of cloth and sluiced away. In spite of his uncompromising crusade against the Nazis, Feodor felt a fleeting fraternal sadness. It was the warrior's bond, Feodor's brief distress that Rehhagel's medal would never be returned to his family.

By close to 3 am Feodor's initial tasks were done. Only then did he turn to disguising his identity. Feodor's NKVD planners had cautioned he would need to live by his wits. But they also emphasised that altering the colour and length of his scalp hair, growing facial hair and the wearing of spectacles, if possible, were central to masking his appearance. Feodor was aware his description would soon be circulated, once the Gestapo had established Hans Rehhagel was an imposter and the bodies of Lothar Hoffman and Gerhard were discovered, with whom the Rehhagel impersonator would be known to have associated at the Reich Room. In Gerhard's bathroom, Feodor rifled through the cupboards. His search was soon rewarded with a bottle of black hair dye. Next he fossicked through Gerhard's bedside tables, happening upon a pair of rimless eyeglasses. Feodor tried them on. The prescription was weak, befitting a man of Gerhard's age, permitting Feodor to tolerate the slightly blurred vision the spectacles induced.

Feodor's final act was to gather the body of Lothar Hoffman and place it on the bed beside Gerhard. Hoffman and Gerhard's discarded clothing he left strewn about the living room. His hope was that the signs of urgent disrobing when combined with the naked corpses in Gerhard's bedroom would suggest death by sexual misadventure, buying him precious time. But as Feodor knew only too well, it would not be long before the investigators turned their minds to the missing Hans Rehhagel.

Tidy up concluded, Feodor returned to the bathroom where he dyed his hair black and shaved his beard but not his upper lip. Once dressed in the double-breasted grey suit, he inspected himself in the bedroom's full-length mirror. On nodding in satisfaction, he donned the rimless spectacles and homburg hat also purloined from Gerhard.

'Good morning, Herr Doctor Schick,' Feodor said to his reflection. 'When your hair is cut short your transformation from Hans Rehhagel will be complete.'

***

By 5 am the summer sun was up. Berlin was a city where people still made their way to work, trying to act normally in abnormal times. Peering through the curtains in Gerhard's front room, Feodor watched for signs of persons on the move. It was a delicate balance between needing to stay in the house long enough for the city to awake from its slumber and leaving his sanctuary without being seen to do so.

Around 6:30 am Feodor saw a janitor emerge from the back door of the pension hotel directly across the street and empty a bucket of wastewater into a drain. Clasping his military carry bag, Feodor waited for the man to re-enter the building. Then, with one last check of the street, he exited Gerhard's house, sprinted to the hotel's back entrance and stepped inside.

Feodor found himself standing in a dusty stairwell. Calming his breathing, he could hear men talking on the landing above, judging it would draw too much attention to walk up the stairs and announce he was searching for the breakfast room. So he waited, prepared to kill anybody who came down the stairs. Eventually, a door closed and the sound of the men's conversation subsided. It was now or never.

Feodor crept up the stairs as quickly as he could, reaching the landing where the men had been talking. To his left was a stairway leading to the hotel's first level, while to the right a set of three stairs descended to the ground floor reception counter. Noting the reception clerk was working with his head down, Feodor pulled his homburg hat low across his eyes and, on taking the three steps to his right, strode boldly across the hotel's foyer and out the front door.

Sighting the Leopoldplatz subway entrance across the street, Feodor headed in that direction, stopping along the way to buy a newspaper behind which he could hide while travelling on the train. His next task as Dr Franz Schick was to try to intercept the German nurse Christel Metternich at the Tiergarten Park as she walked towards her place of work, the St. Hedwig Hospital. If unable to engage Christel by this means, Feodor accepted he would be obliged to rely on the less desirable option of seeking her out at the hospital.

Feodor sat on a park bench positioned to keep watch for Christel, looking out over his rimless spectacles. It was with no little relief that he saw the young woman approach. 'Christel,' Feodor whispered, falling in beside her. The nurse stopped and stared, startled by the seeming stranger and wondering what was happening. 'Don't do anything silly, comrade,' Feodor warned, taking Christel's arm and proceeding to stroll, 'or we'll both end up swinging from piano wire along with our good friend Ernst Thälmann.'

Thälmann was the head of the German communist party. It was Christel who first contacted Klaus Frind to advise of the plan to exchange a downed British airman for Thälmann's life. Things had changed since then, of course—not least for Thälmann. Unbeknown to Feodor, the communist leader had been executed at Buchenwald concentration camp just ten days earlier, shot dead on Hitler's express order.

Christel felt like she was dreaming. But Feodor's mention of Thälmann did cause her to look closely at him. The shock of recognition made her light-headed. 'What do you want?' Christel gasped. 'Is Wilhelmine all right?' she added in a seamless rush, referring to her twin sister held hostage by the Soviets whose life depended on Christel betraying her country.

'Wilhelmine sends her regards,' Feodor said, seeking to stabilise the trembling Christel. 'She said to tell you she is well.' Wilhelmine had done no such thing. But Feodor knew she was safe in an NKVD prison in Moscow where she ate adequately and was subjected to no abuse beyond the prison's rigorous discipline. When Christel did not reply, Feodor pressed on. 'We have no time to waste. You are to contact Klaus Frind by noon today and tell him I will arrive at his house at 5 pm tonight to have dinner with the family. I will be posing as Heidi Frind's nephew, Franz Schick, a Gestapo officer. Tell Klaus to return home early this afternoon to warn his wife of my impending arrival. Accept no argument. Tell him I have come from Moscow to take the Australian airman back there.'

'And what about my work?'

'You should go to the hospital as planned but by mid-morning pretend to be ill. Then go immediately to Klaus Frind and pass him my message before returning home.' With that, Feodor gently pushed the small of Christel's back, urging her to do as requested. 'Now off you go, and don't turn to look at me.'

Feodor watched Christel disappear into the glare of the summer morning, pleased to have completed the exchange with her in a matter of minutes. But now he had over nine hours to kill before he was scheduled to arrive at Klaus and Heidi Frind's house in Kladow. The imperative was to spend the time as unobtrusively as possible until he could get to the house, have his hair trimmed and finalise his transformation into Franz Schick. Feodor's solution was to draw on painful memories of living in Berlin.

In early 1936 Feodor and his wife to be, Adelaida, had come to Berlin from Frankfurt where they met as students. Although lovers by this time, the fact that they were living with Adelaida's parents prevented them from sharing the same bed until wedded. Thus while Adelaida slept in her girlhood bedroom, Feodor took up residence in a garret room in the family home formerly used for storage. But not to be deterred, the young ones set about finding a place where they could be together undisturbed and undetected.

That is why on leaving Christel, Feodor made his way to a cemetery on the Stralau peninsula, a salient jutting into the River Spree in central Berlin. The home owned by Adelaida's parents until the time of their deportation back to Argentina in 1938 was just three kilometres away in Berlin's Treptower district.

Specifically, Feodor went to the cemetery's ancient church, a tall and narrow late Gothic construction with a steep slate roof on which a spire extended far into the sky. There on the belfry's first level, on a bed of straw, Feodor and Adelaida would often spend the early evening during the three-month period preceding their marriage, making love and giggling silently whenever movement could be heard in the small nave below. Feodor knew that the church would be undamaged by Allied bombing—the cemetery was an important target reference point for the RAF Bomber Command raids on Berlin.

After eight hours in his hidey-hole, using the suffering of his thoughts of Adelaida to recharge his will to prevail, Feodor set out for Kladow. A slow train journey to Spandau followed by a twenty-minute bus ride and he was there. Striding confidently and carrying his German officer's leather carry bag, Feodor walked from the bus station, taking in his surrounds as he went, noting in particular as he passed by the Kladow market the presence of several uniformed individuals. At 5 pm he reached the Frinds' house.

***

Heidi's heart was in her mouth as she opened the door to greet the man in the double-breasted grey suit. Feodor smiled broadly before engaging in a chaste hug. 'Franz,' Heidi said loud enough for any listening neighbour to hear, forcing a smile to her lips. 'How wonderful to see you. Dear me, my sister's boy has grown. Come in, come in. We will have a glass of schnapps before dinner.'

Inside the house the dynamic changed. Feodor immediately took charge and was all business. 'My real name and details are not important,' he said, addressing those seated at the Frinds' dining table and speaking English for Adrian's benefit. 'For the purposes of this exercise I am Dr Franz Schick, a special duties Gestapo investigator.' Heidi was baking a rabbit and boiling a motley collection of stunted potatoes. Feodor's mouth watered; he had barely eaten all day. But driven man that he was, he pushed trivial thoughts like hunger from his mind.

'You are to be Antonio Navarro,' Feodor told Adrian, 'a Spanish civilian interpreter. You speak no German and we will converse in English.' With that, Feodor proceeded to detail the prepared cover story of Schick and Navarro travelling to Tilsit on the Lithuanian border to interrogate General Franco's cousin over the Wolf's Lair attack on Adolf Hitler. He finished by describing how Francoist intelligence, when forced by the Gestapo to provide an interpreter for the task, chose a non-German-speaking civilian because of the political distance such an odd appointment created between the intelligence service and the investigation of the Spanish leader's relative. Then Feodor stopped, waiting for questions.

It was Klaus who spoke first, fearful of impediments to Adrian leaving the house. 'Surely that's only half of it?' he objected. 'I mean it's fine to have a story why Spanish intelligence selected an interpreter who doesn't speak German. But what if someone speaks to Adrian in Spanish of which he can't speak a word?'

Feodor smiled amiably. 'Before leaving Moscow I had many discussions about what I should say or do in certain situations.' Feodor laughed, remembering the endless planning meetings in Lubyanka that resolved nothing. 'But in the end it was agreed that some matters defy easy prescription. We might encounter a Spanish speaker, we might not. But if we do, the action we take would depend on the circumstances.'

Klaus, though, was not for placating. 'What about Adrian's nasal drawl, then?' he asked with some aggression. 'His Australian accent will tell any English speaker he is not Spanish.'

'I can only offer you much the same answer, Herr Frind,' Feodor said evenly. 'Should we come across someone fluent enough to detect Adrian's Australian dialect, it might suffice, for example, to say Navarro is a Spanish–English interpreter who has worked the world over, leading to a hybrid English accent.'

A contemplative silence followed as Klaus mulled Feodor's response. 'And identity papers for Adrian?' Heidi enquired after a time, her electing to change the subject signalling she too foresaw that some matters could be addressed only as they arose.

'Certainly, Frau Frind,' Feodor said. 'If someone could kindly bring me a sharp knife.' The document signed by the Gestapo head Heinrich Müller declaring its bearer to be Antonio Navarro was of course sown into the inner sole of Feodor's left boot.

'What does it say?' Adrian asked, examining the incomprehensible to him typed German text sandwiched between the letterhead of a Nazi war eagle perched on a swastika and several official-looking stamps at the foot of the page.

Feodor read aloud from the document. 'It says that Navarro is acting at Müller's personal direction in quote: *the discharge of urgent and vital state duties.* The last paragraph directs that he is to be assisted without let or hindrance by all servants of the Reich.'

'Will that document alone suffice?' Klaus broke in, his voice pitching up. 'Shouldn't he also have a Spanish passport?'

'Müller's authority is absolute,' Feodor said grimly. 'We calculated in Moscow that, as with my identity papers, the letter will have currency for around twenty-four hours in the current climate.' Feodor smiled briefly. 'This judgement was premised on our travel taking no more than a day and the likelihood that those to whom we must explain our presence, most probably mid to upper-ranking military personnel, will be intimidated by Müller's name.' Feodor shrugged. 'Otherwise, we're in the hands of fate.'

The barely perceptible nod of Klaus's head was Feodor's cue to switch his gaze to Adrian. 'This, however, is something that wasn't fully considered in our planning.' The puzzled looks around the table prompted Feodor to expand. 'We in Moscow,' he said, 'understood that being kept indoors for some months would leave Adrian quite pale. We therefore conjured up some simple reasons for this. But now I find his appearance is worse than thought.' Feodor leant close to Adrian and studied him. 'Frankly,' he said, speaking to Adrian, 'you remind me of someone only recently discharged from a tuberculosis sanatorium.' Feodor stroked his cheeks with his index finger and thumb, as was his habit. 'How problematic this becomes remains to be seen.'

Klaus and Heidi both turned to examine Adrian. For the first time they noticed the extent to which he was ghostly pale. Adrian was naturally fair and over the past six months Klaus and Heidi had adjusted daily to the incremental blanching of his face. And although Adrian's features were not in and of themselves a difficulty—owing to Spain's genetic diversity fair skinned Spaniards were not uncommon—his sickly pallor was unusual.

The ever jittery Klaus again took up the cudgels. 'So, what is Adrian to say if asked about his health?' he said anxiously.

Klaus's continued questioning did not annoy Feodor. But he did reason that the German was too on edge to accept there were not ready solutions for all possible scenarios. It was time to end the discussions.

'My instructions,' Feodor said soberly, 'are should we encounter anyone who causes us problems, I am to deal with the situation as I see fit. This will obviously include issues that may arise in relation to Adrian's pallid complexion.'

The others stared at Feodor, drawn to the unflinching hardness in his voice and the deadly resolve it conveyed. A sinister pall settled over the room—the Russian's icy understatement had reminded Klaus, Heidi and Adrian of the high-stakes game they were playing. Feodor sensed their rising apprehension and sought to break the tension. 'As for the many other headaches with Adrian's cover story,' he said dryly, 'we will have to rely on our Gestapo friends continuing to scare the pants off most people.'

The immediate effect of Feodor's irony was to lift the dark mood gripping the house. Klaus poured more schnapps. 'To the communist international,' he toasted, his simple salute infusing Adrian with the knowledge that Heidi's socialism transcended national boundaries. It was why he didn't complain when later informed by his Soviet masters he would be a Russian agent and not one for communist Germany as Heidi had intended.

Soon there were relaxed smiles all around. Heidi wound up her old gramophone player and selected Antonín Dvořák's symphony

Number 9 in E Minor from her record collection. The music's haunting tones and lilting beauty engulfed the partially darkened room. The recording was of four movements and ran for forty minutes. Adrian was mesmerised, which only made more surreal his improbable situation in the company of equally improbable people. He was in another world far from his boyhood in Ballarat in Australia, but equally the sensation was exquisite.

As the music drew to a close, Adrian felt a hand take his under the table. It was Heidi looking searchingly at him. Adrian returned Heidi's grip feeling a powerful sexual surge as he did. He smiled and she smiled back, only to withdraw her hand. The brief gesture was a signal that all was forgiven and Heidi's personal wish for his safe passage rolled into one.

In his Notting Hill flat in February 1994, Adrian remembered that night like it was yesterday. As well he might, for it was the determining moment of his life: the occasion when he first met Feodor, even if unaware of his name at the time; and when Heidi's goodwill set his love for her in stone. As the terrible shame of his life readied to sheet home, Adrian pondered the ultimately destructive influence of those two people. He smiled briefly. In the years that followed, on Saturday nights after unstopping the sherry decanter, he would relive the dreamlike night in Kladow, playing Dvořák's symphony over and over again, conducting each movement with intensifying passion the drunker he became.

CHAPTER 16

Adrian had been part dozing and part reflecting, his head resting on the table at which he sat. While slumbering he'd been thinking that in one way or another his entire life had been dogged by worry and tension. And now the imminent publication of Roger Hardwicke's *Sunday Exegesis* article was one more distressing crossroads. The fearfulness Adrian was experiencing as he waited for Hardwicke's exposé reminded him of an earlier crisis point, the Thursday in the first week of February 1964 when the CIA internal investigations officer Kevin Carstone had come to his office. The American was again in the company of the top floor's James Newcombe, and that the MI6 heavy should have a funereal look on his face portended bad news.

It had been less than a week since Adrian walked across Westminster Bridge with his Soviet controller and told Anatoly he wanted to defect. By now the KGB would be considering the matter. Adrian was torn. On one hand, he fervently hoped that Lubyanka would do something, and soon. But on the other he was also worried the Russians might actually agree to his defection, given his mindset that at forty-two he might not be able to come to terms with living in Moscow.

But for all of Adrian's indecision, it ultimately didn't matter. 'Political reasons,' Anatoly said when later advising Adrian his request to defect had been denied. 'Politburo edict,' he said. 'The USSR's relations with the UK are currently too delicate.' And with that Adrian accepted the outcome, unsure whether or not to be angry but mulish all the same over the Soviet political leadership's apparent indifference to his welfare.

In the interim, the pressure had been building. The weekend after meeting Anatoly on Westminster Bridge and requesting to defect, Adrian had gone about his business trying to act normally. But on two occasions he thought he detected tails, not that he could be sure. The suspected taggers were not the same couple Adrian had sighted earlier, the presumed US embassy husband and wife team working informally for Carstone. The latest sightings—possible sightings—suggested official surveillance, the effect of which was to leave Adrian decidedly on edge. And now to have Newcombe and Carstone standing before him both grimly countenanced was further grounds for concern, to put it mildly.

Newcombe began by playing straight man for Carstone. 'Kevin has some more questions for you, Adrian,' he said gravely.

Adrian clasped his clammy hands and smiled, trying to remain steady. 'Yes, James, how can I help?'

Newcombe did not answer but instead glanced at Carstone, inviting him to speak. 'Why do you go to Manchester so often?' the American asked bluntly, not even trying to act the Southern gentleman. 'And what do you do when you're there?'

Adrian shuddered. His worst fears had just materialised; Carstone was now on a pathway to Sara. Adrian tried to fudge, which was unwise because it served only to feed their evident suspicions. But he was panicked and it was the best he could do in the moment. 'I go there in my own time. That's not a crime, is it?'

'I didn't ask when you go. I asked why you went there and what you do when you get there,' Carstone replied coldly.

Newcombe interjected. 'It won't surprise you to know, Adrian,' he said, 'that we're taking a close look at all aspects of the Nicaraguan op. This allegation by Kevin's source is a very serious matter, that the Sovs went along with the president's ousting in favour of his younger brother all for the purposes of building the bona fides of a KGB agent, here inside our very own house.' Adrian forced himself to look Newcombe in the eye, willing that he should not blink. 'We've come across this propensity of yours to visit Manchester,' Newcombe continued, 'and the fact that you do so without obvious reason. You have no family there, for example.'

'How do you know when I go to Manchester?' Adrian asked in an attempt to deflect and interrupt the line of questioning. 'Have I been under surveillance for some reason?'

Carstone smiled knowingly. Minicabs had only recently been introduced in the UK and, because they were cheaper, Adrian started using them in preference to hackney carriages. But now his bent for economy had backfired. 'Fellow called Reggie Shed,' Carstone said, 'know him?' Reggie Shed was a minicab operator with whom Adrian had formed a loose relationship. Reggie would pick up Adrian at home in Notting Hill and take him to London Euston from where he would catch a train to Manchester. Reggie could be relied on to be waiting when Adrian returned.

'So, you've been checking on my minicab use?' Adrian replied with heat, pleased to be angry because it calmed his nerves a little.

'Yup,' Carstone said, smugly proud of his detective work. 'So, if you'd be good enough to answer my questions.'

Adrian again thought of defection, unaware at the time of the Politburo's veto. The prospect of living out his life in Moscow suddenly didn't seem so bad. But he also knew that before his defection could be arranged, he'd first have to see off this immediate threat. And that was easier said than done. He had exhausted the limited tricks in his spy's rucksack and would now have to rely on Sara keeping her mouth shut. This was not a proposition that filled him with confidence.

'It's a woman, if you must know,' Adrian said, his nerves twitching again.

'Name?' Carstone asked with crisp hostility.

'Sara,' Adrian replied, knowing full well the question that would follow.

'Sara who?' Carstone said, now in the lead and relegating Newcombe to second fiddle in a demonstration of American might over British strategic need.

'Lnu,' Adrian said, before spelling out the letters. 'L N U.'

'Last name unknown?' Newcombe broke in disbelievingly.

'She offers certain services,' Adrian said resignedly, as if not hearing Newcombe speak.

'Of a sexual nature?' Carstone asked, the hint of a leer briefly coming to his face.

'Something like that.'

'OK,' Carstone said, 'where do we find your... er... friend?'

'I write to her care of the Dumbrille Hotel,' Adrian said, grateful for the fact that he never boasted about his spying in any of the letters he sent to Sara. 'She works around there most nights.'

Carstone took notes while Newcombe adopted a disapproving tone. 'This is highly concerning, Adrian,' he said. 'Officers using prostitutes can have significant security implications.'

Adrian began to grasp at straws. 'Well, not in my case, James,' he told Newcombe, striving to sound assertive. 'I'm not married and, as you know, have no family. It would be a different matter if I tried to hide my association with Sara and lied to you. But I've told you the truth without having to be pressured. It's not actually a crime in this country to use prostitutes, you know, so long as they're of age.'

Adrian was astonished to see Newcombe take this on board, it dawning on him in that instant that his masters on the top floor were anxious to find any excuse by which they might avoid a scandal. So encouraged, Adrian tried to exploit the MI6 management's denial. 'It's not as though I talk about my work,' he said. 'She thinks I'm a claims clerk with Lloyd's of London.' It was Adrian's one big, damaging lie. But the harm inflicted was not to Adrian—rather, the ultimate damage was to Kevin Carstone, the price he paid for learning of Adrian's mistruth.

***

That night Adrian fretted, knowing that no matter how much Newcombe might argue to the contrary, Carstone would insist he be surveilled until the facts of his Manchester connection were clear. The two people in the world with whom Adrian badly needed to speak— Sara and his controller Anatoly—were both off-limits. The next morning Adrian felt so poorly that he even contemplated ringing in sick. But he knew he could not because this would give away the extent of his worry. So he hauled himself into the office, feeling at any minute like he might throw up on the tube.

The day passed without Adrian sighting Carstone. At another time he might have believed the American was busily ensconced in the top floor office the MI6 administration had allocated him. But today Adrian could not. He knew only too well that Carstone was travelling to Manchester. After a miserable day he thought would never end, Adrian began to retrace his path home. Fatalistically depressed, he didn't bother to look for tails, in no doubt that someone would be on his back watching to see he went directly to his flat before a monitoring team in a nondescript van parked nearby took over for the night.

Adrian poured a large sherry from the drinks tray in his flat's entrance hallway and stood in the gloom drinking it, shoulders slumped. A male voice coming from the unlit sitting room made him jump.

'Aren't you going to offer me a drink, Mendoza?' It was Feodor, older for sure, with grey flecks now visible in his once blond hair, but unmistakably the same old, imperturbable Feodor. Adrian had last seen him in Moscow in June 1945 shortly before being returned to British hands, nine months after they made their epic trek from Berlin to the Lithuanian border.

The shock of seeing Feodor caused Adrian to think his bowels were going to move. He placed a hand over his mouth and gestured frantically at the ceiling. Feodor laughed. 'There's no microphones in here if that's what you're worried about,' he said. Adrian stared at him, bug-eyed with fear. 'I had someone check ahead of inviting myself in. I've been here since our people left.' Feodor shrugged. 'I'm a little surprised, to be honest, given what Anatoly has reported. I can only assume that in wishing to avoid political attention, your superior, this James Newcombe, has been dragging his feet on taking action.'

'Things have got a lot worse than you know,' Adrian said dejectedly. A sense of exhaustion wafted over him. Now he was prepared to accept his flat was not bugged, the adrenalin rush on finding Feodor waiting in his sitting room had petered out.

'Tell me about the new developments,' Feodor said in a fatherly voice.

Adrian sighed and proceeded to tell Feodor about Sara, how he met her, how the relationship developed, and how he had told her everything. Feodor listened impassively, occasionally nodding. 'The American cunt, Carstone,' Adrian snarled in angry conclusion, 'went to Manchester today. If he hasn't yet found Sara, he'll find her tonight and that'll be the end of it.'

Feodor briefly shook his head in amusement. Adrian rarely used coarse language and his agitated resort to vulgarity was so out of character as to be funny. 'I should think they've already bugged your telephone,' Feodor said matter-of-factly. 'But they were likely unable to do in here today because Newcombe's soft-pedalling left them with insufficient time to have a judge sign the requisite paperwork. And as it's Friday night, they won't be able to install microphones until Monday when you're next at work.'

'I need to defect,' Adrian blurted fearfully. 'You've got to get me out, tonight.'

'I'm afraid even the wheels of the magnificent Soviet state do not turn quickly enough for that,' Feodor replied, aware of the Politburo's edict directing Adrian should stay, and the KGB Chairman's decision not to dispute it, but judging now was not the right time to tell Adrian. 'In the interim,' Feodor continued, 'we need to concentrate on neutralising your friend, Mr Carstone.'

'How will you do that?' Adrian rasped. The tension was irritating his throat.

'I came in from Stockholm last night as Jennsen, a Swedish telecommunications executive.'

'And?'

'Well, if your concubine, Sara, works mainly in the evenings, Carstone will stay in Manchester overnight, almost certainly at this Dumbrille Hotel where you first met her. As I got into the country as the friendly Jennsen, nobody from British security will be taking an interest in me. As such, I'll leave you shortly and take the last train to Manchester.'

'But you can't be sure that Carstone will stay at the Dumbrille Hotel; it's a dump and being an American he'll want something swankier. Manchester's a big city. You may not find him.'

Feodor shrugged. 'Did I ever tell you I studied behavioural science?' he asked conversationally. 'I still dabble in the field,' he added when Adrian didn't answer. 'The point I'm making is that your Mr Carstone displays an unhealthy zeal where you are concerned. He will, therefore, stay where Sara does most of her work, even if he finds it distasteful. I can guarantee it. Why? Because Carstone knows that Sara will be motivated by money more, I am sorry to say, than any affection she has for you.' Feodor leant forward and looked hard at Adrian. 'Have trust, Mendoza. Our American friend will hire Sara, not for sex but for cooperation. Her interrogation will take half the night and then Carstone will want to sleep. Provided I am there by early morning, I think I can locate him.'

Feodor stood in Adrian's darkened hallway, preparing to go. 'Accepting that I can resolve matters satisfactorily,' he said, 'we should meet again on Sunday night.' He held up a hand, knowing Adrian was poised to ask about the current surveillance. 'If MI6 is no longer watching you a car in your street will sound its horn twice at seven sharp on Sunday night. Be listening. Should you hear the all clear signal meet me two hours later at Holland Park tube station.'

With that, Feodor left, not via the front door onto the street where an MI6 surveillance team was sure to be observing from a parked van, but through the rear entrance. Vaulting across a hedge fence, he ran swiftly through the neighbour's small back garden. Minutes later, with no one the wiser, the Russian entered High Street Kensington tube station heading for London Euston from where the overnight train to Manchester would depart.

***

Now at 4:30 am on Sunday 27 February 1994, Adrian waited for Roger Hardwicke's damning disclosure and the moment of truth. He felt the weight of his nearly three score and twelve years like never before. Wearily he recalled that night in February 1964 and how Feodor's optimism about finding Carstone had raised his hopes the Russian would rectify matters on reaching Manchester. But Adrian's cautious confidence was not without a brief flutter of panic once it had occurred to him that Feodor's putting affairs right might involve him killing Sara.

Adrian smiled, remembering how he had bitterly cursed for failing to extract a promise from Feodor that Sara was not to be harmed. But on thinking it through that night his anxiety had eased, aided no doubt by a second glass of sherry. Just as he loved Sara with every fibre in his being, especially when she was in full flow as Heidi, Feodor had loved his wife Adelaida with the same if not more intensity, only for the Nazis to take her from him. Feodor knew better than most the excruciating pain of personal loss. It was not something the Russian would inflict on him willy-nilly. For if nothing else, Feodor knew he was too damaged to cope with the emotional trauma.

Adrian again inspected Feodor's letter. An awful question formed in his mind. If Feodor was aware of his emotional vulnerability in 1964, when despite his shakiness over Carstone, he was still relatively strong, why then had Feodor betrayed him in the twilight of his life, inflicting grievous injury when all robustness was gone? Adrian stared at the torn envelope in his hands. He knew the answer to this and many other questions were inside. And with barely ninety minutes before

Hardwicke published, the time available to read Feodor's letter was fast shrinking. 'Just give me ten to fifteen minutes more,' he pleaded, to whom he wasn't sure. 'Just a little longer, then I promise I'll read it.'

But the words rang hollow in his ears, and he heard them for what they were. Adrian occasionally had been physically brave, especially during the war, but he was ever the moral coward. It was this failing making him want to avoid the reality of Feodor's letter, just as over the years he had ignored the many home truths that, if heeded, might have led to a less troubled life. So Adrian stared into the early morning, knowing he would read the letter only at the last moment, when absolutely he must.

CHAPTER 17

'It's the way he looks at me,' Tonia Newcombe complained. She was referring to Kevin Carstone and voicing her dislike of him. Tonia and her MI6 husband, James, were standing in the kitchen of their Belgravia town house. It was the Thursday night in the first week of February 1964. Earlier that day Carstone and James had quizzed Adrian on his frequent visits to Manchester and learned of his association with Sara. In the hours since James's antenna had been warning of a problem. His solution was to invite Carstone over for an informal dinner to try to head it off.

'What do you mean, Ton?' Newcombe said distractedly. His head was inserted halfway inside the refrigerator. 'White wine, white wine,' Newcombe muttered, 'Kevin wants a glass of white wine.'

'He doesn't look at my face when speaking to me,' Tonia explained, 'only at my chest.' She was waiting for the chicken to finish roasting. 'It's quite unsettling.'

Newcombe withdrew from the refrigerator and looked at Tonia. She held an oven glove to her forehead and was pushing at a persistent wisp of blond hair. Newcombe saw the sign of strain, and the last thing he needed right now was a domestic dispute.

'It's a proven scientific fact, darling,' he said, adopting a mock professorial tone in the hope of humour defusing the issue, 'that women's chests have a physiological effect on men. Unfortunately, Kevin seems to find yours especially attractive.'

Tonia glared at her husband. 'Well, I certainly know that women's chests have an effect on *you*,' she said cryptically.

To this day, James Newcombe did not know if Tonia knew about his affair when they were stationed in France after the war, when she was pregnant with the twins and went home to be with her mother for the birth. His best guess was that being a woman, she intuited it because the good intelligence officer he was he chose a married woman as his mistress, calculating this would limit the chances of discovery. It was during the affair that Newcombe came to realise career was his natural calling. To be sure he enjoyed the thrill of the liaison, but not sufficiently to overcome the niggling worry it risked his professional advancement. After putting an end to the relationship, therefore, once Tonia and the twins returned to Paris, he became the family man workaholic he was today—just as his employer liked.

Newcombe's big breakthrough came in Budapest in 1956 during the Hungarian Uprising and the brutal Soviet intervention to quell it. The ratlines he established ensured the extraction of most of MI6's key assets, the ensuing promotion setting him firmly on the career path. Now at age forty-nine Newcombe was in sight of the top job, the Director General no less, provided he could ensure that Adrian Ashton didn't cause any political palpitations for which he, the head of MI6 organisational integrity, would be blamed.

***

'Recrudescence,' Newcombe said. 'Are you familiar with the word, Kevin?' Dinner was over and Tonia had gratefully left for the kitchen to wash up while the boys talked shop. 'Some use it to describe the recurrence of an undesirable situation,' Newcombe continued when Carstone didn't answer. 'And that's what I fear you might be doing with this hounding of Adrian Ashton.'

'Hounding?' Carstone said aggressively. 'The guy's got more question marks over him than a two-dollar bill.'

'Look, he's an Australian,' Newcombe said, as if that explained everything. 'God help them if he's the best they can do. Ten years ago, he somehow wrangled a spot on our team. He's an odd man with odd ways, one who got lucky in Nicaragua, and we're saddled with him.' Carstone listened, continuing to simmer as Newcombe pressed on. 'I was prepared to put him under surveillance as you requested because of the historically close cooperation between our Services. But, really, you could waste oodles of precious time digging around and still only find that he's an inadequate little colonial who uses prostitutes.' Newcombe sighed, seeking to place emphasis on his closing argument. 'That would be scant recompense for reigniting the trans-Atlantic schism, especially as we both know it would inevitably extend to Number 10 and the White House.' Newcombe was referring to the glut of British traitors over the last dozen years and more and the resulting American ill will, a lingering crack in the Western alliance that had barely healed.

Newcombe was usually as smooth as the proverbial duck's egg. But tonight the obsessed Carstone was impervious to his sophistry. 'You Limeys are something else, you know that?' Carstone said, his anger spilling over. 'You're more worried about what the tabloids print than you are in fighting communism. Tomorrow morning I'm going to Manchester to find this Sara Lnu. When I do, I'm going to have her tell me everything there is to know about Adrian Ashton. And trust me, if it's juicy enough, which I'm betting it will be, I'm coming straight back here, to your Englishman's castle, and dropping the whole steaming mess at your feet.'

The evening was now officially a debacle and all Newcombe could do was perfunctorily offer Carstone more coffee as a prelude to wrapping up. Carstone left, deliberately driving with enough speed to tear up some of the gravel in the driveway. Tonia had gone to bed leaving Newcombe to sit quietly nursing a brandy, thinking. He knew he had neither the time nor likely the persuasion to convince Charles Kilbay, head of the CIA station in London, to pull rank on Carstone and prevent him from going to Manchester. 'But there's more than one way to skin a cat, old boy,' Newcombe said, speaking out loud to the departed Carstone. The bureaucratic powerbroker had just decided that in defence of his ambition to become his agency's Director General, he would use his considerable authority within MI6 to discredit, deflect or otherwise neuter any information Carstone unearthed, no matter how serious. 'I've come way too far to be pipped at the post,' Newcombe muttered as he turned off the light and headed for bed.

***

A little over three miles away in another part of London, Adrian Ashton retired around the same time as James Newcombe. But whereas Newcombe had been gifted the ability to compartmentalise, to set his problems aside and sleep, Adrian possessed no such capacity. He lay awake, fretting about the day's events and thinking how Carstone now firmly had him in his gunsights. He shuddered, not with the cold but with fear. Adrian was often scared but seldom this fearful. The terror rivalled that which drove him to save Feodor's life when it was hanging in the balance during their miraculous journey to the Lithuanian border.

Lying in his Notting Hill bed, Adrian thought of that moment long ago when the deep bond was formed between he and Feodor, when the Russian awarded him the Mendoza honorific. It was an instant in time with its origin in the evening of 25 August 1944 in the house of Klaus and Heidi Frind, the night that Feodor arrived in Kladow. Feodor had just begun to outline departure arrangements.

'I originally thought we might wait in the woods until dawn and take the first bus to the station at Spandau,' Feodor told Adrian, while Klaus and Heidi looked on. 'But when walking here earlier tonight I saw several rural police gathered at the Kladow market. I would prefer to limit the chances of running into a random check by one of their units. We can't support a claim to be local businessmen and our cover as the Gestapo investigator and his Spanish interpreter does not take effect until we're on our way east.' The rural police service had been formed by the Waffen-SS in 1936, its ranks bulging with vicious Nazi zealots. Feodor stroked his cheeks with index finger and thumb, as was his habit when thinking. He turned to Klaus. 'What about the men who picked up Adrian?' he asked.

'I haven't enquired who did the pick up for security reasons,' Klaus replied. 'But they're possibly fishermen because Helmut Dzufer engaged them. He's a fisherman who operates a trawler to fish the Wannsee lakes. He is also someone who I know and trust. I paid him a tidy sum to do the job, to be the sub-contractor, and he made all the arrangements.'

'Tell me more about Helmut Dzufer,' Feodor ordered. The Russian was aware that an hour up river from Kladow stood the Lindenufer pier, adjacent to which was the Spandau railway station. And now a plan was forming in his mind whereby he and Adrian would be ferried to Spandau hidden in Helmut Dzufer's fishing trawler.

Klaus shrugged. 'There's not much more to add,' he said. 'Helmut lives in a cottage on the other side of the woods. We went to school together. After his wife died his only child, a son, was seduced by the Nazi propaganda and left home. Helmut has never seen him again and thinks he died in Russia. He blames Hitler and the Nazis for this. Although not a socialist, that's why Helmut was willing to organise a party to pick up a British airman when I broached the subject with him. But the risks were huge and whether Helmut would want to get involved again, I don't know.'

'I think I could convince Helmut,' Heidi interjected softly from the far end of the room where she was pressing the suit taken from Gerhard's house that Adrian, as Antonio Navarro, was to wear. She had read Feodor's mind. 'I can go to his house right away and ask him if you like.'

'Thank you, Frau Frind,' Feodor said. 'Please do that. Tell Dzufer I will pay him 250 reichsmarks for danger money in return for him taking us to Spandau, leaving at dawn.'

'250 reichsmarks?' Heidi echoed.

Feodor understood Heidi was enquiring as to the source of this sizeable sum. Happy to oblige, he began by describing how he had reached East Prussia disguised as the regular German soldier Hans Rehhagel. 'I had taken medicine to make me ill,' Feodor said. 'The German patrol that found me took me to a military hospital in Königsberg. Later I was transferred to a hospital here in Weimar Germany where to my great surprise the German paymaster corps tracked me down, believing me to be Rehhagel.' Feodor laughed. 'The Gestapo will get quite a shock when it discovers I have been paid Rehhagel's back pay.'

Heidi was grateful for Feodor's explanation. She could now accept his good fortune with a clear conscience, knowing that offering Dzufer generous compensation on top of her existing leverage would guarantee his cooperation. She put down her heavy stove top heated iron and readied to go. 'I will take the shortcut through the forest,' she told Klaus.

Klaus's anxiety, however, was never far from the surface. And Feodor's mention of the Gestapo was causing him to worry about Heidi encountering rural police while she was out. 'Heidi, no,' he said. 'It's past 10 pm and nobody walks around after dark these days. It's too dangerous and Helmut will not be happy to be disturbed so late. In any event, I'm at a loss to understand how you could convince him to help any more than I could.'

Heidi ignored Klaus's misgivings, as often she did. 'Helmut,' she said, addressing Feodor, 'has the key to the boat shed. I'll get it so that you and Adrian can go there before first light and be ready to depart at dawn.' The boat shed was where six months earlier Adrian had spent his first night after being snatched from the civilian search party in the Wannsee forest. Indeed, on reaching the boat shed and awaking the next morning, Helmut Dzufer was the man in the Greek fiddler's cap watching over him.

'Excellent,' Feodor said. 'That would be ideal.' Feodor inclined his head reflectively. 'But to pick up on Herr Frind's point,' he said levelly, 'why do you think you personally can persuade Helmut Dzufer to assist us, especially as he may not appreciate you calling at this odd hour?'

'He won't complain about the time,' Heidi replied vaguely.

Feodor smiled, intrigued by Heidi's evasion. 'And remind me again,' he pressed gently, 'why should Dzufer accommodate us?'

Heidi took a deep breath, exhaling forcefully. 'Because he and I were once lovers,' she said. She looked directly at Klaus. 'Before we were married.' Heidi had answered in German, her intuition telling her not to reveal her long-held secret to Adrian. Klaus bristled before restraining himself. Yet although Adrian saw the exchange, he questioned neither Klaus nor Heidi on it. It was in fact human nature at work in two acts: one of commission, Heidi's protection of Adrian's sensibilities her tacit acknowledgement he had become the son she never had; and one of omission, Adrian's lack of enquiry his maintenance of a purity for Heidi of the type the infatuated reserve for the object of their desires.

By 3 am it was time to go—the summer sun would rise in an hour or so. Feodor's hair was cut short and with it dyed black a radical departure from the blond and wavy mane he wore while posing as Hans Rehhagel. For over an hour the four in the house had been sitting in the dark, each absorbed by their own thoughts.

'After we reach central Berlin later this morning,' Feodor said, standing to leave, 'we will catch the first available train east, ideally to Königsberg. It will be late at night when we arrive. My plan is to find a vehicle, make the 120 kilometre commute to Tilsit in the early hours and proceed by foot until we link-up with the Soviet forces. No more than a twenty-four hour trip in total if we are lucky.' All present were hoping for the best. But as socialists there were no silent prayers, just prolonged handshakes before Feodor and Adrian stole into the night, Feodor with his military carry bag and Adrian a plain suitcase Klaus had provided.

Kladow was still and quiet. Feodor and Adrian inched towards the boat shed, moving painstakingly from one hiding place to another, secreting themselves behind tree trunks or in clumps of grass as they went, constantly on the lookout for posses of rural policemen. At the boat shed they lay in its shadow, out of the moonlight, listening for sounds of human movement. On detecting none, Feodor crept forward, boat shed door key in hand. Once inside, he stood stock-still, straining to hear. In the distance a dog barked but apart from the river's gentle lapping no other sound could be heard. Opening the door, Feodor lobbed a pebble in Adrian's direction. It was the signal he should enter the shed as quickly as possible. Then they waited for the light.

***

The sun was barely up when Helmut Dzufer arrived. Feodor and Adrian heard him walk to the adjoining jetty where he started his trawler's throaty engine before returning to the boat shed, leaving the motor idling. Feodor immediately handed Helmut the 250 reichsmarks. By now the Gestapo would be piecing together the movements of the Hans Rehhagel impersonator, alerted by the real Rehhagel's failure to return to his family in Frankfurt. To dally was to take an unacceptable risk. The Gestapo would have already connected him to the murders of Lothar Hoffman and Gerhard and circulated his description. Feodor's moustache was still a couple of days from forming. But he had Gerhard's eyeglasses, a new hairstyle and civilian clothes, which gave him confidence he could survive all but the most studied inspection, especially with the homburg hat taken from Gerhard's house worn low over his eyes.

Feodor was also sure the Wehrmacht officers with whom he drank at the Reich Room had unquestioningly accepted he was a native of Frankfurt—his targeted references to the city drawing on his student days were intended to create this exact impression. The deception was important for the confusion it created. No doubt the Gestapo would consider the possibility that the Rehhagel imposter was a Soviet agent. But when the investigators took into account his crime was a criminal offence rather than an act of sabotage against the Nazi war effort, this would suggest he was nothing more than an errant German citizen, a fugitive from justice now intent on surrendering to the British and

American forces advancing from the west. For no German, not even a brazen murderer, would want to fall into the hands of the Bolsheviks marching from the east.

Helmut retrieved two sets of oilskins from pegs at the rear of the boat shed. 'Put these on,' he instructed Feodor and Adrian. 'You can't be seen getting on the boat dressed in suits. The skins will make you look like fishermen, at least from a distance.'

Ten minutes later the little red fishing trawler with the single high mast and wide-set bows was underway. The vessel was named *Schatzi*, *little treasure* in English. The journey would take just over an hour. Feodor and Adrian were below deck in the boat's cramped forward section, still in their oilskins and squashed together trying to ignore the pungent odour of rotting fish. Adrian began counting the minutes, grateful for Feodor's insistence they should back into their hiding space so that their feet pointed to the bow and their faces to the hatch through which a zephyr of fresh air flowed.

CHAPTER 18

Adrian vividly recalled Feodor's calm leadership in August 1944 when the Russian led him through the Kladow night to the boat shed where they waited for passage to Spandau on Helmut Dzufer's little red trawler, the *Schatzi*. It was the time when his trust in Feodor began to take root, something that would unfold into unquestioning faith as their epic 800 kilometre journey progressed across a Nazi-held landscape all the way to the Lithuanian border. Ever since, Adrian had marvelled at the contrast of Feodor's ruthless genius with his amiable nature and ready smile. But with Roger Hardwicke's *Sunday Exegesis* article soon to expose him as a traitor, all thanks to Feodor, Adrian admitted he had admired the ruthlessness only because it was exercised for his benefit. The feeling, he decided, was not quite so warm when the boot was on the other foot.

Feodor's train reached Manchester Piccadilly station at 7 am on Saturday 8 February 1964. The morning had dawned icy cold and showery. Lack of sleep seemed never to affect Feodor. Just as well, because sleep would have been elusive seated upright in his second-class compartment in the company of a travelling salesman, self-described, who was boisterously inebriated. And even after the man passed out, his loud snoring presented yet another impediment to sleep. Not that Feodor minded staying awake; he needed to plan.

Feodor surveyed the near deserted Manchester city centre. The Dumbrille Hotel was about a mile away. Pulling up the collar of his overcoat and skirting from one shop overhang to another, he arrived to see a trickle of guests either checking out or making their way to the in-house restaurant for breakfast. Feodor strategically positioned himself in the lobby, halfway between the hotel restaurant and its reception counter. Whether Carstone decided to check out or try his luck at the restaurant, he would spot him. Of course, all Feodor had to go on was Adrian's description of Carstone. But he reasoned that an American in the west English Midlands would not be difficult to spot, CIA agent notwithstanding.

Fifteen minutes later, Feodor's vigil was rewarded. A tall man with neatly parted black hair wearing a fawn trench coat and carrying a grey hat had just marched through the lobby to the check-out counter. The bounce in the American's step told Feodor that Carstone had extracted from Sara the information he needed, craved in fact. And in Feodor's estimation the American also seemed in a rush to leave, as if he had not yet passed on his accrued intelligence. That indeed was the case. As promised the preceding Thursday night, Carstone was intent on getting back to London where he would call at the Belgravia residence of Adrian's MI6 superior James Newcombe and drop the whole steaming mess at his feet.

Feodor waited outside the hotel for Carstone to emerge, judging that the combination of rain and urgency would prompt the American to opt for a taxi. And so it was.

'Manchester Piccadilly railway station,' Carstone instructed the taxi driver through the lowered kerbside window. But as Carstone sought to climb in the vehicle's rear passenger compartment, Feodor stepped forward from the awning under which he had been sheltering. He began to jostle Carstone in competition for the taxi.

'What the fuck?' Carstone exclaimed. Although he liked to project the image of a devoutly religious man, Carstone would habitually resort to profanities when angry or flustered.

'I am before you in the queue,' Feodor said. 'Please show some manners.' The Russian's English was accented. Feodor usually preferred a Swedish guise, but today had chosen to be Czech.

'Goddamnit, man,' Carstone said heatedly. 'It's a Saturday and there's ten other cabs on the rank. Take the next one.'

'So, you are an American who thinks he can push we British around?' Feodor said in haughty accusation.

'You don't sound British to me, buddy,' Carstone spat back.

'I am a British citizen of ten years standing,' Feodor hammed, 'formerly from Czechoslovakia. I demand an apology for your rudeness and suggest that *you* might like to take the next cab.'

'Fucking foreigner,' Carstone fumed, turning away to take the taxi second in line.

It was then Feodor laid hands on him. 'You are not leaving without apologising,' Feodor said. A struggle ensued as Carstone sought to break Feodor's hold. The hotel doorman eventually stepped in, calling for restraint. By the time the second in line taxi carrying the American departed for the railway station, Feodor was seated in the first placed cab giving the driver vague instructions designed to delay their leaving. Carstone waved his fist as his taxi passed by. Feodor smiled, placing the American's billfold wallet in the inside pocket of his overcoat. He had lifted the item as they struggled. A decade earlier, in March 1954, the KGB had morphed off the drawing board and into existence. Its incoming management had stipulated that all officers transferring into the new security agency should undergo refresher training. When it came to lifting items—pick-pocketing as it were—Feodor found he had lost none of his nimble touch.

***

Feodor's taxi took him to a street intersection near Manchester's grim Strangeways prison, in the red-light district of Cheetham Hill. It was now after 9 am and the flotsam and jetsam of the night had vacated the streets.

Feodor watched the taxi depart before walking two blocks to a narrow laneway running parallel to the prison's eastern wall. Soon after he arrived at a two-storey brick dwelling coated in flaking white paint. A weathered sign above the front door announced the presence of a tailor's shop. Feodor entered, ringing the customer alert bell. A short man in a shabby three-piece suit and loose-fitting collar emerged from the shop's interior, a tape measure yellowed by time draped around his neck.

'Sol,' Feodor said, extending his hand. 'It's been a while.'

'Well, I never,' Sol exclaimed in surprise. 'Rosa,' he called loudly to the back of the shop. 'It's Mr Nilsson.'

The woman called Rosa appeared and made a beeline for Feodor, kissing him on both cheeks. 'Mr Nilsson,' she squeaked, 'we never dreamt we would see you again. How long has it been?'

'Ten years,' Feodor replied, laughing and shaking his head.

Taking Feodor by the hand, Rosa led him to a kitchenette at the rear while Sol reversed the *Open* sign on the door to show the shop was closed. Tea was served and reminiscences engaged in. 'Are you still working for… ?' Sol asked cautiously after a time.

'Yes, yes,' Feodor replied, smiling, 'still at the Palace.' He laughed generously. 'The Swedish equerry, ma'am calls me.'

Sol and Rosa clasped their hands in excitement. 'And how is the lady?' Sol asked. 'She must be due any time now.'

'Doing beautifully,' Feodor lied expansively. 'I see quite a lot of her these days. She's in the pink.' Feodor was referring to Queen Elizabeth II who indeed was to give birth to Prince Edward a mere thirty-one days later. But it was not the Queen's pregnancy uppermost in Feodor's mind but rather the reason for his visit.

'I have another small problem,' he said quietly, as if taking Sol and Rosa into his confidence. 'Quite different to the last matter, though.'

Sol and Rosa nodded. They knew Feodor was harking back a decade to when he first met the couple. It started in the summer of 1954 with a report from the Soviet embassy in London advising that a KGB officer, a Georgian, had sought to defect. Worse, the Georgian had told his suitor, MI5—Britain's domestic intelligence service—

of a KGB operation in train to plant a suborned British national in MI6. The Georgian, however, had not yet mentioned names, which was fortunate for Adrian because the would-be defector knew he was the KGB asset in question, even if unaware Adrian was actually an Australian. For all that, the development was something of which Adrian was oblivious at the time. Indeed, not until long after he'd been accepted into MI6 did he learn of the matter and that Feodor had come to his rescue—again.

Back in the summer of 1954, the report on the Georgian's antics caused a flurry of activity in Moscow. At the time the newly formed KGB held high hopes for Adrian, unaware he was destined to disappoint. Feodor had judged the situation as sufficiently serious to personally come to Britain to put affairs right. Usually any Soviet caught trying to defect would be whisked out of London, back to Moscow where interrogation awaited followed by execution. But with MI5 closely monitoring its prospective prize, and the associated risk of it plucking the Georgian from Soviet embassy hands at London airport, an alternative plan was necessary.

Feodor's solution was to choose a city away from London to where the traitor could be lured on the false promise that in the spirit of a more forgiving and enlightened KGB era, he would face only demotion provided he proved his loyalty and reliability by satisfactorily completing an urgent out-of-town job. The duped Georgian would be kept hidden somewhere where the British authorities would not think to look, until the trail went cold and he could be smuggled out of England, to the Irish Republic in the first instance. That's why Feodor initially chose Liverpool. But on finding the British security services lined up three abreast in the Merseyside searching for Irish Republican Army infiltrators, he opted for the less scrutinised Manchester. The selection of Sol and Rosa came from Feodor's decision to concentrate on Manchester's tougher suburbs, those inhabited by people who knew the value of keeping their mouths shut. And in 1954 no suburb of Manchester was tougher than Cheetham Hill near Strangeways prison.

Sol and Rosa had met in Treblinka concentration camp as twenty-year-olds. Young and strong enough to survive the horror of the Nazis, they immigrated to Britain after the war. There they embraced their adopted country. It was the flag in the window of their shop proudly marking the coronation of Queen Elizabeth the year before in 1953 that convinced Feodor to pitch at the couple using the cover of a Buckingham Palace emissary, albeit one born in Sweden. It was a spur of the moment judgement that proved to be spectacularly successful.

'It's the Princess Margaret, I'm afraid,' Feodor had lisped softly to the startled Sol and Rosa in June 1954. 'You might have seen some of the scuttlebutt in the press about she and Mr Townsend. All nonsense, of course.' Feodor took a theatrical pause. 'But there is another chap who's been hanging about. A bloody wog if you'll excuse the expression with links, apparently, to some decaying Romanian house of this or that.' Feodor smiled. 'We want to put this fellow on ice for a few days, perhaps a week, before sending him packing. And to do that we need to enlist the support of a pair of wonderful patriots like yourselves.'

Feodor understood there would be questions to be negotiated. So he deliberately stopped to allow Sol and Rosa to speak.

'But Mr Nilsson, how did you get to pick us?' Sol queried on the couple's behalf. 'Here in Manchester when there must be tens of thousands of suitable candidates in London.'

'Need to avoid the London press,' Feodor replied grimly. 'As for Manchester, I do confess that when going through the list of persons who purchased coronation flags, it being certain evidence of patriotic bona fides, I chose you at random.' Feodor held up his hand as Sol tried to speak. 'And I might also add that I think it was a jolly good choice having now spoken to you both.'

'But we paid cash for the flag,' Rosa said slyly.

'Ah, yes, cash,' Feodor replied with matching coyness before executing a deft segue. 'Stretches the budget a little, but I'm authorised to offer you 500 pounds for your trouble.'

Rosa looked at Sol and Sol at her. Then both turned and stared at Feodor. An unambiguous understanding now existed between the three parties. 'Five hundred pounds will be acceptable,' Sol said gravely. 'Thank you for choosing us, Mr Nilsson.'

'When should we expect our guest?' Rosa asked, beaming.

'Within the next forty-eight hours,' Feodor replied. 'Be aware he might be a little unsteady on the pegs; we'll likely need to give him a jab before he arrives, spot of sedative to calm him down.'

***

Ten years later, the pact sealed in 1954 was as strong as ever. 'How can we help you, Mr Nilsson?' Rosa said quietly. Although polite, her enquiry did have a business-like edge to it.

Feodor withdrew Carstone's billfold wallet from his coat pocket and took a deep sigh as he held it aloft. 'This needs to be found at the scene of a crime,' he said. 'Not any old crime but a specific crime of a delicate nature.'

'Yes?' Sol queried cautiously.

'The outcome I'm seeking,' Feodor said, 'is one where the owner of this wallet appears recently to have used the services of a working lady in this area.'

Rosa understood best. 'That in itself would not be difficult to arrange, Mr Nilsson,' she said. 'I assume there are additional factors required?'

'Alas, yes,' Feodor replied, smiling bleakly. 'And I need them instituted immediately, this morning, in order that the police might make an arrest this afternoon.'

'And our fee?' Rosa said, finally getting to the issue that she and Feodor had been dancing around.

'Ten thousand pounds,' Feodor replied. Sol and Rosa looked on, astonished. In 1964, 10,000 pounds was an extraordinary sum of money. 'You'll have to employ a reliable contractor at short notice,' Feodor explained, 'and also find a girl willing to be the victim. Both will be expensive, especially the girl.'

Sol smiled and extended his hand to Feodor. 'Best you give us the details so we can make the necessary arrangements,' he said.

Late that afternoon, the first edition of the *Manchester Evening News* carried a report of a brutal assault in the early hours of Saturday morning on a prostitute in the suburb of Cheetham Hill. The victim was in hospital in a serious but stable condition and had now provided police with a description of the perpetrator.

'The person who committed this callous act is nothing more than an animal,' a quoted police officer said. 'But an item recovered at the scene along with the description we have makes us confident of an early arrest.'

Arriving at Euston station in London late afternoon that Saturday 8 February 1964, Kevin Carstone was stunned to be summarily arrested as he stepped from the Manchester train. His removal to Bow Street police headquarters was the last straw in what had been a trying day for the CIA officer. First, his wallet had been pickpocketed in a contrived incident outside the Dumbrille Hotel in Manchester; then he had a blazing row with the ticket clerk at Manchester Piccadilly railway station before the nitwit would allow him to pay for passage to London by cheque; and now, in breach of his rights as an American diplomat, he had been unceremoniously hauled away by the London metropolitan police. Compounding matters, Carstone's angry and flustered attempt to explain he had been nowhere near Cheetham Hill early on Saturday morning but rather in the company of a prostitute at the Dumbrille Hotel did nothing to help his cause.

CHAPTER 19

In August 1944 Feodor and Adrian had travelled in silence as Helmut Dzufer's trawler, the *Schatzi*, glided over the flat surface of the River Havel heading for the Lindenufer pier in Spandau. But at the point where the river narrowed, about twenty minutes from their destination, Helmut's whispered voice from above deck broke the stillness. 'A police maritime patrol is at the entrance to the heads,' he said urgently. 'It's stopping all river traffic for checks. Stay quiet and I'll try to bluff my way through.'

Adrian looked questioningly at Feodor, having detected the alarm in Helmut's voice but unable to understand the German he spoke. 'Police ahead, Adrian,' Feodor said calmly. 'We've struck trouble sooner than ideal. Be aware, I may need to move quickly.'

The *Schatzi* slowed and eventually came to a stop. Hard male voices could be heard ahead of the thump of boots landing on the deck. Feodor wasted no time. The maritime policeman who boarded would soon inspect the *Schatzi's* hold where he and Adrian were hidden. Inching forward like an eel, the Russian's upper body was through the hatch when the maritime policeman checking Helmut's papers turned and saw him. Feodor pounced, wrapping his arms around the man's legs, tumbling him to the floor of the boat, causing it to rock violently. With that, Feodor smashed the butt of the palm of his hand against the base of the policeman's nose. The upward blow was a skilled act of unarmed conflict, its precise timing driving a sliver of nosebone into the man's brain, killing him instantly. Feodor's overcoming the policeman took less than a minute but not before his two colleagues in the motorised dinghy alongside had noticed the *Schatzi's* sudden erratic movement.

Drawing their weapons, one of which was a machine pistol, the policemen in the dinghy screamed for Helmut to raise his hands. In that instant, and with a soft plop, a red blot appeared on the forehead of the officer armed with the machine pistol. The weapon fell into the river as the man crumpled. Only then did his shocked companion see Feodor kneeling in the belly of the *Schatzi*, holding the pistol taken from the policeman he had just killed. Panicked, the maritime policeman fired wildly, the errant round striking Helmut in the chest, fatally wounding him. But the man was unable to fire again. Feodor's second shot caught him in the throat, whereupon clutching his neck he stumbled backwards over the dinghy's far side and into the water.

'Quick, Adrian,' Feodor ordered. 'Let's get this tub moving.' Feodor was conscious that vessels down river would have seen the shooting and possibly passers-by on the riverbank as well. He was also aware he could do only two things: one was to get away from the scene as quickly as possible and be disembarked before the incident was reported to the authorities; the other was to hope that the oilskins he and Adrian had donned on departure at Helmut's insistence would prevent eye-witnesses from accurately describing the clothes they wore.

The Lindenufer pier in Spandau catered mainly to small vessels. Feodor throttled back the *Schatzi* as they approached. Two other craft were moored at the landing. Men were visible on one as they tended to its rigging. The other boat appeared to be uncrewed. Feodor would have liked to wait. But he could not. Pulling up directly behind the vessel on which the men were working, Feodor instructed Adrian to hide his suitcase as best he could beneath his oilskin. 'Get off straight away,' Feodor said softly, pointing to a wooded area adjacent to the jetty populated by a thicket of Linden trees from which the pier derived its name, 'and wait for me at the edge of the plantation.'

Adrian scrambled ashore the instant the *Schatzi* stopped and sprinted away, not daring to look back. On reaching the tree line he turned to see Feodor running towards him, his carry bag clutched to his body under his oilskin. The *Schatzi* was no longer at the pier; it was now veering towards the middle of the river, the shapes of two people discernable in its aft section. Feodor, Adrian realised, had opened the boat's throttle, propelling it forward. And the human forms in the *Schatzi* were the slumped dead bodies of Helmut and the German maritime policeman.

Feodor reached Adrian's hiding place from where they watched the trawler's wayward passage up the river. The crew on the moored boat was doing the same thing, distracted as Feodor had intended when setting the *Schatzi* underway.

'Let's go,' Feodor said quietly after ten seconds had elapsed. 'We need to get away and find somewhere safe to change out of these oilskins.'

The plantation was rectangular in shape, running parallel to the river but away from the Spandau rail station, its narrow width bordered on the far side by a pedestrian promenade. It was still early morning but soon people in numbers would be taking to the thoroughfare. Feodor led Adrian through the woods, conscious they were walking in the wrong direction. Halfway along they reached a cobblestoned alley to their left flanked by high walls on either side. A short distance down the pathway they came across a building in ruins. It was the shell of a burned-out synagogue, the Star of David still visible on the building's blackened facade.

Feodor's mind flashed back to pre-war Germany and the Nazi mob violence directed at the Jewish populace and its property. He would now use the Nazis' thuggery against them. 'In here,' Feodor whispered urgently, pointing to the ruins. 'No German civilian will disturb us while we remove our oilskins and clean up.' Shortly after Feodor and Adrian emerged—brows mopped, hair patted down and business suits smoothed—and with casualness belying their urgency sauntered towards the Spandau rail terminus.

For all their disguised haste, however, the times in Germany actually suited Feodor and Adrian. With the war going badly, Nazi paranoia was rife and people were reluctant to become involved in security matters. Hence, reports of the shooting on the river were slow in coming; not until Feodor and Adrian's train was well on its way to central Berlin did the German police, Gestapo and military units halt all rail traffic leaving Spandau. Shortly after, these same authorities began combing the area searching for two men in oilskins last seen heading deep into the trees adjacent to the Lindenufer pier.

***

Sitting in his Notting Hill flat as the clocked ticked towards 5 am on Sunday 27 February 1994, Adrian recalled Feodor adopting the Franz Schick identity upon reaching Berlin's intercity train terminal. By now trains were departing less frequently thanks to Allied bombing and the general chaos starting to grip the country.

'I am a special duties investigator for the state security service,' Feodor told the beleaguered ticket office clerk, flourishing his forged orders signed by the feared Gestapo head Heinrich Müller. 'This is my colleague, Navarro. We have important business in Königsberg and need immediate travel there.' Königsberg, of course, was the capital of East Prussia. The territory abutted Lithuania to the east and was currently connected to Weimar Germany to the west by the Germans' increasingly tenuous occupation of Poland.

'But Herr Doctor Schick,' the clerk protested nervously, 'as of this week there are no longer passenger services to East Prussia, only troop transports. The furthest east you can go is to Danzig.'

The suspension of services to East Prussia was the first of what was to be several forced changes to Feodor's plan. But he had no expectation of things going smoothly. 'That fucking Lohmeyer,' Feodor blustered. 'I'll have the bastard shot and get a new orderly when I'm back. He assured me the trains were still operating to Königsberg.' Feodor took a deep breath. 'All right, give me two tickets to Danzig. I'll speak to the military commander there about getting to Königsberg.'

Danzig was the German name for the modern-day Polish city of

Gdansk. And terminating at Danzig added a further 155 kilometres to the already 120 kilometre trip from Königsberg to Tilsit on the Lithuanian border where Feodor and Adrian were to cross into Soviet-held territory.

The trip started uneventfully. Feodor and Adrian sat in a six-berth first class cabin along with two German officers. Apart from a cursory nod of greeting, the men travelled in silence. But trouble was not far away. It came four hours later at Poznan, rightly a Polish city but now claimed by the Nazis as their own, when two youngish German civilians took up the spare seats in Feodor and Adrian's carriage. The men's arrogant swagger was a portent of things to come.

'We are General Government district managers,' one self-importantly announced once the train was underway. The man was brash, officious and clearly power drunk. He was also intrigued that two of his travelling companions should be civilians, especially as one did not look German, the small man with the unhealthily pale complexion. The man beaded Feodor and Adrian. 'Your business in the east is?' he asked sharply.

'Schick, state security,' Feodor replied with matching abruptness, flashing his Gestapo identification. 'This is Navarro,' he added, directing his thumb at Adrian, 'a Spanish civilian interpreter. He speaks no German.'

'And your business in our jurisdiction?' the man persisted.

'We are not in your jurisdiction, you fool,' Feodor spat contemptuously. 'We're in a German-annexed region.' In 1939 the western expanse of Poland was formally incorporated into the German Reich, while a central zone—technically still Polish territory—was placed under a Nazi administration dubbed the General Government. It was a fine distinction. But in 1941, when Germany seized formerly Russian-held eastern Poland and added it to the area under administration, most General Government officials began to act as if their unrestrained authority extended across all the landmass once comprising Greater Poland.

The man glared at Feodor, stung by the rebuke. An uneasy silence turned poisonous as the two engaged in a staring competition. Eventually the official averted his eyes and switched his gaze to Adrian. '¿Estás mal?' he asked tersely in passable Spanish. The man was angry and humiliated that Feodor should have stared him down. He had now decided on a change of tack, resorting to the language he acquired during a stint living in Spain before the war to interrogate Adrian on his sickly pallor, starting by enquiring if he was ill.

Feodor, however, was primed and ready. 'A word?' he said heatedly, feigning exasperation with the man's continued probing.

'Certainly,' the official replied, determined not to be fazed.

In the train's rocking corridor, Feodor was fiercely assertive. 'I am acting under Heinrich Müller's personal direction,' he snapped, invoking the name of the notorious Gestapo head. 'Navarro and I are enquiring into sensitive matters relating to the assassination attempt on the Führer at the Wolf's Lair. If you do not shut your stupid mouth, I will ensure you are hanging from a butcher's hook by this time tomorrow and do so without compunction.'

The man's hitherto cold eyes briefly flickered with doubt. Seizing the moment, Feodor slammed the official against the corridor wall and squeezed his testicles over his trousers. 'Well?' Feodor demanded, increasing the pressure of his hold.

The official's face turned grey as vainly he tried to release Feodor's iron grip. 'All right, all right,' he eventually panted. 'No more questions.'

Feodor relinquished his hold and roughly pushed the man back into the seating compartment. 'We'll now have a little peace and quiet all the way to Danzig,' he announced. The two Wehrmacht officers nodded in appreciation, grateful that the upstarts had been put in their place. Feodor resumed his seat and closed his eyes as if intending to sleep. But he did not. His mind was on to his next problem—namely how best to kill the two General Government men once in Danzig.

It was night when the train reached its destination. Feodor and Adrian walked behind the officials, watching them as they made their way into the warm Danzig evening. Feodor knew the men would soon make enquiries about the Gestapo investigator and his Spanish interpreter happened upon on the train. That is why he had to kill them as soon as possible. And while this presented untold difficulties, from problems Feodor always had the knack of finding opportunity. Watching for an opening, he was quick to grasp it when it arose.

The chance came in the form of the two men seated in the back of an open-topped Mercedes. A junior uniformed soldier wearing a side arm was placing their luggage in a rear compartment. Feodor strode confidently to the car. 'Our local transport has not arrived,' he said. 'Were you to offer my colleague and me a lift to our accommodation, I will refrain from reporting the earlier obstruction of our investigation on the train.'

'What obstruction?' one of the men queried aggressively.

'Have it your way,' Feodor said. He turned away, counting as he went, the behavioural scientist knowing that if he didn't get a response in the next thirty seconds his gambit was lost.

It came at twenty-eight seconds. 'Wait.' It was the man whom Feodor had intimidated in the train's corridor. He had heard of the Gestapo's brutality in investigating the Wolf's Lair attack on Hitler and decided to be sure rather than sorry. 'If we take you and your interpreter where you need to go, you'll forget our earlier misunderstanding? Right?'

'That's what I said,' Feodor replied coldly. The man nodded, tight-lipped. And with that he and his colleague bunched up allowing Adrian to join them in the back, while Feodor sat in the front passenger seat.

'Which hotel, sir?' the driver asked once Feodor and Adrian's luggage had been stowed.

Feodor looked at him. He was a boy, no more than nineteen with a pimply face. A wave of Russian sentimentality briefly wafted over Feodor; it was a shame the boy would have to die with the others. 'Who said anything about a hotel?' Feodor barked rudely. 'I asked for a lift to our accommodation. Just head south along the Vistula River. I'll tell you when to turn.' That the Vistula River ran through Danzig was virtually all Feodor knew about the city.

The driver licked his lips, casting a quick glance at the two officials. 'Is it far from the city centre?' he asked in a shaky voice. 'There's been trouble in Warsaw and we now have reports of Polish partisans sighted on Danzig's outskirts.'

The boy was referring to the Warsaw Uprising, the Polish Resistance's ultimately futile attempt to drive the Germans from the city. Although the Polish capital was 350 kilometres to the south, news of the unrest had unnerved many German soldiers in Danzig, sparking all nature of alarmist rumours.

'Show some spine, man,' Feodor snapped. 'Our lodgings are not far from here. Toughen up.'

The railway station was only a short distance from the Vistula River. Soon they were on an arterial road running parallel to the waterway, heading away from the city centre. As the car proceeded, the boy driver was becoming increasingly nervous and the Germans in the back seat were beginning to mutter. Suddenly the party came across a sign pointing to the Danzig shipyard, where German U-Boats were built. The heavily fortified facility was in darkness to protect against aerial attack. But seeing the sign was nonetheless of incalculable value to Feodor—the officials understood that secret research related to Hitler's manic quest for super weapons capable of winning the war was conducted at the shipyard. For a few vital minutes this gave Feodor the credibility he needed, enough for the Mercedes to travel another kilometre along the road.

The outline of a derelict industrial plant became visible. It was time to act. 'We're nearly there,' Feodor told the driver. 'Turn off towards the old plant.'

A short distance down the side road, the German in the back seat next to Adrian ordered the driver to stop. 'Where the fuck are we going?' he growled. His instincts that had been temporarily pacified were now alive. 'There's nothing here. This place is in the middle of nowhere.'

'Hold his arms, Adrian,' Feodor said softly, turning to point at the man who had directed the car to stop. The Germans in the car stared, momentarily stunned by Feodor's muted English-language utterance and its ominous threat. Only when Adrian had grabbed at the nominated man did Feodor then deliver the driver a vicious rabbit chop to his Adam's apple, causing the boy to gag. In the same action, Feodor extracted the pistol from the gasping soldier's leather holster, just as the unencumbered German in the back seat wrapped his hands around the Russian's neck. With a well-timed shrug, Feodor shifted his assailant's weight sufficient to turn and fire a shot into the chest of the official with whom Adrian was wrestling.

Adrian was partially deafened by the gunshot and startled by the sight of the dead man in his lap. Feodor's matter-of-fact voice broke his trance. 'Help get this bastard off me, Adrian, would you?' the Russian said. Galvanised into action, Adrian scrambled over the body of the dead German and grabbed at the hair of the official trying to strangle Feodor. With all his might he pulled backwards while Feodor continued to roll his shoulders. The German snarled and spat as Adrian tugged at him. Next thing Adrian's arm was around the man's neck and, with a strength he didn't know he possessed, he wrenched the German from Feodor.

For an instant time stood still, the memory of it staying with Adrian all his life. Here he was in the backblocks of occupied Danzig struggling with a Nazi fanatic while all the while Feodor watched on with the trace of a smile on his face. Only when the driver, on recovering from the blow to his neck, sought to start the Mercedes did Feodor avert his gaze. Slowly, he levelled the pistol at the boy. 'Do you want to live or die?' Feodor asked quietly.

'Live,' the boy croaked, tears on his cheeks twinkling in the moonlight.

'Then shut off the engine,' Feodor said. He waited patiently for the boy to comply before turning back to Adrian who was now smothered by the awkwardly reclined official he'd dragged off Feodor. Feodor placed the pistol against the flailing German's forehead. 'Stay low and still, Adrian,' Feodor directed calmly. 'I'd hate to shoot you too.' With that, the NKVD major shot the man between the eyes.

CHAPTER 20

'Don't forget to sit up straight and look confident at all times, Adrian,' Feodor instructed. 'Remember, we've got to act as if we are very important people.' Fifty years on in his Notting Hill flat, with Roger Hardwicke's *Sunday Exegesis* article set to publish within the next hour, Adrian's muddled mind had darted back to Danzig in August 1944. He and his Russian escort were seated in the back of the Mercedes convertible, a Nazi flag flying from its front left fender. Assisted by the young German driver, they had just deposited the bodies of the General Government officials in the disused industrial plant at the end of the deserted road onto which they drove shortly before stopping.

'Leave their luggage with them,' Feodor said. 'When they're reported missing, hopefully in the morning, those who find them will think they've been abducted and murdered by Polish partisans.'

'But what about him?' Adrian said, pointing discreetly at the driver. 'Won't his sergeant or whoever looks after him be wondering where he's got to?'

Feodor shrugged. 'Possibly. Probably. But let's worry about that later. It's important we get going.'

'We'll need fuel soon, too,' the driver chimed in morosely, surprising Feodor and Adrian by apparently understanding their conversation in English.

The boy could scarcely believe what had happened. One moment he was doing a routine pick up of two General Government officials at

Danzig train station. The next these two others had somehow wrangled a lift, supposedly to their accommodation. Then after being tricked into driving down a dark side road near the U-Boat construction shipyard, one of the interlopers—the man wearing glasses who sat in the front seat—had shot dead both the officials. And now the killer was demanding that he and his colleague be driven 275 kilometres all the way to Tilsit in East Prussia on the border with Soviet-occupied Lithuania. How the boy wished he were dreaming. Because if he wasn't, he was sure he'd be dead within twenty-four hours.

'We'll look for chances to refuel as we go,' Feodor told the driver. 'For now head east.'

Feodor turned to Adrian. 'It's inevitable that we will be challenged along the way,' he said, 'particularly as we're driving at night. But provided we can overcome these obstacles, we should reach Tilsit in seven to eight hours.'

The boy proved remarkably competent in finding the strip of bitumen passing as the highway that would take them towards the East Prussian capital of Königsberg, and was clearly proud of his achievement. It was a pride Adrian would later see in London's taxi drivers as they demonstrated *the knowledge*. But back in 1944, just as the travelling party neared the town of Elblag, at a time when Adrian was daring to hope of unimpeded passage to Tilsit, they came across a convoy of low-loading trucks transporting tanks forward to confront the Soviets massing on the Lithuanian border. Clearly, something had gone wrong. The convoy was at a standstill and blocking the road.

By now it was nearly midnight and for a staff car to be ferrying around two civilians at this late hour was irregular in the extreme. Certainly, the look on the face of the Wehrmacht transport officer waving a torch at the Mercedes directing it to stop suggested he thought so. In the background, Feodor could make out a four-wheel drive armoured car with the cannon and machine gun mounted on its swivel turret pointing straight at the Mercedes. Standing next to the vehicle a dozen or so uniformed German soldiers watched on. In the weak light their callow faces told Feodor the troops were from the bottom of the barrel; their officer apart, they all looked to be in their teens, Hitler Youth adolescents conscripted by the Nazis and given the mundane task of escorting the tank convoy. But rather than a problem, the convoy hold up was the opportunity Feodor was seeking; the sixty kilometres the party had covered since leaving Danzig had left the Mercedes dangerously low on gasoline.

Feodor bounded from the car and confronted the German transport officer. 'How soon before we can pass?' he asked aggressively, thrusting his forged orders signed by the Gestapo head Heinrich Müller into the startled man's hand.

Straining to see by the light of his torch, the German read the orders. Then, much to the amazement of Adrian watching nervously from the back seat of the Mercedes, the officer jumped to attention and saluted. 'A truck's snapped a back axle, Herr Doctor Schick,' he said. 'We're trying to repair it now.'

'I didn't ask what the problem was, you fucking imbecile,' Feodor spat back. 'I asked how long before we can pass.'

'About thirty minutes,' the officer replied. But he'd shuffled while speaking, telling Feodor this meant over an hour.

'For fuck's sake,' Feodor fumed. 'If we get to Tilsit too late for what we've been sent to do, all because you've delayed us, you'll wish you'd never been born.' Feodor glared. 'We're talking here about sensitive matters linked to the assassination attempt on the Führer. You don't seriously think we'd be driving around the countryside at this time of night for the hell of it, do you?'

The exhausted man shrugged, unsure how best to reply. 'Is there anything I can get you while you wait?' he asked. The question was music to Feodor's ears.

An hour later the Mercedes driven by the boy soldier navigated the path through the tank convoy created for it and, skirting the Elblag township, continued in an easterly direction, its fuel tank full to the brim. Adrian could not believe their luck. But in contrast Feodor was grimly tight-lipped, the strain of acting out his Gestapo role for over an hour had drained him.

'Don't get too exuberant, Adrian,' he warned. 'I can confidently predict there will be other problems before we get there.'

Feodor's were prescient words. Just fifteen minutes after the Mercedes had negotiated the convoy, the escort detachment's radio crackled to life. 'There's a stop and detain bulletin out for the men in the Mercedes that just passed through,' the German radio operator yelled from the armoured car. 'I'll alert the garrison at Elblag that the vehicle's in the area and tell them to go and intercept it.'

The troop commander was a thirty-year-old lieutenant and a man touched by Hitler's evil spell, the Führer having once patted his cheek many years ago. Glorious dreams of serving the Reich were filling his mind.

'No, don't contact Elblag,' he told the radio operator. 'We'll go and get them ourselves.' The lieutenant judged that neither the driver of the Mercedes nor the small, pale Spanish interpreter whose papers he had inspected were terribly important, but the supposed Gestapo man was. 'We must take alive the man in the grey suit wearing eyeglasses,' he ordered. With that, eight conscripts piled into a troop transport and set off in micro convoy led by the armoured car carrying their commanding officer.

***

It was two in the morning, Adrian recalled fifty years later. The warm August night had turned chilly. The driver first spotted the pursuers. 'Someone coming up on our tail,' the boy said nervously. 'Fast.'

'Listen to me carefully,' Feodor said, addressing the boy. 'I know you would like to surrender to the authorities in the hope you will go unpunished for driving us. But understand that Germany is falling apart and the Nazis with it. Fine judgements about guilt and innocence no longer apply. They'll kill you without thinking. But if you stick with us, I will protect you when we meet the Soviet forces. Yes, you will spend time as a prisoner of war. But Germany will be defeated within a year and I will make sure you are looked after until such time as you are released and can return home.'

The boy thought about this. Then he tugged down the peak of his cap. 'Let me see if we can outrun whoever is behind us.' Five years on Private Albert Goltz married a Russian girl he met while assigned to a collective farm near Leningrad. Albert and his wife settled in the northern city where they raised their family. The boy who became a man during a dash across Poland to the Lithuanian border never again returned to Germany. But for now, thoughts of a rosy future were the last thing on Albert Goltz's mind. He and his passengers were in the race of their lives—literally.

The first shot from the armoured car's cannon landed wide of the speeding Mercedes. Feodor leant forward from the rear seat and tapped the boy driver on the shoulder. The German was concentrating on the road and cocked his ear in Feodor's direction without turning his head. 'We need to get off the main road,' Feodor said. 'The next side exit you see, take it.'

Shortly after the driver veered left in the direction of the coast to which they had been driving in parallel. Soon seawater could be seen, the low morning moon glistening on it. To their right was an expanse of farming land. A second shot from the armoured car made them all duck. Time was running out. Suddenly they reached a hamlet of no more than four or five houses some with detached outbuildings. The tiny village was deserted. 'Stop,' Feodor yelled. Adrian still remembered the Russian's steely calm in the eye of the storm. 'Run and hide anywhere you can,' Feodor said. 'Spread out while I find a way to neutralise the command vehicle.' Adrian and Albert both understood that Feodor meant the pursuing armoured car, which continued to fire its cannon as it approached.

'How will you do that?' Adrian asked, unable to prevent his voice from quavering.

'To be honest, I haven't the faintest idea,' Feodor said with a loud laugh, leaping from the car and racing into the night.

The outbuildings to where Feodor, Adrian and the German driver Albert fled were of identical design; rectangular boxes of rough-hewn stone rising to the bottom of an apex-shaped, steeply sloping thatched roof finished by rough strips of weathered wood. Inside the barns various farming implements lay next to scattered animal feed, remnants of the previous winter when, as in all winters, the animals were herded at night to protect against the cold.

Albert was swifter than his companions, running to the most distant barn in a cluster of three. Adrian saw Feodor enter the barn closest to the road and, observing the direction to spread out, bypassed it, racing to a structure sited between those housing Feodor and Albert.

The eight German soldiers split into two groups of three and one of two. It was Feodor who one group of three troops first encountered. Feodor's shelter had two points of ingress, a door on the short edge of the rectangle at the front and another centred in the longer edge to its left. Guided by their rudimentary training, the conscripts adopted a clearance formation whereby two crept through the front door while the third soldier lay in wait at the side entrance.

Feodor was crouched in the dark behind a wooden roof stanchion, the pistol he obtained from Albert in his hand. But just as he fired, the soldier at whom he aimed stumbled causing Feodor's shot to hit the conscript's army issue steel helmet, knocking the boy backwards as if punched such that he fell to the ground. The injured German's companion helped his colleague to his feet and together they scurried from the barn. As they went, they and Feodor alike heard the click of an empty pistol. Albert, Feodor realised, had not fully loaded his side arm's magazine.

Meanwhile, the five German soldiers heading towards the distant barns heard Feodor's single shot. Instructions were shouted, prompting two of the outliers to join the three soldiers outside Feodor's building, swelling their number to five. The soldier who had taken a bullet to his steel helmet was dazed and bleeding from a cut high on his forehead.

One conscript was appointed to accompany the injured boy back to the command vehicle.

'What's going on?' the lieutenant asked crossly. 'Why have you come back?'

The uninjured soldier gestured at his damaged colleague, only to be greeted by a cold stare. 'The man in the grey suit who you want to question is in the closest barn,' the conscript reported, seeking to placate the commander. 'He seems to be out of ammunition.' The commander glared some more. 'Two others have joined Scheel at the barn,' the soldier said. 'That means three of our contingent is outside currently. The man can't escape.'

'Well, there will be four of our lot there when you go back,' the commander retorted, exhaling at the sight of the boy's obvious disappointment. 'You are a Hitler Youth soldier who has taken an oath of obedience to serve the Fatherland,' he spat. 'And the man's unarmed, for fuck's sake, you said so yourself. If four armed soldiers can't capture one unarmed civilian, then who can?'

Thereafter, events rapidly escalated. Feodor's barn quickly became the scene of a kill or be killed battle of hand-to-hand combat. This time three of the now group of four conscripts cautiously made their way through the front entrance, while the other waited in the dark night, positioned to prevent Feodor from escaping through the barn's side exit. One of the boys who entered held a flashlight. Feodor was a ruthless adversary, slashing at the torch holder's neck with a rusty farmer's cutlass, the agricultural tool opening up the boy's carotid artery. A second soldier began to wrestle Feodor causing straw and dust to rise from the barn floor until it resembled a snow-like mist. Through the haze, Feodor glimpsed the third soldier preparing to fire. He rotated the writhing conscript with whom he was struggling until the boy was between him and the readying shooter, so that when the third soldier did fire his bullet hit Feodor's human shield in the back. The boy slid slowly to the ground, much like a fainting dance partner. As the shooter prepared to fire again Feodor charged, his momentum causing both to crash to the barn floor. The young soldier was beefy and strong for his age. But Feodor was soon on top of him and had established a chokehold.

The sound of the commotion inside the barn had alarmed the solitary soldier stationed outside. The conscript nervously opened the door to be greeted by the sight of Feodor's back as he sat astride the beefy soldier, choking the life out of him. But inhibited by the commander's instruction to take Feodor alive, the young soldier elected not to shoot the Russian when really he should have. Instead, he wielded his rifle like a baseball bat, the fierce blow toppling Feodor off the German beneath him.

Lying face down and only semi-conscious, Feodor gasped in pain. The beefy boy struggled unsteadily to his feet, rubbing his inflamed neck. Retrieving his rifle, he placed it to his shoulder and took aim at the back of Feodor's head.

'No, no, Heinz,' his colleague yelled, the boy who had clubbed Feodor. 'We have orders to take him alive.'

'Fuck the orders,' Heinz rasped. 'I'm going to kill this bastard here and now.' He cocked his rifle. But Heinz never got to fire. The pitchfork Adrian buried in his back killed him instantly. The young German soldier who struck Feodor stood rooted to the spot, his senses befuddled by the sight of someone stealing unannounced into the barn and killing his beefy colleague. The boy's inertia was his death sentence. By the time he had summed up that his life depended on shooting Feodor and raised his weapon to do so, Feodor was already on his feet and holding Heinz's rifle. Feodor and Adrian watched the young conscript die, blood seeping between his fingers clutched to his shattered chest, a disbelieving look on his face.

***

In Notting Hill in February 1994, Adrian recalled that moment fifty years earlier when he saved Feodor's life, marvelling at how he had been quaking in the middle barn only for his fear to cross a desensitising threshold of sorts. Temporarily fortified, he became clear-headed enough to reason that the absence of firing since last hearing a German rifle shot indicated Feodor was in trouble. Taking up an old pitchfork, he had tiptoed through the dark to the near outbuilding, arriving just in time to see a German soldier creep into the barn. The tense exchange of boyish German voices filtering through the rough stone wall was his catalyst to act. He had entered the building via the door left ajar by the conscript who went inside just seconds before him.

'You, Adrian Ashton, have saved my life,' Feodor said, his eyes burning brightly as he dabbed a kerchief at his head gash. 'In consequence, I propose to call you Mendoza.' Adrian did not know that Mendoza was the Argentine city where Feodor's wife Adelaida had been born. But Feodor's gravity did tell him that the name bestowed a great honour. This was not without justification. In saving Feodor's life, Adrian had made possible the continuation of the Russian's crusade against the Nazis and, with that, perpetuated Adelaida living on in his heart.

'Your coming to my rescue, Mendoza,' Feodor added in solemn acknowledgement of Adrian's gift, 'leaves me eternally in your debt. It becomes, therefore, my sacred duty to be your protector, now and for the rest of your life.'

And so it was, Adrian thought, reflecting how the bond that formed led Feodor to rush to London in 1964 at the time of Carstone, just as he had earlier learned of the Russian doing the same thing a decade previously when neutralising the would-be defecting Soviet intelligence officer, the Georgian who ended up parked with Sol and Rosa in Manchester.

Tears welled in Adrian's eyes; it was his realisation that Feodor's letter would tell him the noble obligation was over. And with that, the distraught Adrian pushed the envelope aside, fearfully unable to accept the end of Feodor's duty—the burden the Russian had voluntarily assumed in the murk of a Polish barn early one August morning in 1944.

CHAPTER 21

Late in the evening on Saturday 8 February 1964, the CIA officer Kevin Carstone was released from the clutches of the London metropolitan police. It had been some time before Carstone was granted his entitlement to a single phone call and more time before the American ambassador in London could rouse the Foreign Office and invoke Carstone's diplomatic immunity.

The time spent in the cells at Bow Street police station had provided Carstone with a chance to think. It was now clear the lifting of his wallet outside the Dumbrille Hotel in Manchester was no random act of street crime, not when the billfold had been used to frame him for an assault on a prostitute. The American knew the spy's playbook by heart; the whole episode reeked of tradecraft, resources and planning. If he wasn't certain beforehand, he was now positive that Adrian Ashton was a Soviet spy and Soviet operatives in England were actively working to protect their source.

Carstone's thoughts turned to Sara Lnu, so-called, and her role in proceedings. He was grateful now to have been sufficiently disciplined to resist the urge to bed Sara, because if he was honest he did come close at one point to ditching his Southern reserve, when late into the interrogation in his hotel room he and she had rested side by side on his bed. Carstone tried to tell himself it was the effect of being alone with a voluptuous young woman on a cold night in Manchester that had stirred his juices. But much as he did not like to admit it, deep down

Carstone knew he had been tempted to make an injudicious decision because of how much it would hurt Adrian Ashton were he to have sex with Sara.

On release from police custody, Carstone had detailed his findings and related conclusions to the American ambassador and Charles Kilbay, head of the CIA's London station, while carefully omitting mention of his near miss with Sara. But it was now almost midnight. It was agreed that Carstone should have the night to rest and first thing on Sunday morning go with Kilbay to give a full account of events to James Newcombe and other senior MI6 managers at an already arranged meeting. With that, the ambassador's car ferried Carstone back to his flat in Pimlico.

Carstone was weary and drank a cup of warm milk before going to bed hoping to ensure a decent sleep. But for some unfathomable reason his eyes refused to yield to his will, stubbornly so. It was not a racing mind or other form of anxiety denying Carstone his chance to refresh but rather an imprecise sense he should not sleep, that it was important he stay awake.

The tap on his door came at 3 am on Sunday, leaving Carstone wondering if this was what he was waiting for, before quickly dismissing the notion. From the darkened hallway, he peered through the front door's fisheye peephole. A tall man of about forty was visible. He carried what appeared to be a flashlight and wore a cheap type of uniform. The man tapped again. 'It's Sammy Pullar,' he whispered, as if aware Carstone was on the other side of the door.

Carstone was perplexed and understandably on edge in view of everything that had happened to him. But equally a voice in his head was oddly insisting he open the door. Carstone rationalised. Surely the man was some blasted janitor whose name he was supposed to know? Cautiously, the American turned the door handle, leaving the security chain attached. The tranquilliser dart fired by the man using the dart gun resembling a flashlight hit him in the stomach, the quick-acting chemical causing the CIA man to pass out.

With that, another man in his early fifties, his hair flecked with grey, walked up the corridor from where he had been waiting out of sight. With practised ease the man who fired the dart gun inserted a thin metal rod into the door chain and manipulated it until it fell free. He and his older companion stepped inside, quietly closing the door behind them. They carried Carstone to his bedroom where they applied a cream to erase the tiny puncture mark on the American's stomach and a strip of masking tape to his mouth.

A minute later the bewildered Carstone woke to find a light shining in his eyes. From behind the glare, a vaguely familiar accented voice spoke. 'The tranquilliser we gave you will wear off quickly,' the older man said. The speaker had, in fact, returned to London from Manchester thirteen hours earlier, on the Saturday lunchtime flight. Since then he had been processing and cross-referencing reams of information in a hotel room. His name was Feodor Timofeyevich Kozlovsky and he was a KGB colonel.

'When you are awake,' Feodor said, turning off his pencil torch and removing the masking tape from Carstone's mouth, 'we have a document for you to sign.'

'Fuck off, you commie bastard,' the CIA man slurred. Hearing the intruder's voice had caused Carstone to wonder if the man was the KGB operative who stole his wallet outside the Dumbrille Hotel in Manchester. The sight of Feodor had confirmed he was.

'Let him rest a few minutes more,' Feodor instructed the younger KGB man in Russian. 'He needs to be as lucid as possible.'

Ten minutes passed, after which Feodor again inspected Carstone's eyes. Satisfied the American was sufficiently recovered, he directed his colleague to take Carstone to the living room where, once the CIA man was seated at his writing desk, Feodor placed a piece of paper before him. Carstone stared at the document, shaking his head in disbelief. The handwriting was his own yet not something he had written. It was an exquisite forgery.

'You're kidding if you think I'm signing this, buddy,' Carstone screamed. Without reading the words on the page he tore the paper into shreds in a series of sharp, angry actions.

Feodor nodded to his underling and the masking tape was re-applied to Carstone's mouth. 'Please keep your voice down,' he said patiently. 'And don't waste your energy tearing up these letters,' he added, 'we have others.'

Carstone mumbled through the masking tape. His words were unintelligible but effectively he was asking why his captors were demanding he sign the paper; if the KGB could perfectly forge his handwriting, a forged signature would suffice.

In that moment, however, the truth dawned on Carstone. The Soviets knew the CIA trained its field agents to leave a warning signal in their signature to indicate if any documents signed were done so under duress. The Soviets, Carstone now realised, did not know his signature trap. In Carstone's case it was for the crossbar on the *t*, the fourth from last letter of his surname, not to extend beyond the length of his name. Conversely, if the stroke on the *t* projected past his surname, the signature would be taken as genuine.

Carstone's conclusion was correct. Faced with tight time constraints, the KGB forgers flown in by Feodor specifically for the job were obliged to rely on an unsigned note left by Carstone in the foyer of his apartment building on the Friday he left for Manchester. The scrawled correspondence was directed to the milkman: *Deliveries for flat 44 to cease until Monday next week please, when you should give me a quart bottle.* And although the note was unsigned, that its text contained twenty-four of the alphabet's twenty-six letters was enough for the Soviet experts to forge a letter as if Carstone had written it. But for all the forgery's excellence, to complete the deception Feodor now needed a sign off from Carstone that did not trigger the signature trap.

Feodor placed another copy of the same letter in front of Carstone. This time the American looked closely at it, noting that the document was a photostat, no doubt made on one of those recently pioneered copying machines. But Carstone's bemusement was short-lived. Horror soon replaced it. The Soviets, he read, were asking him to sign a suicide note in which he admitted to being a violent and depraved sexual deviant. The realisation caused Carstone to squirm. Feodor gently removed the tape from the American's mouth.

'Have you guys lost your minds?' Carstone warbled, rattled now but speaking softly on pain of the tape being re-applied. 'Why would I sign this if you plan to kill me?'

'Suellen,' Feodor answered simply. Suellen McCarthy lived in Columbia, South Carolina. She was formerly known as Suellen Carstone during the five years she was married to the CIA agent, a union that had produced a daughter now aged seventeen.

Carstone looked at Feodor as if he was mad. 'Why should I care about Suellen?' he asked incredulously. 'She took up with some jerk who sells carpet.' Carstone's mouth was dry and he snorted, endeavouring to dredge up saliva. 'I couldn't give a shit. If you want to kill the bitch, be my guest.'

'Suellen hates you, Kevin,' Feodor answered calmly. 'She would do anything to harm you, especially for a fee.'

'Yeah,' Carstone agreed cautiously.

'We could tell her about your first year at USC, the Graceville clinic in Savannah, for example, and suggest she go to the press. Think of the effect on your elderly parents and your daughter if the whole sordid mess came to light. The shame of it all.'

USC was the University of South Carolina based in Suellen's hometown of Columbia. Carstone had gone there as a freshman in 1942, relocating from his birthplace of Charleston. His parents were high-achieving doyens of the Charleston Catholic establishment and determinedly anti-abortion. The expectations they placed on their only son were considerable. But away from home for the first time and free to plot his own course, Kevin found university life to his liking. The parties, women and booze began to feature prominently in his social calendar. Kevin was also physically maturing and soon a contender for a place on the USC football roster. Growing numbers of female students became aware of him, which only fanned his proliferating sexual appetite.

Students at USC in the 1940s usually learned about contraception on the run. Kevin was no different in 1942. For a time he relied on condoms, items that became increasingly scarce during the year as a result of the US entering the war the preceding December. In the absence of condoms, Kevin's alternative became the practice of coitus interruptus. But as Kevin's conquests began to mount, so did his drug-like need for a bigger and better experience, such that often he took no precautions at all. Inevitably, one of his lovers fell pregnant. Kevin suddenly faced a dilemma. The girl in question was not Catholic, and the fact that she was a Southern Baptist made her someone whom Kevin's family would never countenance him marrying.

Fearful of his parents' reaction should they learn of the pregnancy, Kevin's solution was to bully the young woman into agreeing to an abortion, which only added to the imperative that his fiercely right to life parents should know nothing of the situation. Next he took a trip to Savannah in neighbouring Georgia. Kevin, of course, was not the first boy at USC ever to impregnate a female colleague. The student grapevine was alive with information about illicit activities, including where to procure abortions. In the seedy backblocks of Savannah, Kevin soon found the Graceville clinic he was seeking. There and then he made the necessary arrangements paying cash in advance and booking in the girl under a false name.

But by now Kevin's upbringing was eating away at him. Every life, he'd been taught, including that of an unborn child, was precious. In his waking hours, Kevin was generally able to ignore his conscience reminding him of the sin it was to spurn God's gift. The horror of lying awake in the early hours, however, was another thing altogether.

Eventually, Kevin forged a compromise. Lacking the intestinal fortitude to see the messy matter through, he approached a scholarship student from a poor share cropping background called Raymond. In exchange for twenty-five dollars, he proposed that Raymond drive the pregnant girl to Savannah and, after the abortion, take her to a hotel where she would stay overnight to recover. Things more or less went to plan. But the abortion left the girl deeply traumatised. That night in her Savannah hotel room, she made the decision to return home to upstate South Carolina.

That the girl never did resume her studies at USC was of huge relief to Kevin, even if for weeks after his nightmares continued. Chastened, he spent the remainder of 1942 concentrating on his lectures and attending bible classes. But Kevin's verve slowly restored and by his sophomore year his self-confidence had renewed. For his part, Raymond, the driver Kevin had recruited, pledged to keep his mouth shut. And although Kevin occasionally worried Raymond might not honour this commitment, he did think it unlikely owing to Raymond's role in procuring the illegal abortion.

Two more years passed and the abortion matter receded from conscious memory. Into his senior year and Kevin was a university football star with a new steady, the sorority head Suellen someone or other. The two began to promenade royally about the campus, holding court with adjudged equals and treating lesser mortals with disdain.

By this time Kevin never even considered that Raymond might cause him problems. And to be sure, Raymond's part in the abortion precluded him from going to the authorities. But Suellen was also a Southern snob who encouraged Kevin to mock Raymond for his poor background. Now, as Kevin was about to discover, doing as Suellen had bid would ultimately prove to be a costly mistake.

Raymond, it transpires, had befriended a Panamanian student, another scholarship recipient. On the day in 1946 when Kevin and Suellen announced their engagement, a party took place in a university residential college. Raymond and his Panamanian friend, naturally, were not invited. But from across the quadrangle, the two were able to observe the pretentious proceedings. It was too much for Raymond. 'That Kevin Carstone has some gall,' he told his friend. 'He had a girl aborted in his first year here. Paid me to drive her to the Graceville clinic in Savannah because he was too chicken-livered to do it himself. I wonder what his snooty girlfriend would say if she knew about that?'

The Panamanian made no response other than to raise his eyebrows and grunt. Some weeks later he and Raymond graduated, whereupon the two lost contact, never speaking again. Raymond joined the US army. He was one of 450 Americans killed in November 1950 at the Battle of Unsan during the Korean War, a matter duly noted in the USC alumni newsletter.

A decade on as a politician in his home country, one who had succumbed to the KGB's lucre, Raymond's former friend did mention to his controller that, in 1942 while at USC, a man called Kevin Carstone who went on to join the CIA had forced a girl to have an abortion at the Graceville clinic in Savannah, Georgia. Not inclined to discard even the tiniest scrap of information, the snippet was filed away in KGB headquarters in Moscow. Feodor was well pleased when it surfaced during his urgent search of the KGB archive in February 1964, prompting the immediate dispatch to South Carolina of a team from the KGB station in Washington DC with orders to file a detailed report on Kevin Carstone's background within forty-eight hours.

Meanwhile in his London flat, Carstone's head was spinning. He was frightened and amazed at the same time, staggered that the Russians should know about the 1942 abortion at USC. After all, Raymond was dead and the girl involved, so far as he knew, had married and was living a quiet small town life. Carstone also thought about Suellen and how their fairytale romance had deteriorated into acrimony within the space of two years. And how, while their mutual contempt turned to rancid hatred, family pressure made them stay together for an excruciating three years more. But most of all, Carstone wondered what would happen next.

The sound of the older Russian speaking interrupted Carstone's fearful rumination. 'You are in a difficult situation, Kevin,' Feodor said with fatherly kindness, the behavioural scientist in him hard at work. 'Hobson's choice, I believe it is called.'

'What?' Carstone gasped in scared bewilderment.

Feodor resignedly turned up the palms of his hands. 'If you sign this letter properly, your employer will wish to avoid a scandal. It will ensure that no details leak, hence your family will be none the wiser and remember you as a patriot and hero. But if we go down the Suellen path, your name and that of your family will be dragged through the mud. Your parents will be devastated by the revelation that their only son procured an abortion and the church's subsequent ostracism, in the final years of their lives just when they need their faith the most. As for your daughter, she will be ridiculed and humiliated by her peers. Imagine the effect of that on a seventeen-year-old. Ruinous, really, at that delicate age.'

Carstone looked up at Feodor; then he broke, his tears coming in flooding waves. Feodor sympathetically patted the American's shoulder. 'If you sign the paper validly, Kevin, we will make it easier for you.' The Russian held up a small vial. 'I have some tablets here. A little dose that will be undetectable in your body after an hour will be a big help.'

'How will you know if I sign correctly?' Carstone whispered.

Feodor shrugged. 'We won't at first. But if you do, your Service will make no further enquiries for fear of alerting the press to the scandal. Conversely, if you trigger the signature trap, CIA agents around the globe will be seeking answers, press interest or no press interest. We will become aware of this, which of course leads us back to Suellen.' Feodor allowed his voice to trail off.

With that, Carstone slumped in his chair. It was as if all the air had been pumped out of him. Feodor recognised the capitulation. Motioning to his colleague he requested the original version of the forged confession, which he placed in front of the American. Carstone stared at the letter, his entire body trembling. Feodor gently pressed a pen into his hand. Gulping hard, and with a slow shake of his head, Carstone scrawled his signature at the bottom of the page, finishing with a flourish to ensure the crossbar of the *t* in his surname extended well past the last letter.

Without further ado, Feodor gave Carstone a single pill and a glass of water. 'Give him five minutes more,' he ordered his assistant once Carstone began to slumber, 'then do it.'

An hour later the occupants of the flat across the hall from Carstone woke to the smell of gas. The attending fire brigade officers quickly isolated the main. The team leader had seen his share of suicide by gas and next rang an ambulance.

Daylight was breaking when Kevin Carstone was found with his head inside his flat's gas oven. Shortly after the unresponsive CIA man was removed to St Thomas' Hospital, where he was officially pronounced dead on arrival.

CHAPTER 22

Events moved quickly in the immediate aftermath of Adrian saving Feodor's life that early morning in Poland in August 1944. The two stood briefly in the barn's half-light, staring at one another. The Russian's bestowing the honour of the name Mendoza on Adrian, in memory of his murdered wife Adelaida, had combined with his adoption of the role as Adrian's protector to engender a poignantly deep attachment between the two men. But they could not afford to savour the moment for long. There was still much to do, not least of which was to deal with the rest of the German soldiers out there.

Feodor and Adrian did not know how many German troops had been dispatched to the barns in the deserted Polish hamlet. Nor were they aware that of the original eight soldiers, now only three were deployed. The remaining three conscripts in fact were huddled together in a treed area close to the furthest barn in which the driver, Albert Goltz, had taken shelter. The shots coming from Feodor's barn had left them scared and anxious, unaware what was happening but intuitively thinking the worst.

Meanwhile, Feodor elected to act on the one thing he did know— while prone on the barn floor as the beefy soldier Heinz readied to shoot him, he had heard Heinz's fellow conscript remind the boy of the troop commander's instruction he be taken alive. So informed, Feodor turned his attention to the command vehicle, where a total of four Germans were waiting: the commander, his driver and radio operator, and the injured soldier who had earlier returned to the vehicle.

'It's time I tried to hijack the command vehicle,' Feodor told Adrian. 'You stay in here,' he added, pointing to the barn floor. 'If anybody comes inside, shoot them without hesitation.' Feodor made to leave but stopped and turned back to Adrian. 'Except, of course,' he said with a wry grin, 'if it is me.'

Alone in the barn with only four dead conscripts for company Adrian shook with fear, the stimulus that had led him to save Feodor's life dissipated. He dared not touch the trigger of the rifle he held for worry he might accidentally discharge the weapon. Then a loud voice speaking German broke the night. Adrian's heart nearly jumped from his chest as he wondered what the voice was saying and where it was coming from. The voice sounded again. This time Adrian could make out that the speaker was using a loudhailer.

Soon after the rustling sound of persons in kit running could be heard followed by breathless German spoken as the runners neared. Unbeknown to Adrian, the three soldiers hiding in the treed area were gratefully returning to the command vehicle as the loudhailer announcement had ordered. Adrian's survival instincts re-kindled and his shaking hands stilled as he placed the rifle butt to his shoulder, expecting those approaching to burst into the barn. But to his great relief the footsteps bypassed him and kept going.

After a period of eerie silence, Adrian detected Feodor's voice speaking harsh German, as if issuing orders. Then there was more silence. Adrian crept timidly to the barn's side door and looked out. Cloud now obscured the moon and in the jet-black night nothing was visible. A noise close by almost caused Adrian to faint. He froze with terror as the shadowy outline of a figure moved towards him. Then spurred into action by intense fear, Adrian raised his rifle.

Albert Goltz was lucky. Had he not been wearing his distinctive peaked cap, Adrian would have shot him. But just as Adrian's finger began to press on the trigger, the message from his eyes reached his brain. In that same instant Albert saw Adrian in the doorway, raised rifle in his hands.

'Don't shoot, don't shoot,' Albert whispered urgently. 'It's me, Albert.' Adrian stared at him, trembling with shock and surprise. 'Your driver,' Albert hastily added, thinking maybe Adrian had forgotten who he was.

'Did you hear the German spoken?' Adrian hissed.

'The commander told his troops to return to the armoured car,' Albert explained in a gush, panting for breath in his hurry to get the words out. 'He said the fugitives had been captured. Yet later I heard your friend telling German soldiers to go to the rear of one of the houses, over there. That's why I came back to this barn where your friend hid, to see if I could find out what was going on.'

Adrian peered into the night in the direction where Albert was pointing. Next thing the sound of small arms fire could be heard, accompanied by tracer light like lightning on a distant horizon. The two men stood stock-still, unsure what to do. After a time the barely perceptible sound of footsteps on grass reached their ears. They glanced fearfully at one another. 'Mendoza,' Feodor called cheerily from the gloom. 'We must get going. Don't worry about your suitcase. We are no longer in civilian disguise.'

'Albert's here as well,' Adrian replied involuntarily, too confused and bewildered to ask what had happened.

'Good,' Feodor said. 'That saves us time looking for him.' To Adrian's amazement Feodor stepped from the dark and shook Albert's hand, like they were old friends catching up. 'Can you drive the command vehicle, Albert?' Feodor asked.

'I can drive anything,' Albert answered proudly.

'Excellent,' Feodor said. 'Come along, then. I have obtained German uniforms for us to wear.' And true to his word, Feodor had. On reaching the armoured car, all three men stripped down to their underwear, Feodor donning the uniform of the platoon commander, Adrian that of his radio operator, while Albert swapped his uniform for that previously worn by the vehicle's driver.

***

It was nearly 5 am on Sunday 27 August 1944 when Albert coaxed the armoured car into life. It set off with a roar, Feodor's upper body protruding from its turret. Adrian's head, the radio operator's headphones hung loosely around his neck, was just visible above the armour plate.

'What did you do with the German soldiers you captured?' Adrian yelled over the din of the armoured car.

Feodor looked down at the Australian. It was now light enough for Adrian to see the Russian's grim smile. 'If I told you the whole story, Mendoza, you will think me a barbarian. Suffice to say the fact the German soldiers were loath to fire because they wanted to take me alive convinced me that, without undue risk, I could creep up behind the command vehicle in the dark and hold a rifle to the commander's head. This I did, after which I had him use his tannoy to order the rest of the search party to return to the vehicle.' Feodor shook his head. 'We were lucky the soldiers were so inexperienced and badly led. Regular troops with a decent commander and it would have been a different story.'

'You killed them all?' Adrian gasped. He was horrified by the thought. 'They were just kids,' he croaked, stirred by memories of boys of a similar age at the Ballarat orphanage in Australia. 'Just brainwashed boys who had no idea what they were doing.'

Feodor shrugged. 'It's not bloodlust, Mendoza,' he said soberly. 'It's war and terrible things can happen.' A chill ran down Adrian's spine as he pictured Feodor lining up the captured Germans and shooting them. 'Beforehand, though,' Feodor continued in a lighter voice, 'I did have the radio operator report that we fugitives had changed course and were now heading south rather than east. That should buy us a little time.'

Feodor ducked down below the turret. 'We're just on 200 kilometres from the Lithuanian border,' he yelled at Albert. 'Give it all you've got. If we don't make it in the next few hours, we never will.'

For fifty kilometres the three in the armoured car hardly saw a living thing. But gradually, as they sped east, they began to encounter pockets of German troops seated by the side of the road, often around campfires as they prepared food. The men looked exhausted and battle worn.

'We're headed for Model's headquarters,' Feodor told one group at a point where the armoured car slowed to a walk to traverse large potholes in the road. Walter Model was the field marshal commanding the German armies charged with forestalling the Soviet advance from the east.

'Army Group Centre is all but destroyed,' a German soldier said dejectedly. 'They're pushing us back more and more each day. It's chaos up ahead.'

Feodor nodded and with an imperious wave of his hand ordered the armoured car forward. Thereafter, as foreshadowed by the soldier by the side of the road, the traffic congestion increased markedly, drastically impeding their progress. But in the confusion of vehicles going in all directions and harassed soldiers dashing about, nobody questioned their presence.

The baking sun was high in the sky when their luck ran out. Albert had no sooner reported that, according to the vehicle's odometer, they were sixty kilometres from Tilsit when they came across a roadblock policed by hard-faced troops.

'We're looking for Model's headquarters,' Feodor said on reaching the checkpoint, offering the same explanation he had previously used to good effect.

'The field command is now in Königsberg,' the officer in charge spat derisively, clearly unimpressed, 'planning a counter-offensive. You'll have to backtrack. There's a lot of fighting up ahead.' Two hours earlier Feodor, Adrian and Albert had skirted the East Prussian capital.

'Damn,' Feodor replied, pushing back his German officer's peaked cap until it sat rakishly on his head. 'How far ahead is the battle front?' he asked casually.

But the officer was in no mood for chit-chat. 'About twenty kilometres and rapidly shrinking,' he said guardedly. 'Why do you ask?' he added, his question causing his caution to transform into suspicion. Instincts took over. 'Take cover, take cover,' he screamed, waving in alarm to the members of his unit.

It was now or never. Leaning back in the armoured car's swivel turret, Feodor manoeuvred the vehicle's cannon. 'Get below the armour plate, Mendoza,' he ordered. Adrian did as told, amazed at the Russian's ability to conduct himself as if with ice in his veins. The two shells Feodor fired destroyed the barbed wire-clad barrier blocking the road and the sentry box next to it. 'Drive, Albert, drive for your life,' Feodor boomed before crouching on the turret floor.

The armoured car smashed through the roadblock debris. Albert wrestled with the controls as the vehicle surged forward. Small arms fire punctured one of its rear tyres and rocket-propelled grenades exploded around them causing shrapnel to ricochet off the armour plate. Soon the car was running erratically on its back axle, black smoke and sparks billowing into the air. Eventually, the vehicle could go no further. They abandoned it alongside several burned out German lorries and ran into the fields, heading towards the sound of distant shellfire.

'In here,' Feodor ordered breathlessly when thirty minutes later they reached a crater full of water turned crimson by the blood of the two dead German soldiers floating in it, 'and pretend to be dead if anyone comes along. With the Germans in disorderly retreat no one will be stopping to pick up dead bodies.'

Lying face down in the mud on the bank of the shell hole, the cacophony of battle became clearer. The prospect of being caught in a deadly crossfire now seemed all too real. 'What are our chances?' Adrian nervously asked Feodor without looking at him. 'So near and yet so far,' he lamented, answering his own question.

Feodor, however, seemed unperturbed. 'By my calculation,' he said, 'we are less than five kilometres from the front. Our troops will be advancing at about a kilometre an hour.' Feodor inclined his head towards the far-off road where lines of German vehicles were in visibly rushed withdrawal. 'Perhaps even faster by the look of that.'

For four long hours the three lay in the mud of their improvised foxhole, ignoring the summer flies coming for the dead Germans and feigning death with all their might on the occasions when German troops, first in a trickle and then a flood, scampered by on foot.

Finally, they heard Russian voices in the distance, growing louder as the soldiers neared. Not daring to stand on risk of being shot by the point detachment, Feodor raised his head clear of the mud. '*Tovarishes, tovarishes,*' he yelled at the fast approaching men. 'NKVD. NKVD. Major Feodor Kozlovsky. NKVD. Don't shoot. Feodor Timofeyevich Kozlovsky, NKVD Foreign Directorate.' It was at this time that Adrian first learned of Feodor's name.

The face that peered into the shell hole was hard and weather-beaten with wild eyes sunk deep under hooded eyelids. 'Stand,' he ordered Feodor and the others as several of his comrades arrived. Mention of the feared NKVD had dampened the man's natural instinct to shoot first and ask questions later.

'Get me your political commissar,' Feodor snapped at the encircling soldiers, the crispness in his voice conveying irresistible authority. Political commissars were attached to all Soviet units and responsible for the troops' ideological adherence.

The hyped-up soldiers looked at one another. Then the huddle parted as a non-commissioned officer pushed through the soldiers' midst and handed Feodor a water bottle. Adrian could barely believe it. Somehow they had muddled through and done it—the epic, seemingly impossible journey was over. Against monumental odds, Feodor had steered him all the way from Berlin into the arms of the Soviet forces advancing from the east.

*****

Now in 1994, Adrian recalled the look on Feodor's face fifty years earlier as the Russian staff car ferried them towards the Soviet headquarters in Lithuania. Feodor had shown no trace of elation, indeed no emotion at all. Rather, he sat looking ahead his eyes steely and unblinking. 'It's all over, Feodor,' Adrian said, wanting his protector to share in his unbridled joy. 'We did it; we're safe.'

Feodor made no direct response. 'Do you know why I've named you Mendoza?' he said instead. Adrian shook his head. 'My wife was Argentinian,' Feodor continued, a distant look in his eyes. 'She came from Mendoza. The Nazis murdered her in 1938, in Berlin.' Feodor turned to look at Adrian, his face rock hard and unforgiving. 'That's why it's never going to be over.'

Adrian had recognised the same thousand-yard stare when he met the Russian on the night of Sunday 9 February 1964 outside Holland Park tube station, called there from his home as per Feodor's prior instruction on hearing the car horn sound all clear. Much earlier Feodor had crept from a Pimlico apartment building into the cold and dark of the early morning. 'Kevin Carstone is dead,' Feodor said simply. 'He left a signed suicide note admitting to being a violent sexual offender, forced to do so by the discovery of his wallet at the scene of a vicious attack on a prostitute in Manchester.' Feodor paused. 'I understand several pornographic publications depicting sadomasochism and bestiality were found in his flat. His suicide note also admitted he fabricated the allegations against you to obscure his tawdry secret life.' The Russian pouted sagely. 'Your MI6 masters, Mendoza, have gratefully called off the hounds. You can return to the office tomorrow free of suspicion and continue your work for the Soviet Union.'

Adrian listened, spellbound by Feodor's near superhuman capabilities, just as he had been two decades earlier in 1944. 'But how did you rouse Carstone without alerting the neighbours?' he asked, fascinated. 'It was 3 am and by rights he should have been fast asleep. He'd had a busy last couple of days.'

Feodor grimaced as if wrestling with the question. 'Kevin was in pain, Mendoza,' he said finally. 'For years he fought the Cold War for its virtue, safe in the knowledge that the West could never fully subdue the Soviet Union. Kevin, therefore, was unconcerned that the

Cold War would end and deny him the righteousness of fighting it, his moral protection against the consequences for his family should they ever learn of him murdering his unborn child. But after yesterday he came to believe the Soviet Union was on the brink of defeating itself. Once this was clear to me, I knew he had grasped that the events surrounding his arrest were somehow leading to the disclosure of the shame of his youth to his family.' Feodor shrugged. 'Kevin's past, Mendoza, gravely conflicted with his upbringing. He could cope with one or the other but not with the USSR's implosion coincident with the laying bare of his sacrilege. He was trapped. Without the Soviet Union he had no armour against his family's devastation and nowhere to go. He had to end it all.' Feodor stared into the night sky. 'That's why he was waiting for us, subconsciously desperate to open the door.'

'That's preposterous,' Adrian protested. 'Why all of a sudden would he think the Soviet Union was going to self-destruct?'

'Because of you, Mendoza. You and Sara Lnu.'

'Pardon?'

'While in police custody,' Feodor said softly, 'Kevin had ample time to ponder your curious preoccupation with Sara. But Carstone was unaware that in telling Sara your darkest secret, you were actually trying to impress Heidi Frind, since Sara is your surrogate for Heidi. So he reached the rather more apparent conclusion that you had forsaken socialism because of your love for a wayward woman who, at best, is fond of you. In other words, Carstone came to see that at the very peak of your spying triumph, you had placed a one-sided love affair ahead of socialism because raw socialism could never fulfill you.' The Russian smiled wistfully. 'This demonstration of socialism's abysmal lack of substance validated every belief he ever held in the superiority of God-backed capitalism, convincing him that ideological shallowness was guaranteed to bring down the Soviet Union.'

'Even if that's true,' Adrian said doggedly, 'it still doesn't explain why Carstone thought the Soviet Union would disappear virtually overnight.'

Feodor stroked his cheeks with his index finger and thumb. 'It's difficult to identify his exact thinking. But before attending his flat I calculated that Kevin's deep subconscious would be in control, as can happen when the conscious mind is in distress. I based this on a judgement that his focus on the inadequacy of atheistic socialism together with instincts screaming the secret of his youth was no longer safe would feed Carstone's worst fears to the point where he accepted the Soviet Union's collapse was imminent, triggering a perverse subconscious reaction.' Feodor turned a palm of one hand upwards. 'The evidence of his unconscious compulsion to die is in the fact that when we knocked on his door at 3 am, he opened it, something a dominant conscious mind would not permit.'

Feodor looked briefly into the distance before returning his gaze to Adrian, this time with eyes bright and intense. 'Understand, though, Mendoza,' the Russian said gravely, 'Carstone was right to conclude that socialism could never sustain you.' Feodor inhaled deeply, his eyes never leaving Adrian. 'You are also in pain, Mendoza. You live only for the memory of Heidi Frind and not the socialist ideals she rammed down your throat in Berlin in 1944. One day your pain must end, just as Kevin Carstone's did early this morning. When that time comes, it will be my duty to protect you and arrange everything.'

Adrian watched Feodor walk away, a never before experienced, churning knot of terror forming in the pit of his stomach.

CHAPTER 23

Sara Lnu, she of the unknown surname, was a little confused and much concerned. On Friday 7 February 1964, she had spent the entire Manchester night and most of Saturday morning in a room at the Dumbrille Hotel with an American calling himself Rex. Rex was very different to the average punter but no fruitcake. Ten quid an hour for eight hours he parted with, not so much as laying a finger on her, albeit at one stage late into the night when they were both tired and stretched out on his bed she sensed he was tempted to have sex. But he didn't and in the end settled for everything she knew about her regular customer, Adrian from London.

The fact that Rex sought out Sara was now one reason for her concern. Little Jimmy, the hotel's junior porter, came looking for her around nine on Friday night to advise an American had accosted him in the foyer of the Dumbrille asking for 'a hooker named Sara.' Sara was toughing it out on the freezing street and happy to hear of a possible job at the hotel. On her return, she'd been pleasantly surprised to see the tall, quite good looking American apparently keen to avail himself of her services. The Yank gave Jimmy five shillings for his trouble—a crown piece—and politely escorted Sara to his room, while all the while the hotel night staff discreetly looked the other way.

Sara at first was nervous as the lift cranked up to Rex's room. Goodness knows what this fellow wanted; the straightlaced could be the kinkiest. But much to Sara's amazement, Rex helped her out of her overcoat before offering tea or coffee. Real gentleman he was. Then, after handing over ten pounds for an hour of her time, he started. 'Are you prepared to tell me all you know about Adrian Ashton?' he asked. 'If so, I will pay you ten pounds for each hour you spend in here.'

Sara's nose twitched. She cared for Adrian but had always treated her relationship with him as a business arrangement. God knows she had rent and endless bills to pay, as well as clothes to buy. She could hardly bare her backside for Adrian for nothing, as she had consistently told him. Sara decided to filibuster. The more time she could spend padding out her story, the more the American would pay her.

'He lives in London,' Sara began, 'this Adrian,' despite Rex having acknowledged he knew so. 'Not sure where,' she said, 'but inner London I think. Comes up here about once a month. Likes to travel by train rather than fly, always rabbiting on about the minicab he uses to get from his house to the station and back home again.'

Suddenly Rex became cross, reminding her of her old Pop. 'Sara, if you're going to waste my time we won't get along very well. First up, I want to know how you met Adrian Ashton and then I want you to tell me in fine detail what he says and does when he's with you. After that, but only after that, I'd like to hear why you think he does what he chooses to do. *Capiche?*'

The American's use of the Italian word for: *do you understand?* had a hard edge to it that unsettled Sara. Frightened now, she started to talk. First about how by chance she encountered Adrian half drunk on the footpath in front of the Dumbrille back in April 1962, the night he flew in from Iceland where apparently he had been on business. In time she progressed to Adrian's *oddity*, as he called it. 'He doesn't actually fuck me, you know,' Sara said, something in Rex's intensity prompting her resort to base language in an endeavour to show she wasn't scared. 'Some days, he just likes to look at my cunt while wanking in a real strange way. More often than not, though, he wants me to get on all fours and stick my arse in the air. Then he calls me Heidi—an old flame from during the war I gather—while he whacks off in that queer fashion of his.' Sara laughed dryly. 'I have to be in the mood for it those days.'

Carstone masquerading as Rex frowned at Sara's coarseness but otherwise let it go, along with her mention of a Heidi from Adrian's distant past. He was desperate to hear what Sara had to say and didn't want to distract her. Sara went on. Beneath his veneer of a devout southern Catholic, the American privately regarded himself as a red-blooded male, often silently exalting when thinking of the many women he bedded at university and thereafter. His contempt for Adrian grew rapidly on hearing of the Australian's sexual ineptitude and in particular his effete masturbation, this *oddity* as Sara described it. He pressed Sara for every intimate detail, lapping up the minutia in a combination of professional and personal need, only desisting when satisfied he'd bled her of every last shred of information. When two hours had passed, he allowed Sara a break during which she made tea.

But the CIA man was anxious to continue and soon moved to his next topic. 'You said he liked to chat,' Carstone resumed, 'particularly at the conclusion of these bizarre sex sessions.' He looked keenly at Sara. 'What does he say?'

And with that, Sara dropped Adrian right in it. Not that she spoke initially about his boast of being a Soviet spy within MI6, a secret agent who brought down a government in some godforsaken place she had never heard of. The truth was Sara didn't believe Adrian. For that reason she concentrated on the more credible aspects of his story—to her at least—embarking on a long and sometimes circuitous discussion of his tales about his upbringing in Australia before the war, in orphanages and of a place called Ballarat where he grew up.

Carstone listened attentively to every word Sara spoke. But it was clear he wasn't getting very far. After two hours further elapsed, he suggested they take another break. It was 2 am when the couple stretched out on his bed, resting side by side. Sara detected hesitancy on Carstone's part, her long experience telling her he was debating whether or not to make an advance. Sara hoped not. She was too tired for sex.

'I think he works for an insurance company,' Sara said of her own volition, picking up Adrian's story from where she had left it, aiming to take Rex's mind off the possibility of some late night procreation. It was a clever manoeuvre. Carstone rose wearily from the bed to pick up his notebook. 'Although one day last year,' she added, still lying on the bed and looking at the ceiling, 'he arrived up here all chirpy and full of vinegar and tried to tell me he was a Soviet spy who worked for MI6.'

Carstone's back was to Sara. He was only half listening while writing notes. Sara's words hit him like a bucket of ice water. Flustered, excited and animated all at the same time, he turned slowly to Sara. 'He said what?' he asked incredulously.

Carstone had Sara run through that Saturday the preceding August at least a half-dozen times. 'Yeah,' Sara said, 'he had been promoted in the week and was acting very Jack the Lad. I thought he was taking the mick, sort of trying to big-note himself to impress me. So I decided to take him down a peg or two because he's usually a pretty mundane sort of character. It was then he started to tell me he was an ace KGB spy hidden in MI6.' Sara laughed. 'Yeah, he took the bait and just blurted it out.'

'Why had he been promoted?' Carstone asked, knowing the answer but wanting to hear it from Sara's lips.

'Over some government he apparently had personally overthrown. He did say the name of the country but I'd never heard of it.'

'Take your time and think,' Carstone urged.

Sara tried her best. 'Nica something or other,' she mused. Carstone had to restrain himself from leading the witness. 'Some place that was a complete mystery to me, near America I think. Nicaromania?' she said, looking hopefully at Carstone.

'Was it Nicaragua?' Carstone said eventually. He figured Sara was close enough to saying Nicaragua and had decided to reflect in his report that she did.

'That's it in one, Rexy,' Sara said frivolously, following the lead of Carstone's evident elation. Rex might have been Carstone's cover name but the archconservative in him still bridled at Sara's overly familiar liberty. After that, Sara was excused. It was five o'clock on Saturday morning when she ventured into Manchester's wintery gloom.

***

Sara lived in a small flat to the south of the city centre. Drinking tea, she wondered what to do with the eighty pounds Rex had paid her. The more she thought about it, the more off-putting she found it to have earned such a large amount effectively for doing nothing. If there was anyone who knew that people didn't give out wads of cash for no good reason, it was Sara.

Even so, Sara was not about to look a gift horse in the mouth. She pushed the mounting concern from her mind, whereupon she took a hot bath, dressed and shortly before 7:30 am headed for the nearby suburb of Greenheys. Once there she waited a block from the Devine Mercy Catholic Church until a solitary woman in an overcoat and headscarf, one arm threaded through the plastic handles of a carry bag, walked towards her. It was Sara's mother.

An odd conversation ensued with one party, namely Sara, determinedly speaking English and the other Polish with matching resolve. It was cordial at first. 'Loda,' Sara's mother said, addressing her daughter by her real Christian name, 'it's been so long since I've seen you. Come, give me a hug.'

'It's Pop, mother,' Sara replied as she embraced the older woman. 'I can't come to the house. You know how angry he gets.'

'He was heartbroken when you left,' the mother replied, sighing. 'These days he does nothing but drink vodka and dream of going back home to Krakow. He so regrets coming to England. For two years now he has even refused to go to church.'

Sara grimaced, remembering the blazing rows with her father as she tried to forge an English teenage life while he demanded she observe traditional Polish practices. 'I got a work bonus,' Sara said, producing three folded notes. 'Here's thirty quid to go on with.'

'The public relations business must be doing well, unlike the rest of the country,' Sara's mother replied sceptically. Like all mothers, she could sense when her child was lying and intuitively knew that Sara's work was less respectable than Sara liked to pretend. But she loved her daughter and didn't want to know the truth. And she needed the money. The combination of the pittance she earned working Saturdays at the church, preparing it for Sunday mass, and her husband's social security barely covered the costs.

'There was a lot of overtime involved in getting the bonus,' Sara said defensively. 'I worked hard for that money.'

'I'm sure you did, beloved,' her mother replied absently before lifting her head and staring at Sara. 'There are so many handsome young men who come to the church,' she said. 'I do wish you would come back to us, find a husband and settle down with a family.'

'Loda Lichocki does not shop at the Polish meat market,' Sara scoffed, emphasising her birth name. The matter of Sara's return to the Polish community and the church at its centre was always sure to create tension. Indeed, Sara's wish to live an English life and her father's unremitting opposition to this had compelled her to leave the family home in the first place. After which several unsatisfactory group houses, limited employment opportunities and a succession of dead losses for boyfriends had conspired to see Sara on the streets, a profession at which she had toiled for the past five years.

The mother buried the thirty pounds in her bag. She was running late for work and, moreover, had no wish to leave her daughter on a sour note. She kissed Sara gently on the cheek. 'Whenever you are ready to come home, my darling,' she said, 'I will be waiting.' Both women went their separate ways, neither knowing that within weeks the unimaginable would happen, spurred by a visit to Manchester by another American, one called Charles Kilbay, and his close questioning of Sara about the American whom she had met at the Dumbrille Hotel and knew of as Rex.

It was Charles Kilbay, the CIA head of station in London at the time of Carstone, whom *The Sunday Exegesis* journalist Roger Hardwicke interviewed in Trinidad in December 1993. And Sara's return to the family fold nearly three decades earlier, triggered by Kilbay's probing over Carstone, would be repaid years later when on contracting breast cancer she spent her last days in a hospice ward funded by Manchester's Polish community, watched over by Lidia the daughter she'd had with her late husband, Tomasz. In early 1994, the unscrupulous Hardwicke had tracked down Sara on her hospice deathbed and tricked her into providing the confirmation he needed to publish his story exposing Adrian Ashton as a Soviet spy.

***

Back in 1964, after leaving her mother that Saturday morning, Sara returned to her flat around the same time as the KGB's Colonel Feodor Kozlovsky called on Sol and Rosa at their shop near Strangeways prison in Cheetham Hill posing as a Buckingham Palace equerry named Nilsson. Feodor's visit to Sol and Rosa, of course, was to arrange for Kevin Carstone's billfold to be left at the scene of a brutal bashing of a prostitute, the item he had lifted from Carstone as the American left the Dumbrille Hotel that morning. For her part, Sara was worn out. She hadn't slept a wink on Friday night, primarily because until the early hours of Saturday she was undergoing Kevin Carstone's interrogation in his hotel room.

Sara didn't much follow the news, preferring mainly television soaps, with a particular preference for *Coronation Street* seeing as the series was produced in Manchester. It was while watching *Corrie* on Saturday night that ITV broke in to report the news of a man savagely assaulting a prostitute at Cheetham Hill in the small hours of the day. Such stories always put the wind up street workers like Sara because the offenders were usually psychopaths who would go on bashing girls until apprehended. Imagine Sara's surprise then when told by the lady at the corner shop on Sunday morning that according to the BBC Home Service an American suspect had been detained in London over the assault only for the arrested man later to commit suicide.

This really worried Sara. The chances of two Americans hiring prostitutes on a cold Friday night in Manchester were extremely remote. It also revived her apprehension over the vast sum paid to her by Carstone—or Rex, as Sara knew him—for doing nothing other than answering questions about Adrian Ashton. But that notwithstanding, Sara knew her American couldn't have committed the crime because she was with him well into Saturday morning. Even so, the whole thing was very strange and unsettling. For the first time Sara entertained the thought that Adrian's story about being a spy might actually be true.

Now Sara was panicky. All she knew about spies she'd picked up from television and the movies, which effectively meant she knew nothing about spying at all. But right now, Sara believed her life was in grave danger, unaware that neither Feodor nor MI6 had any intention of coming near her: the former because he knew Adrian would not tolerate her intimidation; the latter owing to James Newcombe's downplaying of Carstone's information as conveyed by the US ambassador and Charles Kilbay. Uninitiated as she was, therefore, it was understandable that Sara should begin to contemplate being shot of Adrian and establishing a new beat away from the Dumbrille Hotel.

Sara's fear also brought to mind her mother's recent heartfelt invitation to come back home. The thought of being safe and snug with her loving parent began to gain traction, giving renewal to Sara's long-held maternal wish to have her own daughter. In just a month that seed would sprout with Sara's return to all things Polish, fully blooming five years later with the birth of her daughter, Lidia, fathered by the Polish boy, Tomasz, she had married the year before.

Adrian, naturally, was anxious to hear what had transpired between Sara and Carstone. As predicted by Feodor, he had returned to work on Monday 10 February 1964, twenty-four hours after Carstone's death, to a warm welcome from the MI6 management. That afternoon he wrote to Sara care of the Dumbrille Hotel to advise he planned to visit the next weekend, telling her that as an exception to the rule, he would fly up and take her to Saturday lunch.

'You can say that again,' Sara said when Adrian casually asked if she'd had any recent dealings with an American, trying to make his enquiry sound innocuous. But the question, rather than having the desired effect, only further inflamed Sara's paranoia, convincing her she had to end the relationship right now, there in the restaurant, once and for all. 'Paid me fifty quid to do it front ways, back ways, in my gob, and every other way,' she said. As a rule Sara never mentioned her clients, knowing how much this would hurt Adrian. But now she was excessively graphic in the hope he would get jealous and storm off for good. 'What a studmuffin,' Sara concluded when she judged she'd laid it on sufficiently thick. 'Just brilliant.'

Adrian really should have observed Feodor's perceived wisdom, that Carstone would hire Sara not for sex but for information. But his commonsense failed him, mainly because of Sara's use of American slang to describe Carstone's sexual prowess. Old demons came back to haunt Adrian—first Millie in Grimsby during the war standing him up for an American serviceman, his resentment soon giving way to a sexual tingling willing him to believe the worst, visions of Chantelle frolicking with Andrew Argyll in the Ballarat stables bright and clear in his mind.

'I wish you hadn't,' Adrian snapped, once he'd lost all self-control.

Sara didn't need a second bidding. She jumped to her feet, throwing her table napkin in Adrian's face. 'Don't you come up here telling me what to do,' she screamed. 'I am so sick of you, Adrian, and your *oddity*. Get away from me you insipid little prat. I mean it. I *do not* want to see you again. Not ever.' With that, Sara pranced from the restaurant in contrived high dudgeon, and Adrian—shocked into literal conformity—never made physical contact again.

Thirty years on, Adrian felt the pain of that moment as keenly as if it were yesterday, remembering the many unanswered letters he wrote to Sara—sent, it transpires, into the void created by her abandoning her Dumbrille Hotel beat in the days following their Saturday lunch and return to the Polish fold a month later, after the CIA's Charles Kilbay had found her working the bars in Manchester's Northern Quarter.

As the bitter taste of loss flooded his mouth, Adrian longed to know about Sara like never before. Was she still alive? Had she married? Did she have the daughter she always wanted? And overarching it all, Adrian wondered about her reaction when Roger Hardwicke's article hit the streets in under an hour from now. 'How different it might have been,' he whispered to the night, 'if I'd never become a spy.'

CHAPTER 24

On 3 September 1944 Feodor and Adrian reached Moscow, marking the end of their perilous trek from Berlin. Albert Goltz, the young German soldier who performed so capably as their driver, had earlier been handed to a special NKVD unit with Feodor's strict instruction that he be well treated. Adrian was given a series of medical checks and allowed to rest for a few days. Thereafter, with Feodor by his side, he attended the secretive NKVD graduate school on Moscow's Michurinsky Prospect. Rather than submit Adrian to the usual year-long training program, for which there was insufficient time, the Soviets instead concentrated on teaching him how to survive interrogation once he was handed back to the British authorities in the coming months.

Adrian preferred not to think about the weeks during which he was prepared for his return to the British forces. The period had been very different from the nearly three months he spent at the NKVD institute. But with the Soviet eastern advance proceeding apace as the German defences wilted, the time was fast approaching when it could be credibly claimed he had been found in a forced labour camp. To ensure he was in a condition befitting a camp inmate, Adrian was systematically starved and occasionally beaten, his morale sustained only by his love for Heidi Frind and her assurances given in the house in Kladow that his suffering was all in the name of world peace.

***

By the end of January 1945 the Soviets were less than 100 kilometres from Berlin. The fighting intensified, including around the town of Schwedt on the Oder River in northeastern Germany. It was here the Soviets professed to have come across Adrian as the sole survivor of a contingent of thirty-three persons. This invention relied heavily on the known fact that trains relocating civilian prisoners from Nazi labour camps in Poland to camps in Germany were now often assailed from the air. After Adrian's train was strafed, so the Soviet story ran, thirty-two civilians and the one British airman in their midst had reached the famous Schwedt Castle. When the advancing Soviet forces began their assault on the town, the civilians apparently chose to remain inside only to be killed by the shelling. Adrian, however, had run outside and shortly after was picked up by a Soviet scouting party. In truth, the Soviets had imprisoned the unfortunate civilians in the castle before deliberately killing them with mortar fire.

It was early June 1945 and Adrian and two British military intelligence officers were seated in the British occupation headquarters in Hamburg. Only days before Adrian had been returned to the British forces. For the preceding three months, he had been interned with nearly 100 other British servicemen who earlier came into Soviet hands. The group had been traded to the British in exchange for certain concessions sought by the Soviets in respect of occupation arrangements in Germany.

'In February 1945,' Adrian told the military intelligence officers, 'we were on a train transporting prisoners—all civilians bar me—back to Germany from Poland. Jammed in like sardines we were. When the train was attacked there was bedlam. Many people were killed outright and others bolted in all directions. I ran for my life and ended up in this old castle with a bunch of others. Gypsies I think they were. Then the shelling started. They were all jabbering away and seemed to make the collective decision to stay. I left them to it and ran outside looking for somewhere less obviously a target where I could hide. Sprinting down the street, I encountered a Soviet unit. I thought they were going to shoot me. I put up my hands and yelled: "British, British." Fortunately, they seemed to understand.'

Although the NKVD had specifically tailored Adrian's cover story to take advantage of the highly fluid situation in Germany in early 1945, the Allies understood there were bound to be Soviet agents sent to infiltrate the West among the repatriated military personnel. As such, the British interrogators were closely questioning all returnees. Adrian told his inquisitors how in February 1944 he was shot down over Berlin and captured by a civilian search party, upon which he departed from the truth and entered into the dangerous world of fabrication. In this he was aided both by his NKVD training and the fact that, once in control of Poland and eastern Germany, the Soviets spared no effort in falsifying records and finding former Nazis willing to admit to remembering Adrian, people who had never seen him in their lives.

Adrian was back in London by the time the military investigators had unearthed confirmation of his key claim to have been held for some months in the cells at the Waffen-SS headquarters in Berlin—or rather confirmation had found them.

'We made payments to the civilians who captured Allied airmen,' a former Waffen-SS soldier told the British. 'I recall this Adrian Ashton was kept in isolation in Berlin for quite some months. Some fool thought he was an Austrian and this aroused a lot of interest. Only later, around August 1944, did we discover he was actually an Australian.' The ex-SS soldier laughed. 'But you know us Germans,' he said. 'Once the error was made it infected the entire administrative system. That's why this Ashton fellow ended up being transferred into the Gross-Rosen camp system for civilians rather than the normal POW network.'

Gross-Rosen consisted of around 100 concentration and labour camps. The records altered by the Soviets at the Prausnitz subcamp in Poland reflected Adrian's arrival there in September 1944, when of course he had been nowhere near the place. A former camp inmate, a man untainted by the Soviets, would later tell the British investigators that in February 1945 the Prausnitz internees and those from other subcamps were to be repatriated to camps in Germany. And in that regard the NKVD had ensured appropriately dated transfer orders bearing Adrian's name were placed on the Prausnitz files. 'But the train,' the former inmate said, his factual account unwittingly confirming Adrian's cover story, 'only got as far as Schwedt, from where it was to track south to Saxony. After the bombing many on the train were dead, some had escaped and a number were recaptured by Hitler Youth units sent to look for them.'

Adrian's riding instructions given to him by the NKVD were to demobilise from the RAAF as soon as possible once in England. This was easily achieved, in the main because of a recently introduced Australian government rule permitting voluntary discharge of service personnel who had served overseas for two consecutive years. Adrian had arrived in the UK in the summer of 1943; with his time as a supposed prisoner recognised as service, he just qualified. The bureaucratic process was slow, but by end-September 1945 Adrian was on civvy street. Then the Soviets told him to wait, knowing the mechanism for calling the Nazis to account would soon be in place and confident that Adrian's invented experience in a German camp system reserved for Eastern European civilians would be in high investigative demand.

In November 1945 the Nuremberg war crime trials commenced. Soon after, the office of the lead British prosecutor came calling on the demobbed Adrian. In a matter of days he had been installed as an adviser in the prosecutor's office and brought to Nuremberg, his first tentative step in the NKVD plan to place him in MI6. Thereafter, Adrian passed on information that otherwise the Soviets would have provided through channels. The ruse could not have worked better. Among other things, Adrian's input would later contribute to the conviction and execution of Hans Frank, head of the Nazi General Government in Poland during the war years.

Returning to Germany invoked many memories for Adrian, none more so than those of Heidi Frind whom he ached to see. Nuremberg, though, was nearly 450 kilometres from Berlin and moving about the war-ravaged country under private auspices was practically impossible. But in mid-1946 Adrian did manage to gain passage on a military aircraft taking a British prosecution delegation to a Berlin conference. Fortunately, Kladow was in the British zone of occupation, making it a simple matter for Adrian to go there.

Asking his driver to wait near the boat shed where two years earlier he and Feodor had commenced their epic journey east, Adrian walked to where he remembered the Frinds' house stood, reliving as he did the morning when Heidi's husband Klaus drove him there and urgently ushered him inside. The house was still set in wooded grounds as Adrian recalled, but now a derelict wreck. Clearly Klaus and Heidi were no longer living at the property.

A skinny old man walking an even skinnier dog approached. Adrian pointed directly at the Frinds' dilapidated house. The man muttered without stopping. Adrian ran alongside him, producing an American dollar and a notebook, again pointing at the house.

Back at his accommodation that night, Adrian pleaded a headache and took to his bed where he cried himself to sleep. The words the old man had written on the page, *Alle tot*, meant *all dead*. Adrian woke the next morning determined to discover all he could about Heidi's death, his commitment to the socialist cause running rampant in her memory.

The building that once housed Gestapo headquarters was located just inside the American zone in Berlin. It was to here that Adrian ventured in the company of a German interpreter. The US marines guarding the entrance closely scrutinised their identity papers. But Nuremberg investigators currently held significant sway in Allied circles and Adrian had been able to wrangle an authority to conduct an unrestricted file search. Soon enough he and his assistant were seated in a musty room in the bowels of the building, a file index on the table before them.

'Frind,' Adrian told the interpreter, spelling out the name. 'Any entry after August 1944.'

For six hours, Adrian and his translator traced Heidi Frind's demise. It started with Christel Metternich, the German nurse coerced in 1943 by then Major Feodor Kozlovsky into becoming the Berlin end of the Moscow–Berlin communication chain. Christel, of course, had become inactive in June 1944 when the Allied D-Day landings in France disrupted the network, which is to say the Madrid-based Spaniard Jaume Ascaso, her Berlin cut-out, could no longer travel to Germany. This left Christel unable to pass on the reports on troop rotations and casualty rates she had compiled since last meeting Ascaso and stored with her NKVD meeting schedule in the metal container hidden under the floorboards in her Tiergarten apartment.

***

By November 1944, Christel was deeply troubled by the incriminating information she held and now accepted she would never be able to off-load it. On her return home from work one night, she decided to burn the papers. But once in the cellar of her apartment building, trying to collect enough fuel to light her coal stove, the child of the family on the floor above entered. He called for his father, a staunch Nazi.

'*Fräulein* Metternich,' the father said when he came down, 'what on earth are you doing?'

'I wanted to heat my apartment a little,' the flustered Christel answered.

'With that tiny cup of coal dust?' the man replied, his suspicion now aroused. Christel stared in terror, giving the man his cue. 'Why don't you invite me into your apartment,' he said, licking his lips, 'so that I might help with your problem? Or do you think I'm not good enough for you?'

The moment before Christel Metternich was shot six days later, she reflected on the events that night, wishing she had bowed to the inevitable and told the neighbour to get lost. But clinging to the hope of a miracle reprieve, she did not. Instead, she allowed the man to enjoy her on her sitting room sofa, while all the while thinking of her twin sister Wilhelmine held hostage by the Soviets. But worse was to follow. An hour after leaving Christel naked and distraught, the man returned with three others. Then followed the inevitable discovery of the metal container under the floorboards as the Gestapo ripped her apartment to bits.

Adrian had never met Christel Metternich but on hearing his interpreter read aloud the record of her interrogation he came to admire her profoundly. He now understood that Christel had been part of a conduit for passing messages from Moscow to Berlin and how when Feodor arrived in Berlin to escort him to the Lithuanian border it was she who alerted Klaus Frind. Why then, Adrian pondered, did Christel not reveal the Frinds when subjected to Gestapo torture?

***

'Dietrich Knote,' Christel had gasped. Her face was bloodied, several of her teeth were missing and all her fingernails had been removed with pliers. But broken as she was physically, the real damage to Christel was her wounded spirit. Over the last hour her information had come slowly at first and then in a rush as she gave up: how she'd been compromised by the Soviets at Rostov-on-Don on fear of them executing Wilhelmine; and the description of the foreign-looking man she'd never spoken with but met periodically at prominent Berlin landmarks to hand over information and receive fresh instructions. Now she'd been asked to name those German communists to whom she relayed the Soviet commands. But Christel nominated only Dietrich Knote, head of the Stalinist faction, while omitting mention of Klaus Frind, leader of the rival Marxists. Christel's was a complicated mix of indignation, intuition and a realisation she'd been duped. Indignation that she should have to die this way; intuition that Klaus Frind was a honourable man whereas Dietrich Knote was not; and most of all her understanding that, from its inception, the Nazi dream had been a cruel lie.

In her Moscow cell, Wilhelmine felt a stabbing pain in her chest at the instant when her twin sister was executed. She knew it was Christel and that the Nazis had discovered she was working for the Soviets. Wilhelmine returned to Germany upon her release by the Russians in 1947. But the Nazis were ever thorough—she never did find Christel's remains.

***

Back in the bowels of the former Gestapo headquarters in Berlin in 1946, Adrian's interpreter had just translated the transcript of Dietrich Knote's interrogation. 'Christel's decency in not exposing the Frinds,' Adrian whispered to nobody in particular, tears forming in his eyes, 'ultimately didn't help them.'

The Knote record detailed how the Stalinist claimed a couple called Klaus and Heidi Frind were the true enemies of the Reich. 'The Frinds happened upon a downed British airman,' Knote told the Gestapo. 'Heidi Frind approached me on the Oberbaum Bridge in February 1944 offering him to me for 100 reischmarks. "Sell him to one of the civilian search parties," she said.' Adrian understood this was the day when Heidi had sent forth her letter to Moscow—thereby charting the course for his future life—and that Knote was covering off on the possibility of having been seen with her at the time.

'But I refused Heidi Frind's offer,' Knote's transcript went on, 'because I now understood that she and her husband were not interested in communist principles but only in grabbing power, prestige and wealth for themselves. It's true I was a communist for a long time, but that day was a turning point in my life. I immediately became a dedicated servant of the Third Reich and National Socialism in general.'

Knote followed this explanation by listing every German communist known to him, while denying any knowledge of the fate of the Allied airman Heidi Frind had purportedly offered to sell. Adrian smiled grimly. Knote's dissembling did not fool anyone, even if it did briefly delay his execution. But once the show trials of the thirty-five communists betrayed by Knote were completed in February 1945, with Knote the prosecution's lone witness, the Nazis wasted little time in putting him to death.

As for Klaus and Heidi Frind, Klaus was recorded as shot dead on 1 December 1944 while trying to evade capture; conversely, Heidi was executed by hanging twenty-four days later, on Christmas Day, after being found guilty of sedition.

According to the Gestapo reports, Heidi came under sustained pressure during questioning about the identity of the downed airman. But her response had never wavered, consistently claiming no such person existed and that Knote was lying in an attempt to save his own skin. For the second time within an hour, Adrian felt tears sting his eyes. It was his love for Heidi, raw gratitude that despite her impossible situation she had mustered the fortitude not to give him up.

CHAPTER 25

The Nuremberg trials finished on 1 October 1946. Adrian had been highly motivated in the preceding four months since learning of Heidi's execution by the Nazis. The NKVD had instructed him to look for opportunities to join MI6. But it also cautioned this might not be accomplished in a single step.

Adrian's initial target, therefore, became British military intelligence. From coasting along as one of a rump in the lead prosecutor's office, he began to cultivate certain military intelligence advisers also at Nuremberg. This was logical, even though he was no longer a serviceman. Military investigators had debriefed him after the Soviets returned him to the British command in occupied Germany and understood best what he had to offer.

A month later, once back in London, Adrian was interviewed in a red-brick building in Hampstead, behind the high fence of which several military policemen patrolled. Soon after he emerged as a civilian employee of British military intelligence, aided in this by the glowing references he had eked out in Nuremberg.

'I made few worse decisions,' Adrian announced out loud in his Notting Hill flat in 1994. He was referring to his disastrous foray into military intelligence and the interminable years he was stranded there. Adrian had soon found there to be a significant attitude gap between the senior officers who facilitated his recruitment and the rank and file uniformed personnel on the shop floor. Before long, tedious days were building upon tedious days as it became apparent that the junior soldiers with whom he worked resented his presence in their midst, especially as military intelligence civilians traditionally performed only fringe specialist roles. The bland reports Adrian was given to analyse were of no interest to his Soviet handler, whose disengagement plunged him into a repetitiously mundane existence. And without the status he had enjoyed at Nuremberg, and the access to senior officers it afforded, Adrian found himself sadly lacking in clout on those occasions when he did ask his superiors for more substantial work.

That Adrian's drift should continue for over seven long years had everything to do with politics in Moscow. From as far back as the mid-1940s, the Russian communist party had been agitating for a single entity under its control to replace the various organs of state security. The NKVD's politically connected conservatives, however, intent on protecting their turf, had steadfastly opposed incorporating foreign intelligence collection into a new umbrella organisation to be called the KGB. For his part, Feodor Kozlovsky was ambivalent. Whether the NKVD conducted the Soviet Union's foreign espionage or whether it was a body of another name with wider responsibilities seemed to him a moot point.

But Russian politics of the era moved to the beat of its own drum. And Feodor's monumental effort in steering a downed Allied airman across war-torn Germany and Poland had become etched in Soviet political and intelligence folklore. It was the gravitas of this achievement that convinced the communist party to isolate Feodor. Fed up with the conservatives' resistance to reform, the party apparatchiks reasoned that, while he was in Moscow, Feodor's ready visibility to Politburo ministers reinforced the old guard's political sway. A posting to Stockholm ensued in 1947. Years passed as the Soviet political impasse dragged on—a wasteful, drawn-out hiatus productive of nothing other than Feodor learning how to speak and act like a native Swede. For Adrian marooned in British military intelligence and ignored by decision-makers in Moscow, his hope to join MI6 withered on the vine and he with it.

Then in March 1953 the Soviet dictator Joseph Stalin died. The shackles were off and the politicking intensified. Without Stalin's patronage, the influence of the NKVD conservatives rapidly waned. Pro-KGB elements gained the ascendancy and, with that, those NKVD officers who didn't embrace widespread change were cut loose, or worse. But in June that year, the East German uprising occurred—the worker-led rebellion against the Sovietisation of East Germany. Suddenly, the same pro-KGB elements who had wrested control of Soviet intelligence needed operatives who spoke German and knew the country, and quickly. By the end of 1953, Feodor was back in Moscow, promoted to colonel and installed in a shiny new office. In the time-honoured Soviet way, he had been rehabilitated.

By the time the KGB formally came into being in March 1954, Feodor was firmly entrenched in the organisation. His first directive from high KGB office was that efforts be revived to place the agent Mendoza in MI6. Feodor's plan centred on Adrian, currently becalmed in British military intelligence, alerting MI6 to the presence of a former Nazi living in England under an assumed name. The man in question had been brought up in now East Germany, or the GDR as it was known. Mendoza's task was to convince MI6 that the former Nazi should be inserted into the GDR as a source reporting on Russian plans to stamp out further anti-Soviet dissent.

But it was not the foisting of a double agent onto MI6 that concerned Feodor. Rather, as he told his underlings, the aim of the exercise was to present Mendoza to MI6 as someone with a rare feel for matters German, a by-product of his time there as a captive during the war. In short, Feodor intended that MI6 should come to regard Adrian as a desirable recruit.

***

Two months later, in May 1954, Adrian approached MI6 about a man called Rudolf Matt, who for most of his forty years had gone by the abbreviated Christian name of Rudy. Matt was a former Waffen-SS soldier who had come to the UK in the guise of a refugee called Ludwig Braun. Braun, so-called, now lived alone in the London suburb of Chalk Farm where in his back garden shed he eked out an existence as a woodturner.

Rudy Matt had never met Adrian. But he had been a member of a squad of Waffen-SS fanatics cornered by Soviet soldiers in a pocket in Berlin's Gendarmenmarkt Square in the closing days of the war. Matt was spared the summary execution that usually befell captured Nazi Party militia when the Soviet unit's intelligence officer heard him speak English while unconvincingly trying to pretend he was a Canadian forced to wear an SS uniform. For some obscure reason, Matt had studied English as a child and was borderline competent in the language.

Always mindful of the next war, the war against the West, the Soviets earmarked Matt as someone who could be of future use. It was they who gave him the Ludwig Braun alias and arranged his resettlement in England in 1948. Once there, Matt was ordered to get established and await further instructions. Back in 1948 the Soviets had no preconceived idea as to how or when they would use the German. But by 1954 Feodor Kozlovsky had decided that the former Waffen-SS soldier was capital ready to be spent.

'I was walking down Fitzjohn's Avenue to Swiss Cottage tube station after work on Wednesday night this week,' Adrian said. 'About half-past five.' It was early evening Friday 14 May 1954 and he was seated in a dingy ground floor office in 54 Broadway Street, London—MI6 headquarters. Two others sat across the table from him. 'I usually go up to Hampstead station but occasionally break the routine by going down to Swiss Cottage. Anyway, I was minding my own business when lo and behold I caught a glimpse of a familiar face walking past the station. Couldn't place him immediately, probably because he was in civilian clothes. But in the early hours of yesterday morning the name came to me. Gave me quite a shock when it did. I knew him as

Rottenführer Rudy Matt during the several months I was locked up in the Waffen-SS cells in Berlin.'

'What rank's a Rottenführer, Ronald, a lance jack?' one MI6 interviewer asked the other. The tone of his voice suggested he thought the German too lowly ranked to be of value.

'Yes, I think so, Arthur,' Ronald replied languidly. 'A lance corporal.'

'But he was no ordinary SS jailor,' Adrian countered. 'He was a squad leader and a favourite with his superiors because he would be as vicious as they liked. He hailed from Magdeburg, which is now part of the GDR. Born and bred there I understand. It seems to me there's decent cover in him saying he couldn't adjust to life in England and decided to go home. He's a craven bastard who would do anything to save himself. After all with no British embassy in the GDR, I'd imagine it's difficult for MI6 to independently collect information. That leaves your firm somewhat reliant on our JHQ.'

Ronald and Arthur looked at one another, each appreciating the attraction of collecting intelligence without having to rely on the charity of the British military command. Yet there were also obvious pitfalls. 'But wouldn't people in Magdeburg know he was Waffen-SS?' Ronald said eventually. 'I mean forget about the East German communist party, Werner Ulreich the prime minister and all those sycophants. The Sovs are in charge of the GDR and always will be. They'd delight in hanging this Rudy Matt from his thumbs.'

Adrian's calm surprised him as he pretended to think, a pause Ronald and Arthur interpreted as uncertainty. 'There's the weakness in your scheme, old boy,' Ronald said smugly, breaking the silence.

This was the moment for which Adrian was waiting. He smiled politely at Ronald. 'With respect, Ronald, I've seen the German character up close in all its gory detail. Let me tell you that most of them drank the Hitler soup. Even in the camps, I occasionally encountered gentiles who by rights should have despised the Nazis but were lukewarm in condemning them.' Adrian smiled again. His patronising expression did not escape Ronald and Arthur across from him. It was perhaps

Adrian's finest exercise of the spy's tradecraft because it messaged that he was one of them. 'It's a nuance you can pick up only on the ground, when cheek by jowl,' Adrian continued, his tone now knowledgeable and superior. 'My somewhat unique experience tells me the German people will protect this Matt fellow. The boys who served in the Waffen-SS were their heroes.' Adrian took a deep breath for effect ahead of his finishing thrust. 'And frankly even if the Sovs got wind of his background, I doubt they'd do much if anything to him. Why? Propaganda. He has rejected the depraved West preferring instead to return home and live in the GDR socialist paradise.'

Ronald and Arthur chortled appreciatively. 'Yes, yes, points well made,' they declared. Adrian warmly returned their smiles. In 1954 MI6 recruitment was largely informal, little more than a nod and a wink old boy arrangement for those deemed to be suitable. Now the body language from across the table was telling Adrian that his foot was in the door. Allowing time for a measured disentanglement from military intelligence, so as to avoid being seen as overly keen, he calculated he could join MI6 by July.

'Mind,' Adrian added, now confident and familiar, 'if Matt gets caught spying or is silly enough to own up to being an MI6 asset, the Sovs won't settle for hanging him from his thumbs, either way they'll string him up by his goolies.' More laughter all around, with only the table between them preventing backslapping.

'And tell us again,' Arthur said genially, 'what happened when you reported the sighting of this Matt chap to your lot?'

'Look, I'll be honest,' Adrian replied, as if taking his newfound friends into his confidence. 'All good, solid men the uniforms, but to a man the worker-bee soldier has little time for civilians and even less tolerance for our opinions.' Adrian smiled regretfully. 'I just got told to stick to what I was paid to do, which frankly is not much more than glorified filing. That's why I raised the matter with your liaison officer when he was over our way yesterday afternoon.'

***

And that should have been that. But it wasn't. Since 1950 Rudy Matt's handler at the Soviet embassy in London had been a Georgian man called Usupov. Under Stalin's watch any number of Georgians had joined the security services, Usupov included, a fact reflecting Stalin's own Georgian ethnicity. The KGB, of course, had emerged only in the aftermath of the dictator's death and resultant change in the Soviet power dynamic. But by June 1954, after just three months of operation, the nascent KGB's Georgian complement had already begun to thin. Usupov's tour in England was soon to end, leaving him deeply troubled by the changing landscape at home. This drove his snap decision to approach the MI5 officer he encountered while strolling with his wife in Kensington Palace Gardens one summer's night in 1954. The British domestic security service was charged with keeping tabs on Soviet embassy staff. It did this by subjecting Soviet diplomats to periods of surveillance on a rotating basis.

Usupov didn't know the full details of the ploy to assist Adrian to join MI6. But he did know the real name of the agent Mendoza was Adrian Ashton and that giving up Rudy Matt was the means chosen to assist Mendoza achieve his objective. To that end, Usupov had been told in early May to instruct Matt that, starting immediately and until further notice, the German was to walk every night from his home in Chalk Farm so that he bypassed Swiss Cottage tube station at around half-past five. He was then to complete the loop back to his house, a round distance of a little over two miles. Matt had questions, naturally. But the Soviets ruled the likes of him with an iron fist, leaving the German no alternative other than to accept the direction. Usupov's sole concession was to tell Matt that if other parties innocently enquired about his take up of exercise, he was to claim the walking helped ease his war-induced anxiety.

Back in Kensington Palace Gardens, Usupov told his wife to wait. Licking his lips nervously, he set off in the direction of the MI5 officer sitting on a nearby park bench struggling to look inconspicuous. Usupov's worry nearly bettered him as he approached, terrified that something could go wrong. Soviet embassy couples were usually forbidden from going out alone. But tonight providence had spoken. Usupov had objected to something said by one of the couple with whom he and his wife began to walk—some silly matter but enough for the other duo to return to the embassy in a huff.

'I am a serving Soviet intelligence officer,' Usupov said in stilted English. 'I wish to defect.' He stared at the startled MI5 officer. 'But without my wife,' he whispered. The MI5 man looked puzzled. 'She cares for nothing but Western fashion and spending my money,' Usupov added, prompted by his watcher's frown.

The MI5 officer was young and only recently made operational. But he'd diligently studied his briefing notes and photographic profiles and didn't need to waste time by asking Usupov to give proof of his intelligence status. 'What are you offering?' he queried in accordance with his training.

'Information,' Usupov replied tersely, turning to look at his wife 100 yards away, offering her a limp wave of his hand, an insipid gesture she justifiably ignored.

'An example, please,' the younger man said.

Usupov hesitated. He didn't want to give away too much without a guarantee of defection. 'I have information of an operation underway to insert a Soviet agent into your overseas spy service,' he answered vaguely. 'A corrupted British national.'

'Into MI6?'

'Yes, who else?' Usupov replied irritably, glancing at his wife who now stood arms akimbo, glowering as she watched on.

'OK,' the MI5 officer said, not really sure what to do next. 'Continue with your normal affairs and we will be in touch.'

Thereafter, three key things happened, two of them the very next morning. First, Usupov's wife, angry that Usupov should have caused a scene with their colleagues the night before, shopped him to the embassy for breaching security and having a one-to-one conversation with a British person. Second, MI5 dithered, electing to monitor the

Soviet in the coming weeks and gather more information about him. Only when fully satisfied he was not an agent provocateur would a defection recommendation go to the Home Secretary. The third event took place four days later, once a confession had been beaten out of Usupov and an urgent report relayed to Moscow, leading to the deployment to London of the KGB's Colonel Feodor Kozlovsky to sort out the mess.

And that's how it was in the summer of 1954 that Feodor came to meet Sol the tailor and his canny wife Rosa at their shop near Manchester's Strangeways prison. Sol and Rosa were an inspired selection on Feodor's part; they did very nicely in keeping the drugged Usupov safely hidden from MI5's roving eyes until he could be smuggled out of England, all the while content to accept that the Georgian was a dubious Romanian nobleman sniffing around Princess Margaret. A decade later in 1964, when Feodor needed to neutralise another threat to Mendoza, that posed by the American Kevin Carstone, the couple performed with even greater aplomb in playing their part in framing the CIA man.

CHAPTER 26

Adrian recalled those early days in MI6. As expected, he was assigned to the East German desk from where running of the former Waffen-SS soldier Rudy Matt took place. It was an exciting time as he memorised items of intelligence and began clandestine meetings with his new Soviet controller at a department store on the Queensway in Bayswater. It never occurred to Adrian that the meetings were exercises designed to establish his rhythm and confidence. The information Matt was reporting back to MI6 via a cut-out periodically sent to Magdeburg had been supplied by the Soviets in the first place.

When initially questioned by MI6, Matt had truthfully denied having met Adrian. But the Russians had also repeatedly impressed on the German that if ever interrogated he must never admit to being a former member of the Nazi Party military arm. Confident Matt would conform in the first instance, the Soviets had channelled to the Americans ahead of Adrian's approach to MI6 photographs of certain Waffen-SS units—featuring Rudy Matt of course—knowing these would be shared with the British.

With both his denials dismissed by MI6, the desperate Matt opted to come clean, explaining how he had been sent to England under an alias as a Soviet sleeper agent. But by now Matt's card was marked. His claim to being a hibernating KGB asset, apart from provoking the odd MI6 belly laugh, went over like a lead balloon. So off to Magdeburg the perceived habitual liar was forced to go, with instructions to join a labour union.

After three months in grudging service, Matt's trickle of information dried up. The East German desk in MI6 began to fear the worst, worries that were confirmed a month later when the GDR newspaper *Berliner Zeitung*, in a caption underneath a photograph of a decidedly unhappy-looking Rudy Matt, reported that a British spy arrested in Magdeburg had been sentenced to death. With that, the East German desk dejectedly closed its files—just as Adrian's probationary term elapsed, the point at which the KGB had always intended to terminate Matt to avoid any future risk of the German convincing MI6 he didn't know Adrian from a bar of soap.

Having set Adrian's MI6 career in train, the KGB waited patiently for the quality of his material to improve. But by 1956, after Adrian had been in place for two years, Lubyanka started to worry. Under pressure from Moscow to gee up its source, the KGB station in London made a very odd decision.

'Comrade Mendoza,' Adrian's then controller said. He was a taciturn Muscovite and they were standing on Primrose Hill looking out over Regent's Park. 'It is of concern that you have been unable to obtain a position on the Hungarian desk. We may need to intervene there later this year if the current civil unrest in Budapest continues.'

'I asked for a move to the Central Europe Branch as you ordered,' Adrian said defensively. 'But Warsaw Pact countries are all the rage these days; everyone wants to work on them. They're only taking the young ones who can speak Hungarian, Czech or whatever. The interest level is currently rivalling the number of requests for attachment to the Soviet Russia section.' Adrian wrung his hands. Life in MI6 was no longer as exciting as it had once been. 'But I'll keep trying,' he added lamely.

'Mendoza,' the Russian said, 'we think you are experiencing a crisis of confidence.' The man paused to delve into his carry bag. 'Here, take this,' he said, offering Adrian a brown paper package, 'and put it somewhere safe.'

'What is it?'

The Russian didn't answer directly. 'It will give you peace of mind and act as a reminder that we are all part of the same team,' he said. The man slapped Adrian on the shoulder. 'Buck up, Mendoza. The Soviet Union needs you working on MI6 Hungarian affairs.'

Not until he got home did Adrian unwrap the parcel. It was a Walther PPK pistol. He stood back, stunned. God knows what they expected him to do with it. But it seemed the KGB station had somehow concluded the gun would boost his confidence. In the years that followed Adrian never once considered using the weapon. From the night he'd taken possession of it at Primrose Hill in 1956 and for the thirty-eight years since, Adrian had kept it safely hidden away, snug in its original packaging.

Now, however, it was 5:40 am on Sunday 27 February 1994 and the gun lay on the table in front of Adrian. Next to it, still in its half-opened envelope, was Feodor's letter, which Adrian was yet to read despite many self-promises to do so. Soberly resigned to the catastrophe shortly to come when Roger Hardwicke's *Sunday Exegesis* article published, Adrian took the pistol from the table and inspected it, nodding in prolonged affirmation. The gun, he decided, had undoubtedly been a turning point. Perhaps after all it had been a clever prompt by the Soviets? Whatever, on receipt of his controller's talking to on Primrose Hill, Adrian had made a determined effort to put his best foot forward. For the first time he attended to his MI6 duties as if they were of utmost importance, where previously he viewed them only as a means for collecting information to further the cause of socialism, Heidi's socialism.

Slowly Adrian came to understand the nuanced difference between MI6, with its predominantly civilian staffing complement, and the world of uniformed intelligence. The style and presentation of written documents, he learned, were almost as important to MI6 as their content: to split an infinitive or end a sentence with a preposition was a career killer. Adrian also took a turn in MI6's antiquated watch office, frequently volunteering for the dreaded night shift where he took phone calls from often quite inebriated colleagues overseas who had judged it time to grind their particular axe. A year later, his efforts were rewarded with promotion to sub-director, leaving him still quite junior but a step up from the bottom rung. With that, he was offered the chance of an overseas posting. Adrian was rather attracted to the idea. But the Soviets told him in no uncertain terms his development as an asset depended on him staying in MI6 headquarters where intelligence opportunities were more plentiful. Adrian wasn't especially upset with the KGB; by the time he'd received its response the thought of living for some years in close confines with a bunch of MI6 colleagues had lost its lustre.

Thereafter, Adrian soldiered on with best endeavours. For all his hard work, however, he could never quite match the polish of his better-educated peers, and nor could he socialise with their effortless ease. All too regularly, he found himself in a pub on Friday nights with a group of colleagues, trying earnestly to participate in their conversation but somehow never managing to be heard. Adrian fell into a rut, unable to satisfy his Soviet masters or keep his head above water in the competitive MI6 environment. Then in February 1960 the British prime minister of the day, Harold Macmillan, gave his famous *Wind of Change* speech while on a visit to South Africa. In effect, Macmillan was declaring the UK's intention to fast track the divestiture of its African colonies. In the budget of that year MI6 received a substantial injection of funds in order to establish a presence in each of the newly independent countries soon to emerge on the African continent, primarily to monitor for Soviet meddling in their affairs.

Faced with an embarrassment of riches, promotions took place across the board within MI6. A number of unworthies, Adrian included, were among the beneficiaries. In early 1961 Adrian was appointed as director for East African Affairs. And for a brief period he did provide the Soviets with helpful intelligence on Kenya's push for independence. But the interlude soon passed and Adrian lapsed back into dealing in bits and pieces. When berated by his controller, Adrian argued he had no access to MI6's most sensitive information, which was available only to the senior executive. It was from the handler's report of this excuse that Feodor would later take the idea to use Adrian's Nicaraguan operation to win his promotion to Assistant Director General, at a time when the KGB's financial mandarins were again urging his dismissal.

Adrian sat with his hands behind his head. Time was slipping away and his outing as a Soviet spy just minutes off. Yet Adrian was still resisting opening Feodor's letter. Instead, he thought of how MI6 had relieved him of his East African duties at the start of 1962 and made him a supernumerary, with little he could do other than grumble and fret about the KGB's reaction. It was while sidelined as a supernumerary that he was dispatched to Iceland during the so-called *Cod Wars*. Adrian understood he'd been handed the assignment only because those in charge thought it unimportant. But he could never have guessed that this scrap from MI6's table would lead him to Sara, in April 1962 while delayed in Manchester on return from Reykjavik.

Four months later, in August 1962 after MI6 had abandoned the supernumerary concept, Adrian was made the director of the Central America section, MI6's smallest and arguably least important unit. This was the position he was occupying in late October of that year when he attended a follow-up meeting with his KGB handler at the Connaught Hotel in Mayfair. The day before Adrian had reported he was to head an operation in Nicaragua that MI6 was to conduct on behalf of the CIA. But rather than laud Adrian, the Soviet was scathing. 'We've suffered your low productivity for many years,' he said, not mincing his words. 'And now this Nicaraguan thing has come up, Moscow has decreed overnight we are to use it to get you promoted to the senior executive, to give you better access to MI6's secrets and us an improved return on investment.' The controller shook his head. He was a decorated war hero, contemptuous of Adrian's timidity and transparently at odds with

Lubyanka's decision to assist Adrian gain promotion. 'You should know your friend Feodor Kozlovsky instigated this initiative,' the man said, making no effort to disguise his distaste for Feodor's enterprise. 'You're lucky to have Feodor Timofeyevich in your camp. If others had their way, we would have severed ties with you years ago.'

'What do you mean in my camp?' Adrian asked indignantly, insulted by the Russian's criticism. 'I haven't seen Feodor since 1945 when we were both in Moscow.'

'Perhaps not,' the controller replied. 'But it was he who devised the operation in 1954 to have you reveal Rudy Matt's presence in England to MI6, the former Waffen-SS soldier. Without Feodor's help you would not have gained entry into British security.'

'I see,' Adrian said thoughtfully. He wasn't overly surprised. The Matt initiative had smacked of Feodor's genius.

The controller was now openly agitated and went on when usually he would not. 'You don't see at all,' he said sharply. 'The Matt operation was very nearly compromised by a defector here in our London embassy, a month after you approached MI6. Feodor Timofeyevich actually came to England to sort out the problem.'

Now Adrian was flabbergasted. 'What?'

The controller smiled, pleased to have startled Adrian and happy to leave it there. 'Remember, Lubyanka wants you at the forefront of the Nicaraguan operation, to get your name up in lights in London and Washington.' The Russian took his coat from the bar stool beside him. 'That should save your bacon,' he said dismissively, leaving without a backward glance.

***

The walls rapidly closing in, Adrian well remembered the controller's biting scorn. 'Feodor was so invested in me,' he said sadly. 'The risks he took in getting me to Moscow in 1944 and then coming to my rescue twice again, in 1954 and 1964, while all the while guarding my back from a host of KGB detractors.' He held Feodor's letter before him. 'So why now has he betrayed me?' Large, wet tears rolled down Adrian's cheeks. 'I have to read this,' he whispered hoarsely, clasping the letter to his chest. 'I have to.' And with that, Adrian's tears for Feodor became heaving sobs, then for Sara and finally for Heidi as the flood of interlinked emotions overwhelmed him. Exhausted by the crying, he slumped back in his chair and closed his eyes.

Thwack, the sound radiated on the cold morning air, making Adrian start. It was precisely 6 am and the noise was the flat mass of supple material slapping down on the hard surface of the front courtyard of Adrian's building. Roger Hardwicke had just made good on his promise to personally deliver a copy of *The Sunday Exegesis*.

'It's all over,' Adrian said, looking at Feodor's letter, which had fallen to the floor. He was addressing Feodor, speaking slowly and matter-of-factly as he summarised his life. 'You wasted your time on me. From the moment my birth parents abandoned me, I was doomed to be a failure. I am a pointless person who has lived a pointless existence.'

As if emboldened by his harsh articulation, Adrian plucked the letter from the floor and ripped at the envelope until it was fully open. Inside was a single hand-written page, the text filling all of the front sheet and two-thirds of its reverse side. Adrian read, becoming increasingly confused as he struggled to take it in: *The fall of the Soviet Union and its socialist folly; Adelaida my darling wife; the end of duty;* along with the vaguest of mentions of a time long ago in Pimlico, to the CIA agent Kevin Carstone opening the door to his flat at 3 am.

The more Adrian read, the more frantic he became. Feodor's letter was as disjointed as a giant jigsaw puzzle. Over and over he searched for meaning, before dwelling on Feodor's stark admission that the aching chill in his bones was foretelling of his looming slide into oblivion and, with that, the end of duty. *The simple truth is, Mendoza,* Feodor's letter concluded, *the shadows are lengthening. And in death, I cannot sustain what I tolerated in life.*

Sustain what? Adrian thought, squinting, his brow furrowed as he re-read the Russian's infuriatingly obscure comparison of the responsibilities he inherited upon meeting Adelaida at the Goethe University in Frankfurt in 1932 to those falling to him in a nondescript barn in Poland early one morning in August 1944.

Only after reading the last paragraph three times did Adrian make some sense of the letter. The passage, he discerned, was a description of how his birth parents, Chantelle in Ballarat, his H for Harry crewmates, Heidi and later Sara were all lost to him in one way or another, whereas the Russian had endured. 'Feodor's explaining how he fortified me against the pain of my rejection, abandonment and abuse,' Adrian whispered in soft wonderment, 'just as Kevin Carstone fought the Cold War as his protection against the effect on his family of him murdering his unborn child. Feodor's telling me that without this suppression, I would not have survived for a further fifty years since first meeting him.' But even as the meaning sunk in, Adrian could not believe that Feodor's other-worldly assertion was all he intended to say—that in eternity Feodor could not tolerate Adrian vying with Adelaida for his emotional attention, unlike in finite life where it had been his duty to do so.

Adrian rubbed his eyes. His inability fully to decipher Feodor's letter had caused him to swivel his head and stare at the Walther pistol. And with that, a churning knot of terror formed in the pit of his stomach. Adrian recognised the chill sensation. He had experienced it only once before, long ago on a cold Sunday night in February 1964 outside Holland Park tube station. Eighteen hours earlier, in Pimlico, Feodor had attended to Kevin Carstone. 'Kevin was in pain,' Feodor had said, 'with nowhere to go. You are also in pain, Mendoza. One day it must end. When that time comes, it will be my duty to protect you and arrange everything.'

The words spoken by Feodor that Sunday night made the hair on the back of Adrian's neck stand on end. He sat bolt upright in burning alarm: the vague reference in Feodor's letter—to Kevin Carstone opening the door to his flat at 3 am—was an instruction steeped in the knowledge that his long suppressed hurt would revive with the Russian's end of duty. 'God help me,' Adrian breathed in horrified awe. 'Oh, Jesus. He's saying it's time to end my pain and that the Carstone template is his chosen arrangement.' For an instant Adrian sat stock-still, sensing the imminent arrival of another equally startling revelation. It came with a rush reminiscent of a powerful sneeze. 'That's why Feodor betrayed me to Hardwicke,' Adrian exclaimed, open hand to mouth and wide-eyed, 'to ensure that like Carstone I had nowhere to go and no room to back away from what must be done.'

But no sooner had the paralysing shock of understanding engulfed Adrian than it vanished, overtaken by his astonished certainty that rather than imposing a dire prescription, the Russian in fact was protecting him, guiding him through one last morass, one final troubled night. Adrian sat back, eyes closed and breathing deeply, relieved at long last to have total clarity and grateful for it. The lull, however, was short-lived, broken by Adrian's sudden lurch into the kitchen of his flat. There he tore Feodor's letter into pieces, placing the shreds into the empty fruit bowl, save for one he lit from the gas jet. Only when the paper's charred remains were crunched into ash did he resume his seat in the void of his bay window.

For fully ten minutes Adrian stared into the grey morning, waiting. Then the telephone rang. The wolves were at his door. He was again with Feodor, their backs to the wall. Taking the Walther pistol from the table, Adrian placed the barrel in his mouth. '*Weather over Mendoza*,' he whispered, closing his eyes for the denouement.

The blinding flash inside his head made Adrian think he was dead. Heidi was smiling. 'Feodor,' the apparition was saying, 'knows nothing but death. It's time to be done with him and see if Sara had the daughter she always wanted.' Bewildered, Adrian realised the long neglected pistol had seized. 'Forget Feodor and use your jail time to find if Sara had a daughter,' Heidi patiently insisted, just like the mother he never had. And then she was gone

Shawline Publishing Group Pty Ltd
www.shawlinepublishing.com.au

S L P

**SHAWLINE
PUBLISHING
GROUP**

CPSIA information can be obtained
at www.ICGtesting.com
Printed in the USA
BVHW030749211122
652420BV00018B/532

9 781922 850669